S0-BDP-750

Takeover Time

Novels by Arthur R. G. Solmssen

Rittenhouse Square (1968)
Alexander's Feast (1971)
The Comfort Letter (1975)
A Princess in Berlin (1980)
Takeover Time (1986)

Takeover Time

A NOVEL BY

Arthur R.G. Solmssen

Little, Brown and Company Boston · Toronto

FIRST EDITION

Library of Congress Cataloging-in-Publication Data
Solmssen, Arthur R. G.
Takeover time.
I. Title.
PS3569.058T35 1986 813'.54 86-2869
ISBN 0-316-80370-7

RRD-VA

Designed by Jeanne Abboud

Published simultaneously in Canada
by Little, Brown & Company (Canada) Limited
PRINTED IN THE UNITED STATES OF AMERICA

Some of the people in this book have appeared in earlier stories about the firm of Conyers & Dean. They are older now, but they are just as imaginary as they were before.

1. ATTY #: 003 (Partner)
2. NAME: Anders, Graham
3. BIRTH: 3/10/28
4. EMPLT DATE: 9/1/53
5. DEPT: Corp. (Head)
6. YEAR ADMITTED TO BAR: 1954
7. SUPREME COURT NO.: 4384
8. COLL.: Harvard '50
9. LAW: UPa '53
10. BAR ASSOCS: Phila., Penna., Amer.
11. MEDICAL INS.: Major Med/Blue Cross/Blue Shield
12. LIFE INS.: Basic, Level I ($250,000)
13. DEFERRED INCOME PLAN: Yes
14. LONG TERM DISABILITY: Yes
15. 1978 MACHINE RATE P/HOUR: $160
16. PROFIT SH: .02
17. MONTHLY DRAW: $16,000
18. 1978 RESPONSIBLE TIME BILLED TO 3/1: $98,600
19. 1978 RESPONSIBLE TIME UNBILLED TO 3/1: $26,400
20. PREVIOUS RESPONSIBLE TIME UNBILLED AT 3/1: $76,587
21. COSTS UNBILLED TO 3/1: $12,792
22. RESPONSIBLE BILLS UNPAID 90 DAYS: $26,592
23. FOR DINNER DANCE: Mr. and Mrs. Graham Anders
    12 Juniper Lane
    Haverford, PA 19041
    (Graham and Caroline)
24. PHONES: Direct Line – 2211
    Home – 525-1770
    Emergency (Mrs. Anders' office) – 732-4688

BOOK I

ONE

1978: The Timekeeper

"I'm a bad boy," said Graham Anders, smiling as they sat down.
Ordway Smith, already sitting down, was not smiling.

"You want a drink?" he asked, because the waiter was already at the table.

"Am I going to need a drink?"

"Mr. Anders will have his usual draft."

"Martini for you, Mr. Smith?"

"Right, Tony. Leave the menus."

The waiter disappeared, Graham Anders began to study the menu, and Ordway Smith lighted a cigarette.

"Graham, you're not a boy anymore, and you are not entitled to different telephone service than any other lawyer in the firm —"

"Please, Ordway, would you spare me this business? This stage business? The managing partner calling the naughty boy on the carpet! All I did was politely visit your highly paid business school graduate who is running our law firm, to ask if I could please have one regular, ordinary telephone in my office, a plain ordinary telephone like the ones we all used to have —"

"Sherman Shapp has patiently explained the new system to you, Graham —"

"— even if I pay for it myself?"

"We can't keep track of the calls!"

"Can't use my own telephone! My own telephone will not work until I punch-in the client code!"

"Or your own personal code."

"Or my own personal code, I have to punch-in my own personal code to make my own personal telephone call, my God, Ordway, *what have we come to?* What would your father say? What would my grandfather say?"

"Graham, we just can't keep track of the calls! We have four hundred people making telephone calls day and night and there is no other way to find out whom to bill for those calls, we've got a monthly telephone bill of twenty thousand dollars and this new system was approved by the executive committee, Sherman Shapp sent out a memo weeks ago —"

The waiter brought the beer and the martini.

"I guess we better order," said Ordway, so they ordered.

"Graham, you've just got to adapt yourself. Times are changing. Times are always changing, and people have to change with them. People who don't adapt themselves die. What's the point of bringing up my father? You know as well as I do, my father used Conyers & Dean as a place to hang his hat, to get his mail, to have his bookkeeping and his tax returns done, kept a quarter of a million dollars in the capital account at no interest, kept Ordway Chemical as a client . . . and when people asked him what he did, he could say he was a partner in Conyers & Dean. Had to be something, right?"

Graham Anders drank his beer and said nothing.

"All right, your grandfather: entirely different story. Brilliant lawyer, wonderful man, pillar of the community, one of the people who really built the firm."

"Managing partner," said Graham Anders.

"Managing partner who gave me another chance when I failed the bar exam . . . you know how I feel about George Graham."

"How would he like this setup of yours?" demanded Graham Anders. "Seventy-five thousand dollars a year for an office manager who isn't even a lawyer? Sherman Shapp, for Christ's sake! A law firm run by some *apparatchik* who understands computers. We're supposed to be partners in the best law firm in town but we're clocked on every minute we work — or don't work — like people on Ford's assembly line, like people in a Siberian salt mine — and now we can't make a telephone call without logging into the computer!"

The waiter brought the snapper soup.

"Another drink, Mr. Smith?"

"No, no thanks, Tony."

"Aw, go ahead," said Graham Anders. "You're going to need it before you're through with me."

Ordway sighed as he put out his cigarette. "I hope not! Why don't you bring us two iced teas, Tony. . . . Graham, you're wrong. You're just plain wrong. Your grandfather was always a guy who adapted to things. Look at the changes *they* had to put up with: the Crash. The Depression. Roosevelt. The SEC. The War — half his lawyers gone off to war. Wage and Price Controls, things nobody ever heard of before . . ."

Graham Anders smiled across the table. "He didn't hire a business manager, though. You know what your business manager did last summer? He sent Schuylkill Steel a bill for air conditioning! *Our air conditioning!*"

"I heard about that. You kept your working team in the office all weekend, we had to pay the building to turn on the air conditioning for a whole floor, it cost over a thousand dollars —"

"Well, we had to breathe! Can't open the windows, you know, and then he sends a bill to my client? Ferguson nearly had apoplexy!"

"Well, of course, that was a mistake, he should have discussed it with you first, but you've got to remember that we've become a great big business organization, we just can't run the place like a private club anymore, if we don't establish modern business procedures, if we don't *enforce* modern business procedures, we are going to go broke, Graham. . . ."

Graham Anders felt his mind wandering to other things: how old is Ordway now? If I'm fifty, he's fifty-five. Still has all his hair and all his teeth, rides before breakfast, plays squash before lunch, looks great, looks like he's really made it — and he has. Our rich boy has made it all the way back, and then some. Flunked the bar exam when he got out of law school — must have been in 1949 or 1950, my grandfather never mentioned it, why should he, I was still in college — and now he's the managing partner. The watershed was when he got us fired as counsel to Conroy Concepts Corporation, Charlie Conroy, his biggest client, fantastic wheeler-dealer, symbol of those go-go years, but there were things wrong with Charlie's companies, and at the last moment Ordway refused to close on Charlie's hundred million dollars of debentures, wouldn't put Conyers & Dean on the hook, the deal aborted, Conroy fired us as his lawyers, Ordway was in the doghouse, people said we shouldn't have let him run a deal like that, people said a deal of that size and complexity was beyond him, Ordway's a playboy, should be left to run the Orchestra and the Academy of Music and the United Fund — but they were wrong. He proved he could stand up under pressure. He showed everybody he had guts, and when Ellsworth Boyle stepped down last year, look what happened! Lansing assumed he'd become the boss. Brilliant lawyer. Famous lawyer. Eminently qualified to be the managing partner. Only problem: Lansing is a shit. Even his own boys can't stand him. Have to stop calling them boys, got so many girls now. Have to stop calling them girls, they hate that, they are *women!* Remember? Okay, wake up and pay attention.

"— really wanted to discuss another matter," said Ordway Smith as the soup plates were being removed. "You remember Fanny St. Eustace, don't you? Been a client of ours for years —"

"Fat Fanny Hyde? Sure, she married a friend of your brother-in-law, didn't she? Another peer of the realm?"

Ordway nodded. "Even grander lord than my brother-in-law. And even more expensive. Represents a London merchant bank in New York, with considerable help from real bankers, I'm sure, but they have to spend a lot of money."

"Well, fortunately she has a lot, doesn't she? The Hydes are loaded."

"Some are, some aren't."

"Isn't she Francis Hyde's daughter?"

"Yes, she is, Graham." Ordway looked across the table as the waiter served their sandwiches. Graham Anders still had the European habit of eating sandwiches with a knife and fork, and he began to do that now.

"You don't know what this is about?" Ordway asked.

Graham's mouth was full. Eyes on his plate, he shook his head. Both of them ate in silence. Then Ordway wiped his lips with his napkin, still looking directly at Graham Anders.

"Well. I don't need to tell you about Francis Hyde's career, but his family life hasn't been so great. His wife had a drinking problem, in and out of these places, you know. . . . Finally died, or committed suicide, some people say. The girls were spoiled, they quarreled with him, they married people he knew were after their money — I mean after his money, of course — He is supposed to be retired from Philadelphia Pharma now. Flies around in airplanes, goes hunting and fishing in Scotland and Africa and South America, goes skiing —"

"How old's he now?"

"I don't know — sixty-five or seventy. Good shape, apparently, but the people he grew up with, the other big shots, the men who made it big as he did — they're dying off. He's getting lonely. Last summer he was in Europe, met a beautiful divorced woman younger than his daughters. . . . Now it seems he's going to marry her."

"Hardly a new story," said Graham Anders. "Why are you telling me all this?"

"Graham, will you cut it out? This is *me!* Your admirer, your friend! In the middle of Charlie Conroy's debenture closing, the night before, I was in New York, it was the worst night of my life and I didn't know what to do and I needed you to tell me what to do. I called you at home and I talked to Caroline and she said, 'The joke's on you, Ordway. Graham's supposed to be in New York with you, helping you close Charlie Conroy's debentures.' And where *were* you, Graham? You know Goddamned well who this is that's captured — taken over — Francis Hyde!"

Graham Anders turned away and looked across the room toward the sunlight streaming through the windows. He was surprised that it still hurt so much. This was March, and he had not seen her since Christmas.

Ordway Smith put his elbows on the table, put his hands together, and leaned forward. "Now this is really what I want to talk to you about, Graham. You stay away from her now, is that clear? That was long ago. That's over! We don't want any more trouble with Caroline, and we don't want *any* trouble with Francis Hyde. We've never represented him, unfortunately Bill Pennington has always represented Hyde and Philadelphia Pharma, but a man in Hyde's position can cause trouble like you wouldn't believe. . . ."

The instant he understood what this lunch was really about, Graham Anders switched his mind away. Or tried to. What Ordway has is presence. The boys like him. The clients like him. Everybody in town likes him. We were lucky to have a guy we all genuinely liked, willing and able to learn all about starting salaries and billable hours and DBR computer printouts and how many square feet on the forty-second floor we will need at how much per foot in the fall of 1988, and now he's going to come at me about that premarital agreement Hyde's lawyers want her to sign, because if she won't sign, the Lady St. Eustace and her sister are going to inherit one hell of a lot less money than they spent their lives expecting. Or maybe if she won't sign he won't marry her after all?

Smelling her sweating perfume, feeling her laughing (laughing!) underneath him in the darkness? Oh yes he will!

His heart was pounding. He really wanted a drink. He had to get Ordway off the subject. "Is this lunch about Fanny St. Eustace's inheritance, or is this lunch about my relationship with the firm?"

"Graham, you're terribly important to the firm."

"Still?"

"My God, I'm counting on you at my right hand! You're the head of our biggest department, you're in charge of Schuylkill Steel, you're in charge of the Soap Company, you're in charge of Boatwright Corporation . . . but what's going to happen to our relationship with Boatwright if Caroline ever decides to sell her stock? You've just got everything put together again, Graham: the arthritis seems to have gone away, you're back home with Caroline, your boy is going to Harvard in the fall, you've even married off gorgeous Miss Jersey Cranberries, I hear —"

"Come on, Ordway, what is the point of all this? Our relationship with Boatwright is based on my friendship with Boris Fleischer —"

"— who is well into his seventies, I believe, and what happens when he's gone? What happens when Boris isn't running Boatwright any more? Don't you see what I'm saying? You've got it all now, but if Caroline and Francis Hyde come after you at the same time . . ." Ordway didn't have to finish the sentence. He looked at his friend. "Is she really that terrific?"

Graham Anders had been asked that question once before — by Caroline Boatwright Anders.

TWO

1948: The Girl Scout and the Orphan Boy

The first Francis Boatwright was a young mechanic from Lancashire who had been apprenticed to Stephenson's locomotive works. He arrived in Philadelphia from Liverpool in 1854, quickly obtained a job with M. W. Baldwin, became a locomotive designer and joined the Arch Street Meeting, where he caught the eye of Miss Caroline Fox, the daughter of a banker. One thing led to another. By the time the Civil War began, Francis Boatwright had his own shop and was selling his tough little "Black Beauty" engines to the war-strained railroads just as fast as he could build them. When he died, in 1903, the Boatwright Locomotive Works occupied two hundred acres of brick buildings in North Philadelphia, employed thousands of people, and shipped its steam locomotives to every country that had railroad tracks.

Francis Boatwright, Jr. (1865–1943), was a fortunate man. He was five years old the first time they let him ride out to the farm in Humphreysville (now Bryn Mawr) on the lap of a Pennsylvania Railroad engineer, blowing the whistle at each crossing. He fell in love with railroads *before* he discovered that he would inherit a booming locomotive factory. Locomotives were the most important things in his life, and locomotives were the most important things in the lives of the men who came up under him, the men who were running the Works after the Second World War, the men who refused to face the fact that airplanes were taking the railroads' passengers and trucks were taking the railroads' freight, the men who averted their eyes from their own sales figures, the men who could not successfully diversify into diesel tractors and hydroelectric turbines. . . .

Part of the problem was the Boatwright family itself. Francis Boatwright, Jr., the little boy who rode in the cabs of locomotives, took control of the Company shortly after the Spanish-American War and ran it for half a century. He ran it so well that a rich stream of dividends nourished the farthest branches of the family tree, providing not only the quiet comfort in which most Boatwrights chose to live, but also the ability to be exceedingly generous. Unlike many of their coreligionists, the Boatwrights resisted the charms of Episcopalianism and remained more or less formal Quakers. They did not *thee* or *thou* each other, they drank alcohol and went to war and generally behaved like other people, but whatever formal worshipping they did, they did at Meeting and many of them, particularly older ones, developed a high sense of public responsibility and spent an extraordinary amount of their time and money on good works of one sort or another. By the time Graham Anders came to know the family, every branch had its own pet charities, ranging from the American Friends Service Committee to day-care centers in the black ghettos of Philadelphia to hospitals on African rivers to poetry magazines irregularly issued from lofts in lower Manhattan.

What these Boatwrights did *not* spend their time on was the Locomotive Works, from which their income still derived. Despite his own background, Francis Boatwright, Jr., did not believe in nepotism. *His* son, Francis Boatwright III, the father of Caroline Boatwright Anders, was encouraged to study medicine at the University of Pennsylvania. He first became a surgeon but then veered off into the biochemical research that was to absorb the rest of his life. His Boatwright Institute at the University made two major breakthroughs in the use of X-ray diffraction techniques for molecular biology; one of his teams captured a Nobel Prize. Dr. Boatwright never went near the factories in North Philadelphia, and expressed interest in locomotives only when the subject of dividends arose.

In that respect he was like all of his brothers and sisters and uncles and cousins: they didn't interfere; after Francis Boatwright, Jr., died they let his protégés run the Company; they didn't know or care anything about locomotives, *but the dividends had to keep coming*. The railroad industry was getting sicker all the time. A board of directors controlled by cool, detached, hardheaded businessmen (like Caroline's great-great-grandfather Fox) would have cut the dividend and used the money to move into other fields. If the locomotive men didn't like that, other men would have been hired to replace them, but that didn't happen. The Boatwrights controlled the Board, the Boatwrights had to have their dividends, and so the Company's stock sold down from $125 a share in 1945 to $14.25 in 1960, where it first attracted the attention of Mr. Boris Fleischer.

In 1948, when all of this really began, Graham Anders had never heard of Boris Fleischer. Neither had anyone else. In 1948 Graham Anders was a sophomore, just back from two years with the Army of Occupation in Austria. He was frustrated, he was lonely, he was desperately trying to forget somebody, and perhaps that is why the thing with Caroline Boatwright happened so fast.

In those days, Harvard undergraduates lived in the Yard and in the Houses, while Radcliffe women lived in their own carefully guarded dormitories on the other side of the Common. It was considered necessary to bring them together. The Freshman Mixer, also known as the Slave Market, was intended to exhibit the incoming Radcliffe girls to their opposite numbers at Harvard, but the Harvard freshmen were lost in the shuffle of upperclassmen, law students, medical students, business school students, war veterans, and Older Men with Cars who came every year to inspect the new crop. The more attractive women were cut in on every few minutes, and some of the men stopped right on the dance floor to annotate their little black books.

She picked him up. She had seen him at parties in Philadelphia. She touched his elbow and smiled and introduced herself; would he cut in on her roommate, who was stuck?

Years later she wrote him:

> You know I have loved you from the first moment I ever saw you, in your wrinkled army uniform walking into Louisa McDonough's coming-out at the Barclay, looking tired and forlorn, and you were older and didn't know me and I spent *weeks* plotting how to meet you and finally succeeded at that foolish mixer in Cambridge.

A tiny well-rounded girl with nice brown eyes, flushed cheeks, freckles, jet black curly hair. Not beautiful, thought Graham Anders — but somehow it didn't matter because she radiated something. What is charm? Is it self-assurance? Is it a convincing interest in the other person?

"You're the grandson of Mr. Graham at Conyers & Dean," she said. "You're the son of Gustaf Anders."

"And you're the Locomotive Works."

They smiled at each other, and he went into the crowd to rescue the roommate. Half an hour later they occupied a booth in Cronin's, a Dunster Street beer hall.

"Are you going to be a lawyer like your grandfather?"

"I guess I'll be a lawyer. I hope I can be half as good as he is."

"I understand he brought you up."

"That's right."

"He's our lawyer."

"I know."

"What happened to your father?"

"He was killed in the Spanish Civil War."

"And your mother?"

Anders was uncomfortable. He didn't like to talk about these things, and his friends had learned not to ask. "My mother was killed in an automobile accident. In Naples, nineteen forty-three. She was an actress. She was giving plays for the American troops there. Somebody was driving her home from a party —"

"You're an orphan boy!"

"Well, I'm twenty," Anders replied, even more uncomfortable.

"And you had a mistress who was an Austrian princess."

"She wasn't a princess and she wasn't my mistress, but you've certainly checked into me."

"Do you want to tell me about her?"

"No, I don't."

"Was she older than you?"

"Yes."

"How much?"

"Seven years."

"Was she beautiful?"

"Yes."

"Was she married?"

"Widow."

"Why didn't you marry her?"

"Because she wouldn't marry me!"

"Because she was seven years older and you had to go back to finish college?"

"Can we talk about something else, Miss Boatwright?"

"You miss her terribly, don't you?"
"You cross-examine all your dates this way?"
"No, I don't. I've never been this much interested in a man."

It happened too fast, but Graham Anders did nothing to slow it down. He had never met anyone like her. She filled the vacuum of his life with her energy, her easy accommodation to the rules of life, her troop of girlfriends, and her enormous family with its enormous problems. Caroline Boatwright was the ultimate Good Girl: highest grades in her class, captain of the swimming team, no probation ever for anything, everybody's best friend. She had actually been a Girl Scout! Her directness could be overwhelming and it overwhelmed him on their second date.

They were alone in his room. In those days there were "Parietal Regulations": no dogs, no firearms, no women after eight P.M. "If you're not in by eight, you're too late," they said, but in those days there was more talk than action.

Some "nice girls" did it, but they did it very carefully and only with men they knew well, men they had reason to hope would marry them if "anything happened." It was a time of smelly rubber condoms and lies to roommates and panicky waits for overdue menstrual periods, a time of abortions performed on kitchen tables by hard old women, or in hotel rooms by nervous doctors willing to risk jail to help a friend, a time of babies given up for adoption — a time of guilt. Sex was a dangerous sport. People who really "did it" didn't talk about it.

He planned to take her to a Greek restaurant in Boston and then to an Italian movie. He had walked up to her dormitory, watched her sign out, and walked back with her through Harvard Square, picking up the bottle of gin and the can of grapefruit juice and the bag of ice cubes at different places. He had signed her into Lowell House and brought her up to the empty suite — roommates out in accordance with iron unwritten law. He had mixed the potent Seabreezes in somebody else's glass pitcher. . . .

"These are pretty strong drinks," she said.

"I'll put in more grapefruit juice."

"No, that's all right, I sort of like it — and anyway I was warned."

"About my Seabreezes?"

A nice smile: "About you *and* your Seabreezes."

"What did they say?"

"They said I wasn't sexy enough for you — but I am." She was standing very close to him now, and the smile was gone.

He took the glass out of her hand and put it on the mantelpiece, but he didn't stop looking into her serious eyes. "Too many Seabreezes, Miss Boatwright."

"I don't appeal to you?"

"Oh yeah, you appeal to me a very great deal —"

"— but not as much as your Austrian widow?"

"I've told you that's over! I don't want to talk about that anymore —"

"Then why don't you fuck me?"

His heart missed a beat, and he put his own glass down. In those days women didn't use that word — at least he had never heard a woman use it.

She swallowed as she saw his expression, turned pale, looked down at the carpet, looked back up at him. "You're shocked? I understand you do that all the time up here."

"No, I don't. Do you do it all the time?"

She shook her head and compressed her lips.

"Have you *ever* done it, Miss Boatwright?"

"Why do you keep calling me Miss Boatwright?"

"Why are you acting up this way?"

"I'm trying to attract your attention."

He had to laugh. "Well, you've succeeded in doing that, all right!"

"It's supposed to be what you're mainly interested in."

"What is?"

"You know. . . ."

"You don't want to say it again?"

"No!" A shout.

"But you really want to do it?"

"Yes." Quietly, looking down.

"Now?"

She nodded. "Yes!"

"Why me?"

Her eyes flashed and her face turned a glistening pink. "*Because you're the one I want!* And if you want me, you'll be the only man for me, for ever and ever — but if you keep teasing me one more second, I'm walking out that door and you'll never see me again!"

THREE

1969: You Don't Have to Know the Language

He first met Karin Bromberg one blazing October afternoon at the hunt races near Unionville, in Chester County. How old was he then? What year was that? That was 1969, the year he had to stop running Charlie Conroy's deals, the big bond issue and the acquisition of Bromberg Instruments, because they put him in the hospital.

He was sitting on the tailgate of Caroline's station wagon, listening to the hoofbeats, serving drinks from thermos bottles, squinting into the sunshine at friends who stopped to say hello — particularly younger people from Conyers & Dean who knew that he was just out of the hospital, that this was his first public appearance.

The sunshine warmed him. He watched Caroline efficiently distributing sandwiches and drinks — stoutly tweedy, but really not much heavier than she had been as a girl, cashmere and pearls, same curly black hair showing just a little silver, a handsome cheerful woman who took very good care of him. He felt comfortable and safe with her, protected by her judgment and her strength. If she had heard about Miss Jersey Cranberries she never showed it. She raised millions for the Orchestra, she ran the house, she entertained the lawyers and the clients, she brought up the children. . . . At the moment her only concern seemed to be Susan Boatwright Anders, fourteen, big, interested in nothing but boys. Caroline had been first in her class when she was fourteen; her daughter's indifference to books and to grades hurt and frustrated her. Look at the boy, Anders told her. The boy has inherited your brains. . . .

Anders felt the sunshine. Anders felt the bourbon. Anders felt a fuzzy warm embrace of relief. Without a mother, without a father, now without even the grandfather who raised him, with no old people around, Anders had barely heard the word "arthritis," had only some dim concepts, advertisements showing smiling old ladies consuming aspirin pills — until that summer morning in a St. Paul hotel room when his feet suddenly hurt so much that he could barely stand on them.

He had been out there with a team of underwriters and lawyers, exploring part of Charlie Conroy's empire to get ready for the sale of Conroy's debentures — but suddenly he couldn't walk. Tommy Sharp, not thirty years old, had taken charge. Tommy Sharp picked up the telephone and spoke directly to Charlie Conroy, who sent out his own plane. That same evening Graham Anders was in the University Hospital.

"Inherited *my* brains?" snorted Caroline. "Are you kidding?" But he knew that she was proud of Francis Boatwright Anders, a tiny bookworm with horn-rimmed glasses, a quiet, obedient, dreamy little boy who, some weeks before, had slipped out of a study hall and down to the Merion railroad station, had ridden in to Thirtieth Street, had asked directions, had walked over and then knocked softly on the closed door of Room 942 in the Ravdin Pavilion. . . .

Suddenly, a tremendous clatter in the sky; all heads turned to watch a helicopter gingerly settling into the adjoining pasture, blowing clouds of dust and hay out from under itself.

A helicopter at a race meet? That year it was still a sensation. "I'll bet that's Ordway, with Charlie Conroy's guests," said Caroline. "Ordway's the only one who could have persuaded the committee to allow a stunt like that," and she was right.

Tommy Sharp had been in San Francisco with Charlie Conroy and Ordway Smith. "That's Bernard Bromberg climbing out of the chopper now. Bromberg Instruments, the pocket calculators. He signed our merger agreement with Mr. Conroy, but the deal hasn't closed yet and Mr. Conroy is throwing a blast for the Brombergs tonight —"

"We know about Charlie Conroy's blast," said Caroline.

"Who is that blonde in the slacks?" asked Graham Anders.

"That's Karin Bromberg, that's his daughter-in-law, I don't see his wife at all, Graham . . . , I'm really glad you're back on your feet, we need you at the office —"

"Well, I'm not on my feet, as you can see. They don't want me to walk yet, although the swelling is gone."

Caroline said, "Tommy, I haven't had a chance to tell you how grateful we are that you got Graham home so quickly."

"Well, we really got a scare, when he suddenly couldn't walk that morning. . . . Say, there's Karin Bromberg all alone over there. May I bring her over?"

Later on he never could remember his first impression — only that he heard the loud laughter from the heart before he saw the round, red face, the face of a laughing child . . . wheat-colored hair tied back into a black silk scarf, a dazzling smile that suddenly vanished as she stared defiantly into his eyes — and wouldn't look away.

Chitchat. Ordway Smith has been showing us your countryside, so beautiful. Did you get to know Ordway out there? Yes, a little. He came to ride at our ranch. A ranch in San Francisco? We don't live in San Francisco, we live in Berkeley, but the ranch is across the Bay, in the hills above Sonoma. She seemed to know a lot about horses, asked questions, the others tried to answer them, but Ordway was the expert, they explained. Ordway was a steeplechaser when he was a boy, what's become of Ordway anyway? He's up there on the hillside, said Tommy Sharp. He's watching the race with field glasses. He's not watching the race, said Caroline. He's watching us.

Ordway Smith had somehow persuaded his client Conroy to buy the old Clarence Pickford Hyde estate in Chester Springs, originally called "Hyde-a-Way" by the Hydes, called just plain "the Hyde Place" by the neighbors, a gigantic unbelievable turreted fairy-tale castle, exact copy of the Château de Montmort in the Île-de-France, surrounded by formal gardens, vegetable gardens, orchards, swimming pool, tennis court, stables. . . . all now magnificently restored by Conroy's decorators and landscape designers — and renamed "Conroy House." On this particular night it rang with the sound of people in evening dress, invited for cocktails and dinner to be followed by chamber music, in honor of Mr. and Mrs. Bernard Bromberg and Mr. and Mrs. Robert Bromberg.

Graham Anders didn't want to stand up during the predinner drinking, so he took a glass from a passing waiter and settled himself on a broad white windowsill.

Ordway Smith came over: "Graham, I won't have much chance to talk to you tonight but I just want to tell you that Tommy Sharp is doing a terrific job on this deal — or deals, I should say, we have Bernard Bromberg's acquisition and Charlie's bond issue going at the same time —"

"Ordway, I told you he would."

"Yes, and I bitched about it when you assigned him instead of Ben Butler —"

"Said Tommy treats you like you're ninety years old and not quite bright!"

"Okay, I was wrong, and I just wanted to tell you —"

"Tell me something else: what's the story on this Karin Bromberg?"

"Ah — what's what story, Graham?"

"In the first place, where's she from? She's German, isn't she?"

"Half German, half Dutch. Her mother's Dutch, she was born in Hamburg during the War. Father was a German rocket engineer. Remember Wernher von Braun? Built the V-2 rockets? The Army brought those people over right after the War ended, to keep them away from the Russians. Karin's father was on von Braun's team, so the whole family was taken to Alabama when she was a baby. Then her parents split up and the mother took her back to Europe. That's where she grew up. She was some kind of a singer, I think."

"Where do the Brombergs come in?" asked Graham Anders.

"The father eventually got out of the Redstone project down in Alabama — I guess it ended or something — anyway, he went to work for Bernard Bromberg's company out on the Coast."

"A rocket engineer?"

"Well, I guess he was basically an instruments guy, and that's still Bromberg's speciality, these pocket calculators are just a sideline."

"This Bromberg hired himself a Nazi engineer?"

"That's an odd remark for you, Graham. I don't know that he was a Nazi."

"Okay, agreed. So Karin was sent out to visit her father?"

"That's right, and she met Bob Bromberg, that's Bernard's son —"

"What's he like?"

"What do you mean what's he like?"

"Why isn't he here?"

"He's cool on the deal. I mean, he thought he was going to inherit his father's company and now his father sells it to Charlie Conroy —"

"If he's cool on the deal, what's his wife doing here?"

"Graham, there's Charlie waving to me, we can talk about this tomorrow."

Anders looked across the big living room, watching her being introduced to people, seeing her suddenly looking back at him over other people's shoulders, knowing that she was going to come over and talk to him and that Caroline would see her do that. Take it easy now, that is quite a bundle but you don't do that anymore, that is something like drinking and smoking, if you really have to quit you can quit if you have the will power, it hurts people and you are just going to quit it, and he took a deep breath and a big sip of his drink and thought about Francis Boatwright Anders peeking into the hospital room, and by the time he had made up his mind to get up off the comfortable windowsill, she was sitting down beside him . . .

"Can I come in, Dad? . . . Oh, excuse me!"

"Hey! . . . Sure, come in. . . . My God! Of course, come in, I'm so glad to see you. . . . You know Miss Carpenter, don't you? She's brought me some stuff to read."

"Good morning, Boatie. I'm Laura Carpenter, I used to be your father's secretary, it's nice to meet you. You can sit right over here. I'll move these things —"

"Aren't you supposed to be in school, buddy?"

"Yeah, Dad, but I wanted to see you. You've been sick a long time, but I didn't know you'd be busy —"

"I'm not busy. I'm just lying here flat on my back, trying to catch up on my mail but it's great to see you. . . . Would you like some . . . Could we get him a Coke or something?"

"Sure. Would you like a Coke, Boatie? I think they have ginger ale and Pepsi and some kind of orange drink, and coffee, of course."

"Can I have a Pepsi?"

"Coming right up."

"Well! It's really nice of you to come and see me. You're not going to get in trouble at school, are you?"

"Is that lady really your secretary?"

"No, she used to be. Long time ago. She's got another job and she's going to school now. Wants to learn about stocks and bonds, about investments."

"She looks like a movie star, Dad."

"A movie star? Tell her that, she'll be pleased to hear it. As a matter of fact she was a beauty queen when she was in high school. She was Miss Jersey Cranberries."

"Dad, can you show me what's the matter with you?"

"Can I show you? Sure I can. Just pull this blanket off, over this way, and I'll pull up the pajama legs. . . . Not much to see, is there?"

"Your ankles are all puffed up."

"Yeah, and the knees."

"Can I touch it here, Dad?"

"If you're careful."

"Does that hurt?"

"A little. It's getting better, I think. You see, it's full of fluid. They stick a needle in and they draw out this brown liquid —"

"*Yuk!*"

"Yuk is right, but there's nothing I can do about it except take the medicines they give me and wait for them to let me out of here."

"Ma won't tell me how long you're going to be sick."

"It isn't that she won't tell you, buddy. She doesn't know. The doctors don't know."

"You mean you'd have to stay in here?"

"No, I hope not, but I might have to stay in a wheelchair for a while."

"Good thing you never liked tennis. . . . I don't like it either, Dad."

"Well, you ought to learn tennis. Fellow like you should play a good game of tennis."

"You never did, Dad."

"Listen, buddy, don't take me as an example. I never did most things I was supposed to do —"

"Here's your Pepsi, Boatie."

"Oh, thank you, Miss —"

"You call me Laura, Boatie. What is it your father is supposed to do?"

"He says you look like a movie star."

"Ah, that's sweet of you, Boatie. I wish I was a movie star, but right now I'd be happy if I learn to become a securities analyst."

"What's that?"

"Well, your father will explain what that is. . . . Why don't you stay and have lunch with him? I've got to get back now — I'll stop by on the way home this evening if you want anything. I'll call, okay?"

"Okay, thank you very much."
"It's nice to have met you, Boatie."
"It's nice to have met you too . . . Laura."

"Why did she leave, Dad?"
"She had to get back to her office. She works during the day and goes to school at night."
"Did she want to leave us alone, Dad?"
"Maybe. She knows we don't see much of each other."
"Dad, could you write me a note for my school?"
"Sure. Don't let me forget. Didn't you tell your mother you were coming in to see me?"
"No . . . I didn't think about it until I was in school. . . . Dad, did the Nazis kill your father?"
"What? Who said the Nazis killed my father?"
"A kid on the train. A guy I ride to school with, he said his father told him your father was a famous writer and the Nazis put him in a concentration camp —"
"They did put him in a concentration camp, but that's not where he died, Boatie. I've told you about my father, there's a book about him, his biography, we've got it. It's in German, but you can look at the pictures —"
"I did look at the pictures, but I never understood about it, Dad. Will you tell me about it?"
"Sure! Of course! I guess we just assume that children pick up these things. As a matter of fact, nobody ever told me anything either, I had to find out for myself, much later. . . . My father was born in Germany, in Mainz, that's a very old town on the Rhine, and he was an officer in the German army in the First World War, and he was wounded, and then after the War he went to Berlin and he wrote songs and poems and plays, and then one of his plays became very successful, made a lot of money. *Trompeten*, it was called. Trumpets. There was a song in it, the "Fusilierlied," the song of the fusiliers, it became a popular song, became a folk song. My father suddenly had some money. He was able to travel. When he was in London he met my mother, a girl called Peggy Graham from Philadelphia, her father was a lawyer here, she had quit college and gone to London, she had small parts in plays in London. They got married, lived in London for a while. I was born there. But they moved around a lot, lived in Paris, lived in the south of France, anywhere they wanted to, because

my father was earning a lot of money from his plays and also from some movies he wrote. . . .

"But then the Nazis came to power in Germany and everything changed. My father's plays were against war, against the people who start wars, he'd been in a war, he'd seen what war was really like, people getting burned to cinders, blown to pieces — and all for no reason, you know. He put all that into his plays. . . . Well, Hitler didn't want the German people to see plays and movies opposing war, because he was getting ready for another war, for the Second World War, he wanted enthusiasm for his new army. . . . The Nazis burned books they didn't like, really burned them in bonfires, the Storm Troopers beat people up, arrested them, put them into concentration camps, tortured them, killed them. . . . Well, this was in 1934, we were living in England and my father heard that the Nazis had put his publisher into Dachau, which was their first concentration camp, a model for the others. The publisher was an older man, a close friend. So my father went back to Germany, went to Berlin to see people he knew, tried to pull strings to get his friend out. He misjudged the situation. Instead of getting the publisher out, he got arrested and thrown into Dachau himself. My father was at least nominally a Catholic, from the Rhine, but he had written these plays. . . . I never knew any of this, they never told me a word about it, but when I was in college, this Professor Malachowski who was writing the biography came to talk to me and he showed me this picture they took of my father. . . . I don't know why he didn't put it into the book, but I can still see that picture when I close my eyes. . . . This is more than you wanted to know, buddy." Anders took a deep breath and looked at the ceiling.

"No, Dad!" The boy was leaning forward in his chair. "Tell me what was in the picture!"

"It wasn't really a bad picture, on the surface," said Anders. "In fact they published it in the newspapers to show how well they were treating Gustaf Anders, this traitorous writer. It seemed to have been taken in front of a barracks, and you can see some barbed wire fencing in the background, and these two tall SS men in black uniforms, with death's heads on their caps and swastika armbands, are looking down at my father. My father was a rather small thin man. He is wearing one of these striped pajama-looking prison suits. His hair is shaved off. A white slip with some number on it is pinned to his jacket. He is standing at attention German-army style, with his fingers pressed against his trouser seams and his shoulders thrown back. The SS guards have their hands on their hips and are grinning down at him in the most disgusting way. My father has his chin up and is staring over the photographer's shoulder, no expression at all. . . . I can't really explain it, boy, but by the time I saw that picture I had been stationed in Austria, I knew something about what went on in those camps, they had him absolutely helpless in there, they could do anything they wanted, just the feeling behind that picture. . . ."

"But Dad, what happened to him?"

"They let him out after three or four months. I mean, my mother and my grandfather got him out. They raised holy hell in London and in Washington and with the American Embassy in Berlin. This was in the early days of Hitler's regime. They couldn't hold a man with an international reputation and an American wife with American political connections, and so one day my mother got a call from the American Embassy in London and she took a boat over to Holland and met him at some border crossing point, some railroad station just inside Germany where the Gestapo turned him over and she brought him back to London and put him right into the hospital. He was never really the same again. They messed him up emotionally."

"Dad, you didn't know any of this?"

"Not at this time. I was six years old. They told me he'd been working on a book in France, that he'd been in an accident and they didn't want to talk about it."

"You mean your father didn't report on what happened in the camp? He didn't write about it?"

Anders shook his head. "They kept his friend, the publisher. They explained what they would do to him if one word from Gustaf Anders appeared anywhere — one word about what happened in Dachau. Of course in the end they killed the publisher anyway, but by that time my father was long dead himself. . . . This is all in Malachowski's book —"

"But I can't read it, Dad!"

"Well, my father had a bad time in England. He couldn't concentrate. He couldn't sleep. He wouldn't play the piano and sing songs for me. He would scream at me and at my mother. And he didn't have any money now, because the Germans cut it off. I think they probably had to live on my mother's money, or money my grandfather sent them —"

"Couldn't your father write in English?"

"No. He was a German writer. As a matter of fact, I'm not sure he ever learnt much English, and I know my mother never learnt much German, and it's a puzzle to me how they even talked to each other. I just don't remember that it was a problem. . . . When I was a kid there was a song: 'You don't have to know the language if you know the language of love' —"

"You know the language of love, Mr. Anders?"

"Oh, hi. This is my son, Boatwright, come to see his sick old man. We call him Boatie. This is Miss Bolognese, come to give me a pill to make my face blow up like a balloon —"

"Hello, Boatie, why is your dad looking so blue? We're going to send him home pretty soon."

"Will you tell them to bring another lunch?"

"You want three lunches?"

"*Two* lunches!"

"Right, two lunches. Nice to have met you, Boatie."

"Thank you, Miss . . . Dad, you were telling me —"

"Yeah. Well, we were living in England, a house on Lord Cranborne's place, he was a friend of my parents and he gave them a cottage on his place. Near Sevenoaks, in Kent. But there was nothing for my father to do, and then the Spanish Civil War began — You know anything about the Spanish Civil War?"

"Not much, Dad."

"Well, you don't need to know much about it, but it was terribly important then, I guess about 1936. The Spaniards had a republican government. General Franco and a lot of other army officers made a revolution against the government and they had a civil war — a very bloody terrible war — and people from all over Europe joined in. Hitler and Mussolini sent tanks and airplanes to help Franco. Stalin sent tanks and airplanes to help the Republicans. Communists and Socialists and people who were just against fascism went to Spain as volunteers to fight on the Republican side."

"What happened?"

"Franco won."

"And your father fought in that war?"

"He didn't go to fight, he went as a war correspondent for a Swiss newspaper. But he got mixed up in a very complicated fight between the Stalinist Communists and the Trotskyist Communists — never mind, it's too involved, I don't understand it myself, and nobody really knows what happened. . . . The Communists were all supposed to be on the same side, the side of the Republican government, but actually they fought against each other as hard as they fought against Franco. . . . There were these International Brigades, volunteers from all over the place, English, Americans, French, Russians, lots of Germans, refugees from Hitler, and apparently my father got to know some officers in a German brigade, and one night they took him along on a mission, a mission to kill somebody, a mission to kill a man they thought was a spy. They did kill that man, but they killed my father too!"

"Why did they do that, Dad?"

"Nobody knows for sure . . . but I met a man . . . many years later I met a man, in Austria . . . I think he was there, I think he was in that German unit of the International Brigades, I think he was on that mission, and he said something. . . . I think my father tried to interfere in some way — apparently my father tried to help this man they'd been sent to kill, so they had to kill them both. Nobody knows exactly what happened. My mother just got a telegram from another reporter, a friend of my father's, his body had been found in a street somewhere, a suburb of Madrid. After that, my mother decided to go home, she brought me over here to live with your great-grandfather, in your great-grandfather's house in Gladwyne, and they sent me to Episcopal Academy and I grew up right here."

"But your mother went away again, didn't she?"

"That's right."

"Why did she, Dad?"

"Well . . . you see, she got married again. This John Cranmore was sent to Washington to work at the British Embassy, and he would come up to visit her . . . and then they got married, and then he had to go off to war in the British army and so she went to London to be with him as long as she could but then they sent him off to Egypt and he got killed. . . ."

"But your mother didn't come home?"

"No, she didn't. She liked it in London. Air raids, danger, excitement, people . . . I don't know, she'd been sort of an actress there before, when she met my father in the first place and now, back in London during the war, I guess she still knew people, she got a job with a company that put on plays for the troops, they traveled around and put on plays by Shakespeare and plays by Somerset Maugham for the soldiers, and later when the British and the Americans moved into Italy, this troupe she was in, they went down to Italy to put on their plays . . . and one night she was killed in a car accident. . . ."

"And you were all alone, Dad!"

"No, I wasn't all alone, I was with your great-grandfather, he took very, very good care of me —"

"Dad, hey, do the nurses know you've got that bottle in there?"

"They sure do. . . . You see that plastic thing there? That thing has ice in it. Would you take a glass from the bathroom and put some ice in it and give it to me, please?"

FOUR

1969: The Third Trustee

The hunt races and Charlie Conroy's party for the Brombergs had been on a Saturday. On Monday morning Anders woke up in the empty house on Juniper Lane. Caroline was at work and the children were at school. Anders could not walk very well, but he could drive his car, so he went looking for Karin Bromberg. He knew that her father-in-law had gone off to New York with Ordway Smith and a group from Conyers & Dean to close the deals with Charlie Conroy; he left a note telling Caroline that he was driving to New York to see if he could help out at the closing. Something might come up. . . .

He didn't drive to New York. He drove into the rolling hills of Chester County, he passed the massive renaissance bulk of the Hyde Place, and turned into the driveway of Ordway Smith's beautiful old farm.

Why was he doing it, when he knew it could get him into so much trouble? How was he going to explain this visit if Marion Smith was home? He knew the questions, but he didn't know the answers, he only knew that he couldn't forget the hearty laugh and the breathtaking smile and the steady cobalt eyes that never looked away, and he was amazed to meet someone this young who had read his father's plays, who had read Malachowski's biography of Gustaf Anders, so here he was driving into Ordway's stableyard.

Ordway's daughter Ailsa, a freckle-faced fifteen-year-old who should have been in school, came striding out of the stable in boots and blue jeans and a gingham shirt. "How are you doing, Mr. Anders?" Smiling, polite but puzzled.

"I'm fine, Ailsa. Is Mrs. Bromberg around someplace?"

"Yeah, she's in there, she's taking the saddle off Minnie."

"Your father's mare?"

The girl nodded, put her hands on the door of his car and put her head through the open window.

"Mr. Anders, that lady rides like a son-of-a-bitch!" She looked pale beneath the suntan and the freckles. An angry Indian maid. How had Ordway and Marion produced this dark Kiowa? *"That lady jumped Minnie across the waterfall!"*

"That dangerous?"

"Aw shit, Mr. Anders, the Pickerings' pony fell in, two years ago, and it was swept into the millrace, and they had to *shoot* it!" and then a deeper voice "Well, good afternoon," and there was Karin Bromberg, also in boots and jeans and a tight blue work shirt with the sleeves rolled high above her caramel elbows . . . she looked at him quite seriously, squinting in the bright sunshine, and as she reached up to pull off the black silk scarf and shake out the golden hair he saw that under her arms her shirt was stained black with sweat and her eyes never left his eyes and he was feeling high on the cortisone but all the way deep down inside he knew that this was something new, something that might get out of control.

She came closer, stood beside Ailsa, and stroked the gleaming fender of his car. "Oh, I love these old three hundreds! My father had one."

"Well, I'm old enough to be your father."

"Not quite, I think. Will you let me drive it?"

He had never allowed anyone else to drive it, nor had anybody ever asked.

"You know how?"

"I show you." She walked around to the left side, expertly flipped up the complicated door that hinged on the roof, and climbed in as Anders awkwardly lifted himself across the gearshift into the other seat.

Karin settled behind the wheel, pulled down the door, then suddenly leaned across Anders so that her arm rested on his chest. She felt damp and smooth and she smelled of perfume. "Ailsa — my dear — I think I frightened you, but you should know that I have *never* hurt a horse! Good-bye, and thank you very much for letting me ride Minnie, such a kind, obedient old girl," and then her hands moved fast: ignition, handbrake, clutch, shift reverse and turn, clutch, shift forward and turn, *kah — room!* Anders felt his head snap back as the Mercedes shot out of the stable court and down the long driveway, spraying pebbles.

He had never let anybody drive his car, and he had never seen anybody drive anything the way she drove the winding country lanes that afternoon, her eyes on the road, both hands gripping the wheel except when she moved one to shift, her two front teeth biting down upon her lower lip. She roared past every car they encountered, sometimes missing an oncoming car by inches. Other drivers honked in fear or in fury.

"You worried?" she asked, her eyes on the road.

"No." That was true. He wasn't worried, but he knew he ought to be. Why wasn't he?

"I've never hurt a horse and I've never wrecked a car."

"Ever been arrested?"

She faced him, a sudden smile. "*Many* times." Eyes back on the road. "Goddamnit!" A frown. She couldn't get around a pickup truck bouncing bales of hay. "Can't you show me where we can really *go?*"

They were not far from that stretch of uncompleted superhighway, eight miles of empty cement snaking across some of the most beautiful landscape in the world. It was closed to traffic, but Anders knew a dirt road across a cow pasture, where the cement trucks went in.

There was a gate, and this time the gate was locked, but Karin took the screwdriver from his glove compartment, quickly removed the whole latch assembly, then stood back and held open the wire gate, grinning like a naughty child, as he drove the car through. . . . One minute after she was back behind the wheel, she had the needle quivering above 120 miles per hour, where the dial is marked in red.

He didn't look at the road. He looked at Karin. Her expression was changing. She seemed to be drifting into an ecstatic trance, as if the vibration, the roaring engine, the wind — and the possibility that a tire might blow out — were doing something to her body. Her mouth was set, eyes open too wide, lips compressed, red face getting redder, breasts heaving. . . .

"You're going to run out of road here in two minutes," he said quietly.

She nodded, opened her mouth to draw breath, took her foot off the gas, waited for the car to slow down, made a huge U-turn driving right across the center strip, and pressed the gas pedal to the floor again.

She rolled to a stop just in front of the wire gate, took the car out of gear, applied the handbrake and pushed up the door, but she did not get out. Instead, she expelled her breath, slumped back into the seat, and closed her eyes.

The soft breeze blew dust off the dirt road. Under the hood the engine idled a deep dark rumble.

Her eyes still closed, she reached out and took his hand. "Could you just hold me for one moment?"

So Anders took her in his arms, feeling her heart pounding against his chest, feeling her wet face against his face, feeling his blood rising — but also in another part of himself hearing the voices in the overlooking farms and manor houses telephoning the state police, so he took her shoulders and held her back a little and looked into her face and said, "I think we'd better do this someplace else," and she opened her eyes and smiled her heartwrenching smile and said: "Will you buy me a *big* glass of beer?"

Double B Ranch
R.D., Sonoma, California

14 NOVEMBER

Sehr geehrter Herr Dr. Anders!

(You are sure your secretary does not open your mail??)

(You said write auf Deutsch but I really don't believe you can read it any more so I will write auf English but you must promise *please!* that you will tear it up and throw it away as soon as you have read it. A man of your advanced age and *strenuous* lifestyle may drop dead at any moment and who will read the letters in the drawer of your desk?)

You did not think that I would really write and I tried for two weeks not to write but as you discovered I'm not so strong and want very much to talk to you again.

Well, as to business matters, the collapse of our merger with Mr. Conroy's company has made things better out here. Of course Bob and his mother were against it all along and Dad I think had second thoughts about Mr. Conroy, after they signed their agreement. Dad is so accustomed to being the boss of his world that he would find it terribly difficult not to be the boss and he realized the more he came to know Mr. Conroy that all the talk about being partners was really only talk because there can be only one boss.

I don't understand the whole story about why Ordway Smith would not allow the deal to close. Our lawyers think he was probably right, but it might have gone otherwise if Graham Anders wasn't sick. (I don't tell them he is not so sick as all that!)

You said I can talk to you if I want to talk to somebody. It is a strange feeling. The second I saw you at the horse race, sitting on the tailgate of the station wagon, and looking across your glass into my eyes, that second I knew — well maybe I only felt a shock, like you recognize somebody even if you have never seen them before? but that day when I got into your 300 SL and sat beside you, then I really *knew!* It is like a loud engine, a compressor or something like that, you gradually don't hear the noise any more until it stops and then the silence feels so marvelous and that is how I felt when I drove away in your car — and all the rest of that day with you.

You asked why did I marry Bob? Long story. I told you I wanted to be an opera singer. I had lessons all my life, I went to a special school when I was sixteen, then I even got a job in a little opera house. Coburg in Bavaria. You know we have opera houses in every little town. But of course it was only in the chorus, and why should I sit around these little towns singing in the chorus? They have wonderful opera in Hamburg, but I was not good enough, and I didn't want to stay there anyway because my mother had married a man I did not like at all (Gottfried Gesstler, he rebuilt his father's factories after the war and is very rich again but I have never liked him) so I visited my father in California. But I was not so close to my father either. My father was what you call a "cold fish," really only interested in his work, my mother left him when I was very small and took me back to Europe and I only saw my father on such visits, every few years. He was always nice and polite to me, but really not like a father. Then I met Bob at a party in Berkeley and he was so enthusiastic for me, he took me to dinner, he took me dancing, he took me to parties, he introduced me to his family, he sent me flowers, he told me I was the most beautiful girl he had ever seen and kept on and on that I must marry him and finally I thought Why not? He looks good and he loves me. His father seems to like me too. There are so many interesting things to do in San Francisco and in Berkeley and the Brombergs know a lot of musical people and artists and university people. Maybe I could sing here too? I liked their style of life here in California and I could ride the horses on Dad's ranch and swim in the pool and play the piano and did not have to go back to singing in the chorus in places like Coburg or Wiesbaden or to marry somebody my mother and Herr Gesstler want me to marry — so that is why I married Bob.

For a while it worked the way I thought it would. We did have a good life. I did have the little girls with Bob. They are good girls and I take good care of them. But with Bob it has not worked. He is a weak person and he doesn't like himself. I don't know why. Perhaps because Dad is such a strong person, as you saw a big strong heavy man, an aviator in the war, a man who started his own company and made it successful and pushed Bob so hard to be successful too but always finding things wrong, always telling Bob he does this wrong and that wrong — all his life until it has driven Bob nearly crazy. He should not work for his father. He should get away from his father and start a life of his own, but he can't seem to do that either.

So Bob inside himself has gone his own way and I have gone my own way. We live in the same house but we live different lives and I spend more and more time out here in these windy warm dry hills. We have a beautiful place here, an old big house built by Spanish ranchers before the Americans got here. Ordway Smith and Tommy Sharp visited me here and Ordway had a good exciting ride with me but Tommy Sharp did not approve, I think. I play the piano when I am alone or listen to my records and now I have you to write to.

Now I will come to the hard part of this letter: I think you know how much I want to see you again, but you may not want to see me again when I explain that I told you 3 lies and I must tell you that I have had to tell lies all my life and do it very easily — but this time seems to be different because I don't want to see you again until I "confess" — as to a priest?

Lie No. 1: "I never lost a horse." The Smith girl was so angry I had to say that. When I was about the same age she is now I was on a point-to-point race up in Holstein and I tried to get around another girl by galloping along a railroad track (strengstens verboten!) and my horse slipped and broke a leg and ribs and they had to shoot it. (I broke two ribs also!) And last year, out here, I had another accident with a beautiful arab gelding Dad had given me — I thought we could clear this deep ravine in our mountains out here. We *had* jumped it before, but this time a rock slipped under the rear hoof and we fell *into* the ravine thirty feet . . . all right, enough!

Lie No. 2: "I never lost a car." My mother (really Herr Gessler) gave me a little red MG two-seater for my 18th birthday but it had an oil leak and I did not check the oil often enough and I drove it very fast on the Hamburg–Kiel Autobahn without oil and destroyed the engine. I used to do my shopping in Berkeley in a VW Squareback and I made a mistake trying to pass some old lady in a station wagon who was crawling along these steep curved roads we have in the hills above the town and I could not get around the curve — I was going too fast to make the curve — so we rolled off the hill — *bad* Karin! But I think you saw that I am a pretty good driver — usually.

Lie No. 3: Well, this is the only important one, the terrible one, the other thing that you guessed and I said No, he is like a father to me, I call him Dad because the little girls and Bob call him that, he has been more of a father to me than my own father was, but of course it is true as you guessed. How could I answer to you Yes, it is true and expect that you would ever see me again? Now you know why you must throw this away as soon as you have read it, because you think of your partners or your wife or your children reading this someday and knowing why I feel you are the only person I can talk to about this.

How did it happen? I cannot explain, even to myself. I was lonely. He was kind. I was weak. He was strong. He is a man who always gets what he wants, but this time I know he feels terrible guilt and it is hurting him inside — so badly that he cannot sometimes do any more what he liked to do so much, and I *know* all this is going to end in *disaster* unless I find a solution.

* * *

Change of Tempo: my mother announces she and Herr Gesstler are coming to New York, between Christmas and New Years. You know of course the Brombergs are Jews. I was worried at first how they would feel about me but they have been good to me (except Bob's mother not entirely) and, of course, I came here in the first place because my father worked for them. However, Herr Gesstler's father, as everybody knows, was an *early* supporter of Adolf Hitler, gave money to Adolf Hitler as early as 1927, during the war had prisoners from concentration camps working in his factories, was even put in jail by the British after the war, and the Brombergs definitely do not receive Herr und Frau Gesstler out here — so when my mother comes to America I go to see her in New York or whatever island they may be sunning themselves on and usually bring the girls along.

Why should Mr. Anders be interested in all this family history? Because I will be at Hotel Carlyle from 26th December to 30th December and Bob is taking the girls to Hawaii this year, and my mother just today wrote that they are *not* coming to New York that week after all, but I have not told that to anybody — except you.

This is the longest letter I have ever written, and I don't know exactly how to end it.

MAY I SAY YOUR FRIEND?
K.

P.S. Should you wish to write me, please

address me c/o Carola von Stumm
8324 Buena Vista Drive
Berkeley, CA 94708
(*old school friend*)

He knew perfectly well that he shouldn't go, but he went.

He could walk by then. She wore a black beret and a black fitted wool coat and boots of soft black leather, and she took his arm and they walked east on Seventy-sixth Street through an evening of gently falling snow, and neither of them said a word.

She took him to a restaurant she liked. They had no reservation but were put at the best table. He sat close beside her in the banquette. Her cheeks still glowed from the cold, and he thought she was the most beautiful woman in a room full of beautiful women. The waiters seemed to think so too.

In the darkness, sliding smoothly beneath him and gasping into his ear, she suddenly began to laugh.

Startled, he stopped.

"Ah no, don't stop, dear!" She moved urgently but he could still feel her laughing.

"What's so funny?"

"I'm happy, I laugh when I'm happy, you're making me happy, Oh do it, do it, do it, do it, do it, do it. . . . Yes!"

Later: "You've never been with a woman who laughed?"

"Not just at that moment, no."

"Strange. When you feel so wonderful, so happy, why shouldn't you laugh?"

"Well, no reason, of course. I guess we think of laughter as being caused by something funny. Maybe we take love too seriously. . . . Hey, listen, I don't think I can, right now —"

She slid across his body. "I think you can, dear. With me, you can," and she was right.

Still later: "Can you stay another night with me?"

"Well, I said I'd be home for dinner tomorrow."

"There is a beautiful concert at Carnegie Hall, only Handel and Bach, arias and cantatas, if you could come with me . . ."

"I'll see what I can do."

She was already asleep, her lips against his throat.

She had ordered orange juice and coffee and rolls from room service. They ate in silence for a while, reading sections of *The New York Times*.

When he looked up from his paper, he found her staring hard across the table, a strapping, red-faced young woman wrapped loosely in a navy blue bathrobe with white polka dots.

"You feel it too, don't you?"

He drank some coffee, then nodded.

"That we have been having breakfast together for years?"

"Yes."

"What are we going to do, Graham?"

"About what?"

"About our lives."

"I don't know what we're going to do about our lives, but you'd better tell me what you want to do about today, because I'll have to make some telephone calls. . . ."

She knew her way around New York, and the people in the art galleries and antique shops of Madison Avenue knew her. He followed her in and out of these establishments as she inspected a Spanish refectory table from the eighteenth century, a charcoal drawing by Käthe Kollwitz, a Pascin etching of a tiny silvery nude —

"You like her?"

"She's beautiful."

"May I give her to you? A souvenir?"

He took her arm. "Let's go to lunch."

"I can't give you a present?" Touching her breast against the back of his hand.

"Where would I put it? And whose money are you using?"

"You don't worry about that!"

"Well, I do worry about that! Where do you want to eat?"

The first thing she said when she awoke was: "Do you have to go now?"

"No."

Up on her elbow in an instant her face above his. "You can stay another night with me?"

"Yes," he said, and she kissed him softly, for a long time. Then she got out of bed and walked to the dresser. They had bought two long-stemmed wineglasses, a bottle of Chablis and a bottle of Cognac.

"I forgot to put the wine in the refrigerator," she said. "Will you drink some Cognac now?"

"Why not?"

She disappeared into the bathroom with the wine, then returned, poured one glass half full of Cognac and carried it over to him.

"What did you tell them?"

"I said I had to stay over and spend the evening with Boris Fleischer." He took the glass and she slid in beside him.

"Who is Boris Fleischer?"

Anders took a sip, gave the glass back to her, threw his head back on the pillow and stared up at the ceiling.

"Who is Boris Fleischer? Good question. Boris Fleischer is different things to different people. I guess I could say he's become one of the most important people in my life."

"Want to tell me?"

"Want to hear about it?"

"One of the most important people in your life?" She put the glass on the bedside table and curled herself around his flank. "I want to learn everything about your life."

He tried to remember how long it had been since he felt such a sense of release, such a relief from pressure; his body was utterly relaxed while his mind was wildly stimulated. He wanted to talk.

"All right, this has to do with Boatwright Corporation, that's the company my wife's family began, they made a lot of money until after the Second World War and then the railroad business got bad and they couldn't sell enough of their locomotives and the prices of the Boatwright stock went down — and kept going down. In 1960, I guess it was, this mysterious Mr. Fleischer first appeared. He bought a lot of Boatwright stock and asked for a seat on the Board, and they wouldn't even talk to him."

"Why not?"

"Well, they didn't like him and they were afraid of him. He had a bad reputation. He had been a Rumanian grain speculator before the war. Jewish. By some miracle he managed to stay out of the German concentration camps — although I later found out that his whole family was killed. After the war he was in American DP camps in Germany, then got himself into Palestine just before they set up the State of Israel, but then he didn't like Israel — he told me once they set up a new Sparta for themselves and he wasn't a Spartan — and somehow he was able to get to New York."

"And of course he made a lot of money," said Karin.

"He made a lot of money. He was a brilliant man, starting over I guess for the third time, willing to work hard night and day, willing to take risks that would scare the hell out of more sheltered people, a man who had been forced to adapt very fast to changing conditions just to stay alive. He learned our rules, and then he played our games a lot faster than some of our people were used to, and he won the games, and the people who lost the games didn't like him very much. To put it mildly. He'd get hold of one company, load it up with debt and use the money he borrowed to buy the next company, then he'd borrow more money on the credit of the first two companies to buy a third one, and by 1960, by the time he came after Boatwright, he'd accumulated a pretty impressive pyramid."

"Sounds like your friend Charlie Conroy," said Karin, moving her damp thigh.

"No," said Anders. "Maybe the way they got started isn't too different, but underneath they're very different people. Charlie got to the point where he was just buying companies to buy companies, he lost interest in running companies. Boris Fleischer doesn't do that; Boris likes to buy sick companies and make them well — like a doctor."

"But the Boatwrights wouldn't talk to him?"

"Wouldn't talk to him. So he started a proxy fight. Tried to persuade the stockholders to vote for his slate of directors. But we beat him. We still had the votes. The Boatwright family held on to their shares, voted their shares against his slate, and the Philadelphia banks that held a lot of shares in trust accounts, they stuck with the old management, and so we beat him off. That was the summer of 1961. But we knew damn well that it was only a temporary victory, because the stock price was down, all the people in the family and the banks, they were just sick about it, our heritage is going down the drain and all that, and we knew that if Fleischer came back and put out a tender offer he would be able to get control. It was just a question of time, or a question of how soon Fleischer could raise enough money to do that. But then a very strange thing happened."

"Something with you?"

"Yeah, with me. Of course I was in Conyers & Dean, I was sort of in charge of this whole fight against Fleischer, then when we beat him that summer they told me to take a vacation, and just at that time a friend of mine, a law school professor, got me invited to attend a law seminar in Salzburg, in Austria. Took me along. Place called Schloss Fyrmian, right outside Salzburg. A little eighteenth-century palace, on a lake."

"Oh yes, a beautiful place. I have seen it."

"It was a sentimental trip for me, because I'd been a soldier in Salzburg when I was eighteen, I was right there when they started the first seminar in 1947, I knew the girl who owned the Schloss —"

"Another German girl?"

"Well, never mind about her, she hasn't got anything to do with this —"

"But with your life? I'm learning about your life, I thought."

"You want to hear about Fleischer?"

Her breasts moved against his shoulder. "Yes, dear. Go on with Mr. Fleischer, please."

"All right, one night toward the end of this seminar in Schloss Fyrmian, we put on a sort of amateur show. They call it a Bierabend, they serve beer to the audience. People from the different countries put on little shows, anything they can do, making fun of the professors, things that happened during the seminar . . . the thing is a lot of fun, turns into a party. . . .

"Another thing: they often have guests at the Schloss. The seminar is dependent on contributions, from foundations and from rich people, and of course people who have given money, or who have been asked to give money, they like to be invited for dinner if they happened to be in Salzburg, as you say it's a beautiful place — well anyway, on this evening, as usual, there were some guests for dinner and they were in the audience of this show down in the great hall after dinner —"

"Were you part of the show?" asked Karin.

"Right, I was in the show, singing and dancing and carrying on, having a fine time, and when the show was over and the audience was milling around in the hall — great big hall lit only by candelabra — I felt somebody tug my elbow and here was this little man. Little man with thick glasses. Business suit. Never seen him before, apparently one of the dinner guests. Some big gun from somewhere. So he asked was I Graham Anders from Conyers & Dean? I guess somebody already told him that. Then he said, 'You don't remember me, do you?' Well, I didn't remember him. So he says: 'I've heard a lot about you this last year, but I only realized this minute that we've met before, a long time ago, and right here in this Schloss!' He says: 'It was 1947, in a snowstorm, I was with some people who came across the Untersberg in a snowstorm. The Austrian police? the American sergeant? You remember that night?' Well, of course I remembered that night but I still didn't know who he was, why was I supposed to know him? So he smiles and says 'I'm Boris Fleischer!' "

"You have never met him before?" asked Karin. "You had never seen his picture?"

"No, I told you they wouldn't let us talk to him or meet with him, and he never allowed himself to be photographed — and if I had seen a photograph I wouldn't have recognized somebody I only saw for a few minutes, in a snowstorm, fourteen years before. Fourteen years!"

"What did he mean about the snowstorm?"

Anders turned away, expelling his breath. They had not bothered to close the curtains. It was dark outside now, and the lights of the city illuminated the ceiling. Down on Seventy-sixth Street, cars honked.

"The Untersberg is a little mountain outside Salzburg, it's on the border between Bavaria and Austria. The Austrian police woke me up in the middle of the night, they had caught a group of people — men, women, little kids — who had come from a camp for what we called 'displaced persons' up near Munich — Jews trying to get to Palestine. Only we weren't supposed to let them get there. We were supposed to arrest them and put them back into a camp. Well, the Austrians were scared to handle Jews, this was right after the war, remember — just wouldn't do it, couldn't do it without Americans, so they woke me up in the middle of the night. . . ."

Anders stopped. He didn't know why, but he suddenly didn't want to remember this part anymore. The scene with Major French?

"What's wrong, dear?" Karin lay on her side, watching him.

Well, he had been right and Major French had been wrong, so why not tell her the story?

"What year were you born?" he asked her suddenly.

"In nineteen hundred forty-three, why do you ask that?"

Why indeed? thought Anders. "You don't want to hear all this ancient history," he said. "The point is, we didn't put them in a camp, we let them proceed on their trip, and after all those years Boris Fleischer remembered my face, and somehow that night, in the candlelight among all those people, he and I became real to each other, not just abstractions like the Raider or Boatwright's Lawyer, we had an opportunity to talk, to get to know each other. . . . We did some things in Salzburg together. Went to the opera. Walked around town alone. Got to know each other a little. He convinced me that he didn't want to destroy Boatwright, that he wanted to get it back to earning profits, get it out of locomotives and into things where money could be made. And maybe I convinced him that I could get the Boatwrights to listen to him. When he was leaving Salzburg I went out to the airport and we had a talk. He suggested an armistice in our war."

"A peace treaty?"

"A peace treaty in the form of a five-year voting trust. He said he would put up his stock into the trust if the Boatwrights would put theirs in too, and then the voting trustees would control the company. So I told him that wouldn't work. Who would the trustees be? He suggested one for the Boatwrights and one for himself. I told him that wouldn't work either, because the Boatwrights wouldn't trust anybody he picked as the third trustee, or anybody he agreed to. And you know what he said?"

Karin's teeth gleamed. She took the glass from his hands and sat up to drink. "I think I can guess. He asked, 'Will the Boatwrights trust *you* to be the third trustee?' "

He brought his arm all the way around her smooth broad back. "You're pretty smart."

"Finish the story."

"Story is still going on, but you're perfectly right. We finally worked out a voting trust, with enough stock to control the company, with Fleischer himself as one trustee and my wife's Aunt Susan Boatwright as another trustee, and me as the third trustee. And without going into all the business details, Fleischer managed to turn the company around, he got us out of locomotives and into tractor trailers, he sold a lot of the real estate for very good prices, he bought a little pharmaceutical company in California, an oil drilling equipment company in Oklahoma, a couple of cable TV companies, he hired smart young men to run these things and if they did well he paid them so much that they became millionaires themselves, and by the time the trust ran out, Boatwright stock was worth more than it ever had been — at which point the banks and most of the Boatwrights bailed out."

"Your wife's family sold their stock?"

"Most of them did. Wanted to diversify. Didn't want all their eggs in one basket, in Boris Fleischer's basket. But Caroline never sold one share, and neither did Aunt Susan, and when her Aunt Susan died, she left her shares to Caroline."

"So your wife controls the company?"

"No, she and Fleischer together control the company. They each have about ten percent of the stock and the rest is scattered among thousands of other stockholders. But so far it's worked pretty well, because she's let Boris run the company the way he wants, and as long as she holds her stock nobody is likely to bother him."

"And you're the lawyer."

What happens if we lose Boatwright? Nothing happens. You've spent your life in the firm, and we would have lost it way back in '61 or '62 if it hadn't been for you. Cut me back, though. Oh, might cut you back a little, who cares? Caroline can't spend her income as it is.

Caroline can throw you out on your ass, though.

Never happen. She knows how much I love her.

You've got a funny way of showing you love her.

She knows how I need her to take care of me.

Better listen to what people keep trying to tell you, buddy.

The train entered the tunnel.

SEVEN

Waldorf Towers

The older Boris Fleischer became, the more he looked like a parrot, thought Anders as they shook hands. Fleischer was completely bald now, peering through heavy black-rimmed glasses that magnified his dark intelligent eyes. He wore, as always, a white shirt, a navy blue double-breasted pinstripe suit, and a dark silk necktie.

"Happy Birthday, Boris!"

Fleischer smiled shyly, showing some gold. "Thank you for coming on such short notice. Not a birthday party, but I do appreciate it."

Boris Fleischer spent most of his life in this beautiful library now. People came to see him. The presidents of the many Boatwright Corporation subsidiaries came, one at a time, and sat in the straight-backed Louis XV armchair on one side of the six-legged oval marquetry library table that supposedly had belonged to Madame de Pompadour, and made their reports. Boris Fleischer sat in the matching chair across the table, listening with folded hands. Sometimes he got up and walked around the room. Sometimes he asked questions and people were relieved when he did that, because most of the time he just listened, thanked them for coming, and showed them out the door. Decisions came later the same day, or sometimes the next day, from Boatwright's corporate headquarters a few blocks down Park Avenue. Fleischer did not believe in meetings. He believed in collecting all the information that was available and then making decisions. He read a great deal: the mail and newspapers and reports one of his secretaries brought over every morning, and the books that he purchased on his walks, the books now filling his mahogany shelves on three walls of the library — books in French and German and English, books on history, on philosophy, on economics, on art, on every conceivable subject that attracted his attention. While reading he would listen to his records — mostly Bach.

He lived alone except for the old Spaniard who cooked his meals, took care of his clothes and received his visitors. It was Victor who came in now, white hair, white jacket, carrying a clinking tray with glasses and ice and vodka and caviar and the things one eats with caviar.

"Come, sit down, please." Boris Fleischer took Anders by the elbow and guided him to the corner at the window. They settled into the leather club chairs as Victor put the tray on the coffee table, fixed their drinks and disappeared.

Anders was thirsty. He picked up his glass and raised it in a toast. "Cheers, Boris. Happy Birthday, again, and many more of them."

"Thank you, I have one little vodka with you, and then it is Perrier until dinner, to please the doctors. They think I want to live forever." They drank and looked out across the lights of the city.

"You're all right, aren't you, Boris?"

An expressive shrug. "The body, at this age, what can you expect? Things don't work as they did, one expects it. But the mind? One had hoped for finally more peace of mind."

Anders frowned. "Peace of mind? What do you mean, Boris? Things are going very well, aren't they?"

Fleischer looked back over the tops of his glasses. "For whom?"

"Well, for you." Anders was startled. "For Boatwright. For all of us."

"For all of us? We had to close the plant in Pittsburgh last month, you knew that? We simply cannot compete with the labor costs in Hong Kong and Taiwan."

"That plant has been losing money for years, Boris. You knew this was going to happen."

Fleischer nodded, said nothing, looked out of the window. Anders had become accustomed to these contemplative silences. His grandfather had taught him that you don't always have to say something just because the other person doesn't. He put caviar on a piece of black bread, added chopped egg, ate it, and then drank some clear icy vodka.

By the time Anders had done all that, Fleischer's mood had apparently changed. He turned back and smiled and said: "For you things are going well now, in any case?" and in that second Anders decided to meet the threat head-on — and before the second vodka.

"Things are going very well, Boris, but I'd like to take this opportunity to ask your advice on a business matter."

"My advice? Well, certainly. How can I help you?"

"Boris, I'm sure you know what an important client Boatwright is for Conyers & Dean. Always has been, and I most certainly hope it will always be. But I'm beginning to wonder if we could give you better service if we had an office right here in New York, right in midtown around here somewhere. . . ."

Are you crazy? Anders asked himself, watching Fleischer's face. How can you go out on your own and make a suggestion like that without consulting anybody else in the firm? A New York office? Well, other firms are doing it. Why shouldn't we? But Christ, *the cost!*

Fleischer considered the idea and asked questions: Would lawyers from Philadelphia be moved to New York? (Not at first. Anders had a classmate who was unhappy in his Wall Street firm, who had in fact suggested something like this a few months ago. He was of course, a member of the New York bar, he had a couple of good clients who would follow him, a few young lawyers who would follow him. . . .) But eventually some of the Philadelphia people who had always done Boatwright's work would be moved? (Sure) Who?

By now, it was clear that this was not the reason Anders had been summoned to New York. It was a new idea to Fleischer, and not, Anders noted with relief, an idea of pressing interest.

Victor removed the scarlet lobster shells, placed finger bowls, poured champagne, served asparagus vinaigrette, and disappeared again. The dining room was almost monastically plain: flat white walls, four chromium-and-cane Bauhaus chairs, a round rosewood table; a big green plant beside the window and a magnificent orange Bonnard of a woman bathing provided the only color.

Boris Fleischer had finally come to the point. On his seventy-fifth birthday, he seemed suddenly afflicted with melancholia. A man who had survived the German occupation of Eastern Europe, the Russian occupation of Eastern Europe, the American occupation of Germany, the British occupation of Palestine, the establishment of Israel, business failure in Israel, immigration to the United States, then twenty-five years of constant battle to establish a solid business success . . . this man suddenly sounded drained of energy and courage.

"What is going to happen to this country?" Fleischer stared across the table. "This country is the hope of the world, but what is going to happen? We close the plant in Pittsburgh because we have to close it, so we put nearly a thousand people on the street. Are they going to find new jobs? They are *not* going to find new jobs! What will happen to them?"

"Well," said Anders, trying to placate him, "We've always had a certain amount of unemployment, except in wartime —"

"A certain amount? What is that? Five percent? Ten percent? In the first place, before we even reach the factory workers, you have a whole class of people who never have been employed and who never will be employed, who are *unemployable!* Totally useless people, do nothing but commit crimes and produce more people like themselves. Remember when we had the power failure here in New York? Elevators stopped, everything stopped, the lights went out, these people came running out of Central Park, thousands of people came running out of the Park and smashed into the stores of Fifth Avenue. . . ."

"Is that really new, Boris? They had riots here in New York in the Civil War, they had riots in London in the eighteenth century, they've always had riots in Paris, they had riots in Rome —"

"*Rome! Rome!* Rome is exactly right!" Fleischer leaned forward. "Thousands, millions of unemployable people who must be fed by the state with tax money extracted from the people who do work, who do save their money, who do invest their savings . . . millions of unemployable people who cannot read and cannot write, millions of unemployable people who are not parties to the social contract, do not feel themselves bound by laws they did not pass, millions of unemployable people who will rise up and take what they want the moment that the lights go out . . ." He stopped because he was out of breath and slumped back into his chair.

"Boris . . ." Anders hardly knew what to say. A man who had lived with forged identity papers in cities where the SS combed through the tenements, who had floated across the river Enns on an empty gasoline canister to escape a Russian border patrol, who had supported himself by trading stolen diamonds for American cigarettes in Munich nightclubs, who had led a dozen people across the Alps and the Mediterranean to a country that didn't exist, who left that country when he felt that he was a stranger there too, who appeared in Cleveland, Ohio, with a net worth of two hundred dollars and persuaded the creditors of a bankrupt water pipe company to let him reorganize it . . . "Boris, this really isn't like you! Sure, we've got social problems in this country, terrible problems, but my God, compared to the things you've seen, the things you've been through . . ."

Fleischer shook his head. "Something must be done. You have now a chaotic situation in this country. The inflation is almost out of control because the American people spend all their dollars to buy oil from the Arabs, the dollar is going down and down — do you realize the German mark is worth more than *half a dollar*, can you believe it? So what will they do to control inflation, to strengthen the dollar? They will have to raise the interest rates to bring down the inflation, and what happens then? Then we have to close more plants, people operating on borrowed money will go broke, more and more people will be out of work, what will they do?"

Victor was serving strawberries with whipped cream and pouring the coffee. Anders didn't know what to say. Was it simply age? Was it something that would respond to the right medicine?

"You know approximately the population of this country?" asked Fleischer.

Anders guessed about two hundred million.

Fleischer nodded. "How many blacks?"

Anders had no idea but suggested fifteen million.

Fleischer shook his head. "Twenty-two million seven hundred thousand in the 1970 census, probably closer to thirty million today. How many Jews, do you think?"

"Boris, I haven't the slightest idea." Anders was becoming worried by the direction this conversation was taking.

"Five-point-eight-million. So the blacks are approximately between eleven and fifteen percent, the Jews maybe from under three percent perhaps up to four percent, perhaps a little more. Now that is people. But if you take the property? All the assets in the country? Stocks, bonds, real estate, commodities, bank deposits, cash. . . . What percent do you think is held by the four percent, what percent do you think is held by the fifteen percent?"

"Boris, you know I don't know that, you don't know that, *nobody* knows that —"

"Make an estimate!" Fleischer seemed to hunch forward, glaring at him.

"No, I will not make an estimate, Boris! And I'm really surprised that you of all people are upsetting yourself in this kind of speculation, compared to the things that you've seen —"

"It is because I have seen the things that I have seen," said Fleischer.

"I have seen how things begin, perhaps I have developed . . . how to say it? A special nose? A special ear? An extra sensitivity to the causes of violent social change? I don't like what I see here, Graham. The next leader of the black people will not be a Martin Luther King, not a Mahatma Gandhi either!"

"What should be done, Boris? And who should do it?"

Fleischer shook his head. "What should be done? What should be done? There should be a plan, an economic plan for the country, a plan that provides work for all the people."

"But you just said yourself that a lot of them are unemployable. Either unemployable in the first place, or like our people in Pittsburgh, they can't compete with the Chinese. So what would the plan — this plan of yours — what would a plan provide for that?"

"Education," said Fleischer. "The people must be educated, in the first place to read and write their own language, in the second place to learn something that is needed."

"Well now, Boris, we've been over this before, haven't we? Remember when you closed the Boatwright Locomotive plants in 1962? Old Miss Susan Boatwright tried to finance a program to retrain those machinists —"

"That would have been a drop in the bucket! Miss Boatwright wanted it done with private money, through the Quakers in Philadelphia, quite an impractical program, and very expensive —" Fleischer shook his head. "Much too expensive for one company. This kind of thing must be done by the Government for the whole country."

"I'm not sure I agree with you," said Anders. "But of course if you think it has to be done by the Government, then you're in the political arena —" Anders smiled. "Boris, why don't you go into politics?"

Fleischer emitted a sigh. "No. . . . I don't want to go into politics, I can't go into politics, of course, but I am so terribly worried about this country! If what happened in the other places happens here? The people here are not acquainted with grief. They have not seen terror. Cities destroyed . . . There has been no war in this country since 1865. . . . You know, this is really an island. There is no place left to go, and I see the water rising." He took off his glasses and sat silently rubbing his hand across his eyes. Without the glasses his eyes looked so much smaller, unfamiliar, and Graham Anders was actually relieved when he put the glasses on again, rolled his napkin into the silver ring and pushed back his chair. "Have you finished? Victor will serve your Cognac in the library. I'm afraid I still have some legal work for you this evening."

SECURITIES AND EXCHANGE COMMISSION
Washington, D.C. 20549

SCHEDULE 13D

Under the Securities Exchange Act of 1934

Boatwright Corporation
(Name of Issuer)

Seagull Corporation
(Name of Person(s) filing Statement)

Common Stock (par value $1.00)
(Title of Class of Securities)

88750-1
(CUSIP Number)

William Rogers Pennington, Esq.
Openshaw, Prescott, Pennington & Lee
123 South Broad Street
Philadelphia, PA 19107
(215) 770-1212

(Name, Address and Telephone Number of Person Authorized to Receive Notices and Communications)

March 15, 1978
(Date of Event which Requires Filing of this Statement)

"Jesus Christ Almighty, Boris!" Anders was horrified to notice that his voice was shaking. He began to flip through the hefty document he held in his hands, taking a deep breath. His voice never shook. It was okay to show other emotions, but not fear. What was there to be afraid of, anyway? It was just the shattering surprise, this sheaf of photocopied papers resting like a time bomb in one of the drawers of Madame de Pompadour's table. . . .

"Boris, I must say! They drop a 13D on you by registered mail at nine o'clock in the morning and you show it to your lawyer at —" glancing at his watch — "nine-forty that evening? Or have you talked to anybody else?"

"No," said Fleischer, settling comfortably into the other chair. "Why should I talk to anybody else?"

The Securities Exchange Act of 1934, or rather the Williams Act amendments adopted in 1968 precisely to defend established company managements against people like Boris Fleischer, requires that any person or any group that buys five percent of the stock of a public company file with the SEC and mail to the company detailed disclosures of Schedule 13D: Who are these people? Where did they get the money? What do they want?

Seagull Corporation? Who are these people? Anders noted from the cover of the 13D that whoever they were, they had retained another Philadelphia law firm. Why?

Item 2. Identity and Background
(a) Name: Seagull Corporation
(b) Address: c/o Corporation Trust Company,
Wilmington, Delaware. . . .

Seagull Corporation had been organized under the laws of Delaware about two weeks ago for the purpose of investing in the stock of Boatwright Corporation. It had no officers; some faceless lawyers were its incorporators. Forty-five percent of its stock was registered in the name of Bell & Co. nominee for First Hudson Corporation, One Chase Manhattan Plaza, New York, NY 10005. The *beneficial* owner was Kielwasser & Co. N.V., a corporation organized under the laws of the Netherlands Antilles. Kielwasser & Co. in turn is owned by a group of private investors listed in Appendix A. . . .

Anders turned to Appendix A, to find a list of names and addresses. The names meant nothing to him. The addresses were all the same:

c/o Hansa Nordamerika Bank A.G., Ferdinandstrasse 27, 2000 Hamburg 1, Federal Republic of Germany.

Anders turned back to Item 2. Fifty-five percent of Seagull's stock was owned by Brandywine Investors, Inc., 123 South Broad Street, Philadelphia, PA 19107. Brandywine Investors, Inc., was a wholly owned subsidiary of Chester County Management Co., Inc., same address. Chester County Management Co., Inc., was a wholly owned subsidiary of Philadelphia Pharmaceuticals Corporation, which was listed on the New York Stock Exchange. A table showing all of the officers and directors of Philadelphia Pharmaceuticals Corporation was attached as Appendix B, but Anders, feeling his pulse beating in his throat, didn't need Appendix B; he already knew the name of the Chairman of the Board of Philadelphia Pharmaceuticals, so he flipped the pages back to Appendix A for a more careful look at the clients of the Hansa Nordamerika Bank.

When he raised his head, he saw Fleischer was silently watching him.

"Boris . . ." Should he allow himself such a remark? "Boris, you're worried about a black revolution in Central Park? I think maybe you've got a different sort of 'blacks' knocking on your boardroom door. I think we may be looking at the SS!"

Fleischer raised his eyebrows but said nothing.

"Boris . . . I find it very hard to say this, but I think maybe you'd better consult somebody else about this — another law firm."

"Why?"

Anders felt the adrenaline washing the vodka and the Champagne and the Cognac right out of his brain. "Boris, I'm afraid this has something to do with me personally."

Fleischer nodded. "That was my feeling. Do you want to tell me about it?"

"Boris, they only have to give you ten days' notice every time they buy. There could be another 13D in tomorrow's mail! Haven't you talked to the brokers? Is the volume up? Haven't they noticed —"

"Oh yes, they have noticed, many telephone calls, it will be in the *Journal* tomorrow."

"And you didn't tell me about it until this minute?"

A shrug. "Is there such a hurry? Read Item 4."

Item 4. Purpose of the Transaction

Seagull's purpose in purchasing shares of Boatwright is to acquire a significant invest-

> ment in Boatwright. While Seagull has no present intention of acquiring a majority interest in Boatwright, Seagull intends to review its investment from time to time and may, depending upon Boatwright's business and prospects, general business conditions in Europe and the United States and other factors, change its position in the light of the circumstances then prevailing. In the meantime, Seagull may continue to purchase shares of Boatwright, but as part of its periodic review, Seagull may propose to Boatwright's management merger or similar transactions, or Seagull may decide to make a tender offer.

"Same old bullshit," said Anders. "That's what everybody says. That's what we'd say in their position."

Fleischer suddenly slid forward in his chair, putting his elbows on the table and his chin in his hands.

"Graham, they know, I assume, that I control about ten percent of our stock, and your wife has about the same, so even if they make a tender offer for all of the stock . . . at a forty or fifty percent premium over the market now, what would that cost them? And knowing there is twenty percent they can't get, and certainly another five or ten percent who will stick with us. . . . Do they really think they can freeze us out? I don't understand this, Graham. Who are these people and what do they want?"

BOOK II

EIGHT

Parties

She said the words quietly but quite distinctly, in the darkness: "Kühles Blut und warme Unterhosen."

She was in her bed, he was on the floor beneath it, and her husband was climbing the stairs. The words mean "cool blood and warm underpants" and they said that in the German army and his father had said that to him whenever he got upset about something but he had not heard those words since he was seven years old and now he was forty-five years old — too old for bedroom farces.

The door opened. "You awake?" Bob Bromberg sounded angry.

"Mmmm?" The bed moved as she turned, heavily, pretending. She was wide awake, a girl who recognized Mercedes engines in her sleep: her husband drove one, her father-in-law drove one, and now here was Anders who drove one, too, but of course his wasn't in front of the house. She had fetched him from the railroad station, or rather from a side street near the railroad parking lot, because Bob was supposed to stay in New York tonight. . . .

They had separate bedrooms. She claimed that she had not slept with Bob since they moved here from California. . . . The bed shook again, her feet hit the floor, she was walking away and they began to talk out in the hall, whispering so as not to wake the little girls.

Naked, trying not to shiver, Anders remembered an ancient Peter

Arno cartoon in *The New Yorker*. The wife, sitting up in bed, stretches out her arms to welcome her husband, who is running in the door with hat and overcoat and suitcase — but on the near side of the bed we see a man in striped pajamas sliding underneath it, where he is discovering *another* rather frightened-looking man (in polka-dot pajamas): "So, Bitterman, our paths cross again!"

Well, at least there wasn't anyone else under here, but in real life it didn't seem funny. Especially without pajamas.

There was a patch of moonlight on the floor, six inches from his foot. He lay there and looked at the hair on his legs, his white hairy legs in the moonlight. This was crazy. He had a wife who loved him. He had a daughter who loved him. He had a son who loved him. He had Laura, twelve years younger, who loved him. He was a department head in the best firm in town. His arthritis had gone away. His world was in order . . . Why this dangerous unfunny burlesque?

As he walked in the front door, Anders could hear what was becoming a familiar and tiresome quarrel.

"Mother, pu-leeze! Will you not even *listen* to what I'm trying to convey to you? Oh hi, Daddy, won't you ask Mother to just *listen* to me, *please?*"

They were in the library. Susan Boatwright Anders lounged across both arms of the deep easy chair with her hands in her pockets of her very tight blue jeans, glaring at her mother. Caroline, who still had her raincoat on, was sitting at the desk, opening the mail with a long silver letter opener and not paying much attention to Suzy.

"Is this another fight about another party?" asked Anders.

"This is another discussion about crashing parties," said Caroline, glancing up at him and then back at the mail.

"You *see*, Daddy? Crashing parties! That's a word from the . . . 'forties or something, twenty years before I was even born, I mean *Jesus Christ*, nobody today even knows what that *means!* When you crash someplace you go to sleep or you pass out. . . . People do not send out written invitations today if they want to have a few people over to dance or something, no matter what they may have done in your day, they just tell people to bring their friends —"

"A hundred and fifty friends arrive," said Caroline, still opening envelopes. "A window is smashed. Furniture is broken. The neighbors call the police, who find that everybody's smoking pot. Six boys and two girls are facing criminal charges. Elaine Hamilton and Deedie Gump are suspended from school — "

"M*other!* Those people are seniors, they had college boys at the Hamiltons' —"

"Where's the party tonight?" asked Anders.

"In Paoli," said Suzy.

"She doesn't even know the name of the people," said Caroline.

"What difference does that make? Are you afraid I might meet the wrong kind of people?"

"Oh stop that," said Caroline. "Graham, I could really use a drink."

"On my way —"

Suzy followed him across the hall and into the pantry. "Daddy, I thought I'd get some support from *you.* If I have to have a *written invitation* every place I go, I might as well be grounded. It's ridiculous!"

Anders put two glasses on the drainboard, opened the freezer, and took out a handful of ice.

"Well, I must say if you don't even know where you're going —"

"George's brother knows where we're going."

"George's brother knows. Well, why don't you ask him and tell your mother?"

"Daddy, I can't ask George's brother. I don't even know where he is right now."

Vodka. Vermouth in Caroline's vodka. Sharp knife? Lemon.

He looked into his daughter's angry face. A tall broad-shouldered girl with Graham eyes and straight black hair. Nothing of Caroline's heavy-breasted roundness, of Caroline's curls. Did my mother look like this when she was a girl? Boys coming in the doors and windows? Which one was George, anyway?

"If you don't know where George's brother is, how will you find out where the party is?"

"George will find out."

"How?"

"Daddy, you're *cross-examining* me. . . . Daddy, now you're laughing at me! I don't think there's anything funny about this!"

"Well, I do," said Anders. He kissed her cheek and slapped her tight rump. "Now beat it. I want to have a drink with your mother."

"You want me to hang up your raincoat" asked Anders as he put her drink on the desk.

"That's all right," said Caroline, her eyes on the card in her hand.

"Mr. and Mrs. Robert Bromberg request the pleasure of our company . . . in Ardmore? Aren't these the people Charlie Conroy brought from California that time? What are they doing in Ardmore?"

"This is the son. Bromberg Instruments has bought Horizon Semiconductor, out in Wayne, and the son's been sent here to run it. . . . I told you about it, they retained Ordway —"

"You did not tell me about it. The son's wife is the big classy blonde who was traveling with her father-in-law? The one who insisted on speaking German to you in front of people who don't speak German?"

"I don't remember that —"

"I remember it quite distinctly." Caroline looked at him over the edge of her martini. "When was this? When did the Brombergs buy this company?"

"Just within the last year. I really don't know that much about it."

"A corporate acquisition? Wouldn't that be in your department? Who handled it?"

"Tommy Sharp. He knows them from the time Charlie Conroy —"

"How big a deal was this?"

"Just under twenty million, I think."

"Cash or stock?" asked Caroline.

"Bromberg stock."

"But why did they come to Ordway with it? Ordway represented Charlie Conroy when Charlie tried to buy them —"

"Apparently old man Bromberg was impressed with the way Ordway behaved when Charlie's deal collapsed, the fact that Ordway wouldn't close when something wasn't right —"

"And now Bromberg junior and his wife are living a mile down the road? How is it they're inviting us before we've invited them? Shouldn't we have invited them first?"

Anders took a drink. "Well, they're Ordway's clients, after all, it was up to him and Marion —"

"What you're saying is that Ordway and Marion have already had them, but they didn't include us. Is that the story?"

"I have no idea."

"Bullshit," said Caroline Boatwright Anders as she pushed back her chair to get up, but he stepped behind the chair and put his hands on her shoulders.

"What's the matter?" he asked.

She leaned her elbows on the desk and held her head in her hands. He felt a deep sigh.

"You mad at me?" he asked.

She shook her head. "I'm mad at myself."

He was stroking her throat. "Why? Because you didn't get involved with a more normal-type person in the first —"

"Would you love me more if I was long-legged and gorgeous?"

He stood above her, so he could not see her face. "What do you mean? You're the handsomest woman I know!" He slid his other hand down and began to unbutton her blouse.

"Stop that, Graham, the children could walk in. . . . I didn't say handsome, I said gorgeous, like Mrs. — *Graham!* Was that your first drink? . . . Ah, darling, please, no . . . Not in here . . . Graham, please, you've got to lock the door and let me take my raincoat off!"

The sun was up now, but the grass was wet and slippery. Ordway Smith held the mare back so that he could keep his eye on Karin as she took the arab gelding over the last ditch. She made it with two feet to spare, sat back, and began to canter up the long slope.

Ordway remembered his first ride with her, in the brown Sonoma hills above the Brombergs' ranch: dry dusty grass, western saddles, and the most dangerous riding he had seen in his life. He remembered one glimpse of her face contorted with unbearable pleasure — as she jumped this same horse across a fifteen-foot ravine. They were her horses — or her father-in-law's horses — and he kept up with her on that one wild ride, but he had no intention of doing it again, certainly not right here on his own place in Chester County. . . .

At first, the idea of letting Karin board her horse in the Smiths' stable caused an uproar with Ailsa ("That lady is *nuts*, Pa, that lady jumped Minnie across the waterfall! If you think I'm taking care of *her* horse . . .") but Karin gave Ailsa a black terrier puppy that melted Ailsa's heart, Karin took Ailsa along on shopping trips and stimulated an entirely new interest in expensive European blouses and skirts and sweaters, Karin refrained from dangerous stunts . . . and by now her sleek cream-colored gelding had been living in the Smiths' stables for months. She went riding with Ordway these summer Sundays at six o'clock in the morning.

Getting old for this, thought Ordway, as Minnie also cleared the ditch but had to be kicked a little to catch the gelding as they flew up the hillside. Both Minnie and me! Graham is younger than I am, and I don't see *him* up here at the crack of dawn after that party. Wow!

"You want me to drive?" Marion had asked when they finally walked out to their car, but Ordway felt fine.

"That was the best party I've been to in *years*," he had announced as they drove away. "Amazing what interesting people they've collected so quickly."

"Just a little ostentatious."

"Ostentatious? She didn't even have caterers! That dinner was all cooked right there in the house. She cooked it herself."

"That's what I mean. Ostentatiously simple. Simple jars of caviar. Simple crayfish from Louisiana, white asparagus from Germany, fraises-de-bois from France, three gorgeous au pair girls to serve and clean up and then dance with the gentlemen. Just your simple little folk festival."

"Aw, come on now, it was a hell of a lot different from most of the dumb dinner parties around here —"

"Sure was! The hostess at the piano, leading the barbershop quartet —"

"I thought we sounded pretty good."

"You sounded drunk! A bunch of middle-aged men singing songs from their childhood and gazing down the piano player's cleavage."

"Graham Anders wasn't drunk. They sounded terrific when they sang that song together —"

"Yes, and did you notice Caroline's face watching them sound terrific? He's going too far this time, Ordway. You've got to do something."

Karin reined in when she reached the wood at the top of the hill and Ordway came up beside her. Both horses were snorting comfortably.

"That feels good, doesn't it?" she almost shouted. "It will be a beautiful day." Her expression changed. "Are you unhappy about something?"

"Just a little hung over, Karin. That was quite a splendid feast you put on — and it only ended a few hours ago."

"Fresh air," she said, and touched the gelding with her heel. "Fresh air and sunshine." They moved the horses single file into the path, ducking their heads to avoid the dew-dripping leafy branches. When they came to the fence separating Ordway's land from Charlie Conroy's, Karin slid to the ground and approached the gate.

"No, Karin! I've told you, we don't ride over there anymore."

She turned to look up at him. "Oh, what nonsense! He probably isn't even home, and he never goes outside, he will never see us —"

"That's not the point," said Ordway. "Charlie passed the word that I was not to ride across his land anymore, and I'm not going to do it whether he finds out about it or not!"

She had one hand on the gate latch while the other held her horse. "Up to you, my dear friend. I'm going to canter down the hillside for a few minutes —"

"*Leave that gate alone, Karin!*" He got off his horse and moved toward her, pulling Minnie along. Both horses heard the new pitch in his voice and both horses began to dance about with their hind legs. Karin frowned. Her lower lip came out in the suggestion of a pout.

"I want to talk to you about a couple of things," said Ordway, now face to face with her. "In the first place, when you're riding with me, or even when you're riding alone out of my stable, you don't ride where I don't ride. Is that clear, Karin?"

She glared at him for a moment, then suddenly turned into a scolded child, compressed her lips, examined the tips of her riding boots — and nodded.

"That's not really what I wanted to talk to you about," Ordway continued in what he hoped was a more friendly tone. He took a deep breath. "I want to talk about Graham Anders." She looked up and frowned again. "I've known him all my life, Karin. He's my best friend in the firm, but I have to tell you that he does this all the time."

The gelding snorted and pulled his head up, but Karin didn't turn as the bridle pulled her arm. "Does what all the time?"

"What he's doing with you."

"What is he doing with me?"

"Come on, Karin! You should have seen what the two of you looked like at the piano, roaring out that German marching song —"

Karin's face turned red. "That's no marching song, that's the Fusilierlied from his father's play *Trompeten* . . . his father *wrote* that song!"

"Well, it certainly sounded like a marching song to the rest of us, but whatever it was, whoever wrote it . . . watching the two of you belting out all the words by heart . . . Karin, he likes women very much, women like him, but he's been happy with Caroline for over twenty years —"

"A splendid marriage!"

"It works! She hasn't looked at another man since she was eighteen years old, she accepts him as he is — and he needs her. He needs her desperately. His parents died — his parents were killed — when he was a boy, his grandfather brought him up, his grandfather died. . . . Caroline Boatwright fell in love with a very lonely guy. She gave him a family, she gave him a place in the world, she's strong as iron — and he needs her. Really, Karin, I've seen this happen before. We had a secretary in the office, most beautiful girl you ever saw in your life, went to college and came back to work for him, finally quit and became a damn good securities analyst, married some nice young man — he still sees her when he feels like it, but he keeps all that away from Caroline, he keeps all that away from his children — and he always goes home!"

"This is different."

"What makes you think so?"

Karin suddenly grinned. "Because I know myself . . . and I know the words to his father's song!"

The whispering stopped. Footsteps. Doors. Water running? Light from the hall washed away the square of moonlight. Her legs appeared, and then her face. "Still under there, my dear?"

He rolled out, stood up with a grunt, and grabbed the clothes she held for him. "Where's Bob?"

"In the shower." She turned toward the sofa, picked up a sweater and began to pull it over her head.

"What are you doing?" he asked, tucking his shirt into his trousers, stepping sockless into his shoes, idiotically wondering how he could get a photograph of Karin dressed in nothing but a black angora sweater.

"I'm going to drive you to your car." She stepped into a skirt and pulled up the zipper. "Come, hurry please!"

She took his hand and pulled him out of the room, along the hall, past the closed door to Bob's room, and down the little back stairs to the kitchen.

"Are you nuts?" he whispered. "It's only a mile, I can easily walk it. . . ."

"It doesn't matter, and I have to tell you something." They were already climbing into her dusty black Porsche.

"But it isn't necessary. . . ."

She turned the engine on. Bob's car was blocking the driveway. Without a second's hesitation, she put her head out of the window and began to back the Porsche across the lawn and into the street.

"I don't understand why —"

She switched on the headlights and roared up the hill. "You don't understand why I want to be with you five minutes more and with him five minutes less?" She touched the tape deck and the car filled with the contralto of Maureen Forrester, Bach's cantata *Schlage doch, gewünschte Stunde!*, so they didn't speak until she pulled up at the parking lot barrier. And stopped the music.

"You don't need this, do you?"

Anders didn't look at her because he was still putting on the socks he had stuffed into his pockets, putting on his shoes for the second time. . . . As he opened the door, she grabbed his arm, so hard that he could feel her fingernails through his shirt. "You won't be so uncomfortably interrupted again. Bob agrees to the divorce, finally! He is moving out his things tomorrow."

Anders stared through the windshield. Was he glad? Shouldn't he be pleased to hear that?

She held his arm. "No kiss?"

"I'm sorry." He closed the door again and put his arms around her and kissed her on the mouth. She reached for his hand and put it between her thighs. "Heisses Blut," she murmured. "Heisses Blut, und *keine* Unterhosen!" and this time he laughed, feeling her laughing in his arms, wondering what his father would think of that expression: hot blood, and *no* underpants.

NINE

The Day the Painters Came

On this particular Monday morning, Ordway Smith thought he was finished with the daily management conference, when Eleanor Leaming came stomping back into his office, furious.

Eleanor Leaming had been Ellsworth Boyle's secretary for fifteen years before the firm officially made her what she had been all along — the office manager — and by now she could handle the most touchy problems and the most temperamental lawyers without help, but this morning she stood with her legs apart in front of Ordway's desk, folded her arms across her bosom, and said: "Graham Anders is playing games over in his department and I'm just not going to put up with it anymore —"

"What do you mean? What's going on over there?"

"The painters are in his room. You know we decided to do one office at a time on that side of the building, they've been over there for two weeks, every attorney and every secretary was told two weeks ahead of time which office would be painted which day, it only takes them one day, we've got that little conference room on that side reserved just so every attorney can work in there the day his office —"

"Well, why does Graham have a problem with that?"

"He claims he wasn't told, his secretary's out sick, he's been out in

Los Angeles all week on one deal and he says she has the papers for some other deal spread out on his work table and the painters put a drop cloth over his papers and I don't know what he said but they just walked off the job and what kind of an example does that set for the younger lawyers and *how am I supposed to get this place painted?*" She was fighting back tears now, so Ordway Smith stood up, and walked around his desk to get his jacket because he wasn't going to have this kind of thing going on around here, and Graham Anders leaned in the doorway with his hands in his pockets. He looked contrite.

"I'm sorry, Elly."

"You're sorry? What are you, some kind of child? How am I supposed to get the office —"

"I found the painters down in the coffee shop and I apologized and they're back at work."

"They're back at work?"

"Indeed, ma'am. They are."

Eleanor Leaming expelled her breath and shook her head. "Boy, you are really something!" She turned and stalked out of the room.

"Also cost me fifty dollars," said Anders to Ordway Smith, who was still regarding him unhappily, but then Ordway's secretary came in: "Mr. Anders, they're holding a call for you in Conference Room Thirty-one North —"

"Way over there? Why don't they just put it in here on your other line?"

Ordway's secretary had been with the firm for a long time. She looked Graham Anders straight in the eye and pursed her lips. "You want this call in Conference Room Thirty-one North, Mr. Anders. They're holding it for you."

A hoarse whisper: "Whatcha doin'?"

"Where are you?" he asked.

"In bed. Sore throat. Whatcha doin'?"

"Well, I don't know what I'm doing! I've been in California for a week, I can't get into my office because they're painting it, my secretary isn't here, I'm sitting in an empty conference room wondering how the hell I'm supposed to do any work —"

"Want to have lunch? Up here?"

"Where's your husband?"

"Vancouver."

"What's he doing in Vancouver?"

"What's he ever doing? Selling pills. I'll make some spaghetti. Pick up a bottle of Soave and some Italian bread. I think I'm out of garlic. Pick up a garlic, too."

"Am I going to get a dinner plate thrown at my head?"

"You deserved that! Listen, I'm sick and I'm bored and I haven't seen you for a long time, but I'm not asking you up here for any three-ring circus, okay?"

"Sure you want to see me?"

"Would I ask you up here if I didn't want to see you, you son of a bitch? Don't forget the garlic." Laura Carpenter hung up.

There was no reason he shouldn't feel at home in her apartment. He had known her since she was twenty, in progressively nicer places, holding progressively better jobs. He had given her many of the pictures on the walls and many of the books, and if she hadn't thrown them out in her most recent fit, there should still be a razor and a toothbrush and a clean shirt and a T-shirt and a pair of socks concealed in different places — beneath her lingerie, inside her leather boots — to cover the nights he could claim to be out of town when her nice young detail man really was out of town.

Anders used to tell her that he didn't have a jealous bone in his body. He had seen her through countless courtships, affairs, infatuations, three broken engagements; he was quite prepared to see her through this and any other marriage. Her husband was a graduate of the Haverford School and the University of Pennsylvania, a pre-med who had not quite made it to medical school. He traveled about the country explaining his employers' new pharmaceuticals to doctors who were supposed to prescribe them for their patients. He had introduced himself on Sixteenth Street, after he had walked into a lamppost while staring at her. Such a thing had not happened to Laura for several years and it cheered her up. He owned fifty regimental neckties, played squash at the Racquet Club, took turns washing the dishes, invested half of his after-tax income in Philadelphia Pharma stock, and had trouble with premature ejaculation. The week they had returned from their Bermuda honeymoon, Anders was teaching a seminar on securities law in New York; Laura came over to spend the night in his hotel room. The whole thing seemed in comfortable balance until something happened.

Anders never did find out what happened. Laura had worked at

Conyers & Dean for years, and he could only assume that one of her girlfriends had seen the blonde in the Porsche and the sable jacket who sometimes dropped him off in front of the building, or had overheard his partners worrying about him. . . .

In any event, the last time he visited the apartment there had been furious questions about a German chick, screams, a glass of Vouvray thrown in his face, a Meissen plate crashed against the wall beside his head — then tears, and orders to get the fuck out of here.

Anders was incredulous. "Why, you can't even *remember* how many men you've been with; you tried to count them and you couldn't even remember!"

"That's different. You're married!"

"So are you!"

"Shut up. I hate you. I've put up with your sainted Girl Scout and your sainted children, nothing must ever bother them or disturb them, but I've got to be alone every weekend, every Christmas, every New Year's Eve —"

"You're married!"

"Shut up! You let me marry this — this little kid, this *squash player* — so you wouldn't feel guilty leaving me alone, but I've been a good sport all these years, I haven't called you at home no matter what was going on in my life, I damned near went out the window a couple of times, but I never called you, I accepted the fact that your wife comes first, your children come first, I played by the rules — but if you think I'm going to be the senior girl in some harem of yours, you've got the wrong chick, Charlie!"

She had opened the door to the hall and repeated her request that he leave, but now he was back.

"Don't kiss me, I'm infectious." Her voice was hoarse and her nose was red but she looked good in a quilted blue housecoat, her long thick platinum hair pinned up. Anders went into the kitchen and put the wine into the freezer. A spaghetti machine was extruding spaghetti, vibrating with a tremendous racket. He stood behind her in the tiny kitchen as she manipulated the controls of the machine, which sounded like a cement mixer. He put his hands over her breasts and kissed her damp neck.

"Cut it out!" she shouted, but continued to work the machine without disturbing his hands until there was enough spaghetti and she turned the machine off.

"How's the German chick?" she asked in the sudden silence.

"What German chick?"

She turned her head to look at him. "Up yours, Graham. Where did you put the garlic?"

There was a comfortable familiarity to the feel of her smooth hot body between the smooth cool sheets, sliding efficiently through her favorite attitudes like a dancer doing a ballet exercise. She permitted only a few minutes of what she called "fooling around."

"I said no three-ring circus, remember?"

"How about a one-ring circus?"

"That's what you're going to get," she said and climbed over him, grasping him firmly, impaling herself, covering his face with her breasts and commencing a hard, slow, steady pumping. She didn't laugh, she didn't cry out, she didn't sweat; she panted into his ear and very gradually increased her speed. A trace of afternoon sunlight shone above the closed curtains, making patterns on the white ceiling. Drowsiness, from the wine. Should he go back to work this afternoon? Back? Didn't do any work this morning, thinking suddenly of the computers. How am I going to bill forty hours this week? Well, you worked at least twelve hours every day in Los Angeles, forget it, and just as she reached the very edge, she gasped, as always: "Tell me you love me!" and as always he told her he loved her, grabbed her buttocks, and let himself explode.

When he woke up she was padding around the room, picking up her clothes, brushing her hair.

"Still built like Miss Jersey Cranberries," he said, folding his hands behind his head.

"How would you know? That was before you met me."

"I've seen your picture."

"You never saw my picture bare-assed. Matter of fact, I weigh six pounds less than I did then."

"Looks good to me."

"How much does the German chick weigh?"

"What German chick?"

"Okay, old boy, you can get dressed now. The circus is over."

"Why? Is Harry due home?"

"No, Harry's not due home until tomorrow, but this is a fuck-and-run session, I can tell."

"What do you mean by that?" He was indignant.

"I mean you didn't expect to hear from me today, so you haven't covered yourself, so you've got to get out of here. Also this is Monday, so you've got your department meeting, remember? Come on now, brush your teeth and take a shower, I don't want you to get in trouble with the Girl Scout or with C&D — and one more thing, you dirty old man." She sat on the bed and put her cool, carefully manicured fingers on his chest. "Don't get yourself shot, okay?"

It was almost three-thirty by the time Anders walked out into the puddles and the April sunshine of Rittenhouse Square. Back to the office? Anders could feel the computers clicking out the time he wasn't working, each hour of his life divided into tenths to be logged into the daily time sheets: 6 minutes = .1 unit, 12 minutes = .2 units, one hour = 1.0 unit, so the interlude with Laura had blown away not only 3.5 units of his life but also $560 of Conyers & Dean time. . . . But you haven't done anything all day that you can bill to any client! Suppose we write the whole day off? Eight times $160 is $1,280 of Conyers & Dean time, and if you *could* have billed it, applying the .45 profit factor, you would have made $576 for the firm. . . . *Cut this out!* This can drive you crazy.

She was right about his department meeting at five o'clock. He had been out of town all week and had nothing to say. Why do we need these meetings all the time? "Because lots of people like to hear themselves talk," George Graham had said at his own dinner table, a generation ago when George Graham was running the firm, when there were no departments and no committees, and one partners' meeting a month was considered plenty.

Should he call somebody — Butler or Sharp or one of the older partners — and explain why he couldn't come? Drank half a bottle of Soave and don't feel like it? Never apologize, never explain.

Anders walked up Seventeenth Street, crossed Market Street, climbed down into the grimy underground railroad station, and boarded a train carrying students, shoppers, unemployed executives, and retirees. A person in Anders's position was not supposed to be on a train this time of day, and especially not without a briefcase. Sure enough, he had barely settled himself behind his newspaper when a heavy body wedged into the other seat.

"My God, Graham, you haven't had a heart attack or anything, have you?"

Morris (Mo) Patterson had been a law school classmate of Ordway Smith's, or at least had started law school, had flunked out in the days when they cut half the first-year class, but had since supported himself very comfortably in the stock market.

"No, I'm still in harness, Mo." Never explain.

"Well, the fact is I have to see old Mrs. Tavistock in St. David's, client of your firm, come to think of it. She wants to revise her portfolio, and some of these old gals, you know, they like a little personal attention, and it pays to give it to them."

Mo Patterson kept talking. Anders made the right noises at the right places. At Merion a shouting crowd of boys in Episcopal Academy blazers climbed on, but Boatwright Anders was not among them. At Haverford another crowd of schoolboys got on, and Anders got off.

He walked up the street, crossed Montgomery Avenue, and entered the parking lot of the Cricket Club. He walked along the rows of cars until he came to the battered old 300 SL, which was even more conspicuous than usual: under the left windshield wiper was a single red rose.

He put his car behind the house so that people would not see it from the street, and when he came in through the kitchen door he heard the piano. Finger exercises. He crossed the parquet floor of the hallway and turned into the big, sunlit living room, which blazed with paintings and flowers. Karin was sitting at the piano with Dolly, her six-year-old. The sun streaming through the tall french windows behind them made their identically golden hair shine, and the radiance in Karin's face as she looked across the piano at him made Anders stop in his tracks, made Anders suddenly wonder if he had passed some point of no return.

Dolly stopped playing and grabbed her mother's arm. "You know what my mama did?" she shrieked. "You know what my mama *did?*" and Anders took the rose from behind his back and held it up, and the little girl jumped off the piano bench, grabbed the rose, and began to gallop around the room, her little plaid skirt flying.

Anders sat down beside Karin. "Thank you very much."

"Oh, you're very welcome." She wore a gray pleated skirt and a navy blue sweater and pearls. Smiling, she stretched her arms and leaned back lazily. "Mr. Anders has no work at his office on the first day back from California?"

He told her about the painters.

She turned to the girl, who was still skipping around the room. "Dolly, don't make such a noise, please! Why don't you find a little vase for Graham's rose? He will want to leave it here, I think." When Dolly had dashed out of the room, Anders put his arm around Karin and kissed her mouth.

Leaning back against his arm. Raising her eyebrows. "Mr. Anders brushes his teeth after lunch now?"

He kissed her again, feeling her warmth through the sweater, feeling her breathing under his hand, feeling her turn toward the keyboard.

"You know this song?"

Boom-boom da boom-boom, she played the black keys, with her left hand only, boom-boom da boom-boom, and sang in her smoky contralto:

Denn wie man sich bettet, so liegt man, she sang

Es deckt einen keiner da zu, and turning to face him again: "You understand that, still?"

He understood it, from the very first chords: You lie in your bed as you've made it, and nobody covers you up!

Boom-boom da boom-boom, she played on the black keys, *Und wenn einer tritt, dann bin ich es*, she sang

Und wird einer getreten, dann bist's du!

"That's Brecht and Weill," said Anders, feeling himself swept away and drowning. If somebody does the stepping, it's going to be me, and if somebody gets stepped on it's going to be you!

"That's Brecht, that's Weill, that's also Mr. Graham Anders, I think, perhaps your theme song, my dear?" but now the telephone rang in another part of the house. Karin continued to play, looking down at the keys now, biting her lips. A moment later, shoes clattered across the parquet, Anders withdrew his arm and Dolly pulled her mother's head down, whispering into her ear.

"What is it? Who has invited you? Why are you whispering? It's not a secret!" She hugged the child and smiled across the golden head at Anders.

He was in the kitchen, putting ice cubes through the electric crusher when she returned from delivering Dolly.

"Where is everybody?" he asked. "Where's Didi?" Didi was the ten-year-old. "Where's Greta?" Greta was the Swedish girl who took care of the children.

"Didi spent the weekend with Bob in New York and she isn't

coming home until tomorrow, so I told Greta she could stay out all night. May I have some vodka too?"

She took his hand, held it against her cheek, and closed her eyes. "Oh dear, it's good to be with you. How long can you stay?"

"Want to give me some dinner?"

"Oh, I would *love* to give you dinner, but on your first night home?"

"No, I got home Saturday, and Caroline has some kind of function in town —"

Karin put her hands on his shoulders. "My dear, it's a special treat, we can make love *before* dinner!"

Her divorce was final. Why shouldn't he be in her bedroom in broad daylight — well, twilight — if that's where she wants him? Children not home . . . She liked mirrors. One whole wall was a mirror in which he now watched her stepping out of her skirt, looking solemnly across the room at him. Dirty old man? He took off his coat and his tie and his shirt. If the shoe fits . . . Might be dead tomorrow! He pulled his undershirt over his head.

"Will you come over here, please?" She smiled, almost shyly, and took his hand. Frowning, she unbuckled his belt and unzipped his fly and pulled his pants and shorts down with one powerful two-handed movement and put her nose and her forehead against his stomach and pushed so hard that he fell back across the bed and had to struggle to remove his pants and shoes and socks while she attacked with her mouth . . . and then suddenly stopped doing that and brought her face close to his and stared into his eyes.

"Miss Cranberries!"

"What?"

"Your little bathing beauty queen from New Jersey who used to be your secretary and your lover, and she is *still* your lover!"

"What are you talking about?"

"You taste of garlic, my dear friend! You can brush your teeth, but garlic comes through your skin, and you told me once she cooks spaghetti for you, spaghetti with garlic sauce —"

Anders rolled on top of her and pulled her sweater off, holding her wrists together with the sweater as he kissed her on the mouth: "Garlic! Baloney! May have been garlic in the scallops I had at the Club," and then he was comfortably between her thighs and inside her, thinking never explain, but hoping this would work because he wanted her desperately now, he wanted her so much that it was the only, *only* thing —

"You know what's very nice?" she asked into his ear as he freed her wrists from the sweater and she wrapped her arms around his neck and her legs around his back. "That no one will come up those stairs and make you jump under the bed!" and he could feel her laughing.

"You know what I will give you for dinner?"

"What are you going to give me for dinner?"

"Spaghetti, with garlic sauce."

"All right."

"That's a joke! You had her before you had me, I have no right to ask questions and you will not hear more about it. For dinner we will have a crabmeat omelet and a bottle of very good champagne, and strawberries, but I must tell you that you now smell very strongly of *me*, so perhaps you should take a shower while I cook."

He slid his car next to Caroline's station wagon, turned off the ignition, climbed out, and closed the garage. There was a light on in the kitchen. Boatwright Anders, wearing a navy blue school sweater, was sitting at the table, reading a book. He took off his glasses and smiled.

"Hi, Dad, I've been waiting up for you."

He looks so small, thought Anders. Why is he so small? "Kind of late, isn't it? Everybody else in bed?"

"Yes, they're asleep, Dad, but I wrote this assignment for English and Mother said I could stay up and show it to you."

This was unusual. The boy rarely asked for help, and Graham Anders, who had no happy memories of his own homework, never volunteered. He had been drinking on and off since lunchtime: why stop now? He went into the pantry, poured himself two fingers of Scotch, returned to the kitchen and sat down at the table. "Okay, what have we here?"

"We're supposed to write an essay, Dad. An essay is a short piece that makes a point in an interesting way. Could you tell me what you think of this?"

"Sure." Anders swallowed some whiskey and took the paper-clipped, typewritten and carefully corrected sheets.

FORM I — ENGLISH
MR. WAYNE

Is It Ever All Right to Lie?

by

FRANCIS BOATWRIGHT ANDERS

We are always taught that lying is bad. The 9th Commandment that God gave to Moses was "Thou shalt not bear false witness against thy neighbor." That kind of lying is always bad, because that kind of lying hurts the other person. But there are other kinds of lying.

Beginning at the bottom of the scale we find the kind of lies we all tell, to spare another person's feelings. We call these lies "white lies."

When somebody asks you do you like his father's new car, most people will say "Oh, that's a hot car!" even if they really think a two-tone Mercedes is gross.

If a girl asks you if you like her new dress, she does not want to know if you really like it and if you tell her that you don't like it you will hurt her feelings for no reason. We believe that this is not "bearing false witness." We believe that a white lie is all right because it makes your neighbor feel better.

White lies *are usually about little things, like cars, or dresses. Going up the scale are more serious lies, but they are still told because the truth would hurt the person you are telling the lie to more than the lie will hurt him.*

Another and more complicated white lie is the placebo. *This is a pill that is made out of something neutral like sugar or salt or vitamins, but the doctor tells the patient that this pill will get the patient well. The doctor may prescribe this kind of a pill if he thinks the patient's problem is really* mental, *so that the patient will get well because he thinks the pill is making him well. The doctor is really lying to the patient, but lying for a good reason.*

Suppose you are a doctor and find out that your patient has cancer and will die from that no matter what medicine you give? Do you tell him and make him suffer even more from worry? That is another exsample of where it is all right to lie.

Suppose the patient does not ask the doctor "Do I have cancer?" and the doctor does not tell him? Is that different than if the patient really asks "Do I have it?" and the doctor replies "No, you don't." It is easier on both of them if the patient does not ask, but it probably means the patient already knows the answer, but does not want to be sure.

Now we reach the top of the scale. In her book The Diary of a Young Girl, *Anne Frank writes this in Amsterdam on Thursday, November 19, 1942: "Countless friends and acquaintances have gone to a terrible fate. Evening after evening the green and gray army lorries trundle past. The Germans ring at every front door to inquire if there are any Jews living in the house. If there are, then the whole family has to go at once. If they don't find any, they go on to the next house . . ." In the end, the Germans did catch Anne Frank and killed her, but the people who protected her and her family as long as they could were lying every time the doorbell rang.*

These are only a few exsamples. The answer to the question that is the title to this essay is: Sometimes.

Anders quickly finished his whiskey, because he felt his eyes filling with tears; he wanted the alcohol inside and he wanted a few seconds to regain his composure.

"What do you think, Dad?"

Anders took a deep breath and then expelled it. "I think it's terrific. Very, very good!" He took out his handkerchief and blew his nose, really fighting for control.

"You don't think it's too short?"

Anders shook his head. "A *short* piece that makes a point in an interesting way. Fits the bill exactly. Are you interested in a couple of mechanical nits?"

The boy came around the table and stood beside him.

"Some teachers might mark you down for starting a sentence with 'but.' " Anders turned and smiled. "But I wouldn't. 'Gross' is also a word he might circle, and I would agree with him. Trendy slang in a piece that's otherwise completely free of it. You can think of a real word that has the same meaning and would be stronger. And 'example' doesn't have an *s* in it. That's all I have. A fine job, kiddo."

The boy seemed pleased as he gathered his books and papers but then, just as Anders was reaching for the light switch, he asked: "Are you okay, Dad?"

They looked at each other. "What do you mean?"

"Evans Frick saw you on the four o'clock train."

"What? Who's Evans Frick?"

"A guy in my class. He saw you on the train, that time of the day, so I thought maybe your arthritis came back, but then you weren't home —"

"Oh no, I'm not sick, Boatie, I had to go out to St. David's and see a client about her will, an old lady who wants to change her will —"

"So then you stayed and had dinner with her?" The boy looked relieved.

Anders just nodded and turned off the light. "Good night, boy. I hope Mr. Wayne likes your paper as much as I do."

In the total darkness of his dressing room, Anders took off his clothes for the third time that day, thinking he didn't plan this; when he got dressed this morning he was planning to spend the day going over the closing papers for the steel company acquisition, and he slipped into the big double bed in the silent bedroom.

According to the digital clock it was only 11:47, comparatively early, but Caroline always said hello if she was awake. He couldn't hear her breathing, but that didn't mean anything because she usually slept in silence —

"Can I just ask you one question?" said Caroline in the darkness.

"Wow, you scared me! I thought you were asleep."

"No, I'm not asleep, Graham. I want to ask you a serious question."

"Okay."

"What do you really truly deep inside think of a woman who will drive into the parking lot of a club she isn't even a member of, with a couple of small children in her car, and put a rose on the windshield of a car that belongs to a man she knows is married to somebody else, a man the little children know is married to somebody else? What do you think of a person like that?"

How do you answer a question like that?

You don't. You have to lie there in the darkness and wait for the rest of it.

"I know you're not going to talk to me about it," said Caroline. "I sometimes think it might help if you could bring yourself to talk about it, but you take the attitude that if one doesn't talk about the problem the problem isn't there, and I haven't forced the issue . . ." She paused. "I haven't ever pressed you about these things because I know it won't do any good, you can't change the way you are, and if I want you — and I think you know how much I want you, Graham — I've got to take you as you are. . . ." Under the covers she suddenly reached over and took his hand, so quickly and firmly that he couldn't draw back. "Graham, this one is different from all the others. This one *isn't* going to let you live your life the way you've always lived it, this one isn't going to play by the rules. One of those children in the car was Betsy Butler —"

"Ben Butler's kid?" Anders had not meant to open his mouth, but it shocked him now to think of the children watching. The children watching?

"That's right. So Sally Butler knows about it, which means that Marion Smith knows about it, so Ben and Ordway both know about it by now, and also my sister was playing tennis, and the minute she was finished, somebody came up to her and told *her* . . . so this sweet little gesture is all over the firm and all over town."

Silence.

She held his hand. He had to say something. "Do you think anybody really gives a damn?"

"I give a damn!" She squeezed his hand.

"Oh, now look . . ."

"No, Graham, *you* look! This woman is deliberately putting me into an impossible position, fixing it so I can't look the other way no matter how much I'm willing to. Can't you see that? She doesn't want to be another girlfriend, she wants to be your wife and she isn't going to rest until she *is* your wife, and I just want to know if you want to be married to that kind of person."

"Oh, sugar —" Caroline, who never cried, was crying now, so Anders pulled her over and put his arm around her, tried to wrap his arms around her plump soft body, but she twisted away from him and sat up in bed.

"Graham, I want you to listen to me." He felt her take a deep breath. "I've been thinking about this all evening, and I've come to a decision."

Anders rolled over onto his side. "What decision have you come to?"

Another deep breath. "I can put up with girlfriends if I don't have to know them or see them, but I can't put up with this kind of public show that Karin Bromberg is performing right here in front of all our friends and neighbors, and you can't expect me to put up with it, either, so I'm asking you to move out! I'm not suggesting a divorce, I'm not suggesting a formal separation or anything like that. I just want you to figure out who you want to live with. Move into one of your clubs for a while — or move in with her, and see how you like caviar for breakfast and teenage au pair girls for dinner —"

"Caroline, please don't —"

"See how you like all that continental flash and glamour as a steady diet! See how you like receiving that poleaxed husband when he comes to visit his children! See how you like living in a household that's dependent on that sad old father-in-law in California . . . that sad old man who apparently paid twenty million dollars to send her out of his life and into ours! Perhaps he knows her better than you do, Graham. The body of an over-ripe peach and the soul of a ten-year-old spoiled brat!"

Anders felt himself falling backward in empty darkness. "Caroline . . . don't kick me out. I need you!"

"Graham, I don't want you out, I want you here beside me more than anything in the world, but I don't know any other way to bring you to your senses. *I want you to grow up!*" As she talked she turned around against him. Her long chaste nightgown had bunched up under her arms, and he was absently stroking her flank.

"Everybody tells me to grow up," he said, into her hair. "I think maybe it's a little late for me to grow up, but stunted as I am, I do believe to be married to the only person I want to be married to —"

"If you only *knew* how hard I've tried to believe that, but my sister says —"

"Being twice divorced, your sister is the real expert on marriage," said Anders, and felt her chest expand with what sounded more like a laugh than a sob. This instant change in her mood aroused him.

"Graham, don't make me laugh, this isn't *funny*," but then her hand discovered what he was also noticing with surprise. She grasped him quite firmly, then rearranged her legs so that suddenly he was behind and inside her. "This doesn't change anything," she said into the pillow. "This is just animal appetite, I am *not* going to let animal appetite control my judgment, Graham, you smell of Scotch!"

"Just had a drink with Boatie."

"What did you think of his essay?" This is how she liked to do it: fast and hard, but almost secretly, under the covers, while talking about something else. "What did you think of his essay on lying?"

"I thought it was splendid. I thought it was very, very good, and I told him so." He tried to pull the nightgown over her head.

"No!" She clamped her elbows against her ribs. "I thought . . . I thought he argued . . ." She was breathing heavily now. "I thought he argued in favor of lying!"

"No, he didn't." Anders could hardly believe what was happening. She said it doesn't change anything? "He points out the examples where it's better to lie than to tell the truth."

"It's never better to lie than to tell the truth!" announced the Girl Scout, as she came.

TEN

The Seagull

GOTTFRIED GESSTLER

FERDINANDSTRASSE 27
2000 HAMBURG 1
TELEFON: (040) 11732

August 1, 1977

Mr. Francis Hyde
c/o Hotel Ritz
15, Place Vendôme
Paris 1er, France

Dear Mr. Hyde:

Perhaps you are surprised that I did accept your invitation to "write me a letter". Please forgive me if I do not address you by your first name despite your request: for a German of my generation it is difficult to address an older person by his first name. As we come to know each other I will learn.

The purpose of this letter is to arrange that we *do* come to know each other better, and quickly. Our meeting at the Air Show was *most* interesting to me but too short and of course too many other people and I would very much enjoy talking to you as we say "under four eyes" about the problem I mentioned to you:

I have recently sold (to an investor from the Middle East whom I named to you) one of the shipyards my family has here in Hamburg for several generations. The payment in Deutsche Mark would create a considerable German tax problem for us, but as part of the arrangement in obtaining permission for the sale from the German government, it was agreed that the taxes would not be assessed upon those proceeds reinvested into the economy within twelve months. Our lawyers were able to convince the authorities that it would be quite impossible to correctly invest such a sum directly into the German economy within such a short period, therefore it was agreed that 1/2 of the proceeds may be invested in other West European or in North American economies *if* taxable dividend income plus "significant technological or business opportunities" will flow back into the German economy from such investment. That does *not* mean go into the New York Stock Exchange and buy a block of IBM! That means obtain a business — or a sufficient voice in a business — so that it can be operated in a way to bring real benefits back to Germany.

You said "investment bankers" and of course we are doing that, but in my experience a personal contact with a man in your position is more effective, and that is the reason why, when I was introduced to you at the Gulfstream reception the thought like lightning hit me: My God, suppose we can put our Pharma Leverkusen together with Mr. Hyde's Philadelphia Pharmaceuticals? They have had a splendid working relationship with the Prototesterone licenses over the years. . . .

I want now to assure you that I completely understand why you do not welcome an investment of this size in your company, and I give you my word that I will make no such attempt.

Nevertheless, I would deeply appreciate your advice and possibly other ideas that you might have for joint cooperative profitable investment in the United States, and therefore I am writing this letter to ask if you would do my wife and me the honor of joining us on our quite comfortable 30-meter schooner *Möwe* for a few days *at any time* convenient for you this summer before you return home. We keep the *Möwe* at Kiel and sail her mostly in the Baltic although we have been in Ireland and Brittany and Spain and Corsica and Greece with her — not always all the way on board! But we do always take our splendid Thailander cook along and I can promise you excellent meals. We should be quite alone except of course the crew and possibly my wife's daughter, who has lived some years in your city, may be visiting us later this month but the ladies will not be interested in our discussions.

Please do telephone me at the number above at your pleasure. If you can join us, I will of course meet you at Hamburg airport. It is only a short drive to Kiel.

With respect, and anticipation of your visit, I am sincerely,

GOTTFRIED GESSTLER

Frau Gesstler wasn't listening. In her first marriage the talk was always war and rockets and the differences between living in Germany and living in the tropical heat of Alabama; in her second marriage the talk was making money, avoiding taxes, buying companies, and the threat of Communism. . . . Frau Gesstler had learned to smile as the gentlemen lighted her cigarettes and to think about other things. . . .

Thank God the weather was holding up. It was always more pleasant to have the dinner here on deck, and tonight there was so little wind that they hardly needed the blue and white awning, but earlier in the day the wind had been just right and they made the run from Kiel without using the noisy smelly diesels at all. They had dropped anchor in an excellent spot right in the middle of the basin, they had washed and changed clothes and started on some good icy Danish aquavit with a little herring and then Phitar had served his special steamed bass with black bean sauce which you would not expect to be served on a German yacht and white asparagus very late in the season. The sun was just setting behind the church tower, the little hurricane lamps had been lit, the crêpes Suzette were a success, another glass of brandy?

The belt of Frau Gesstler's slacks was too tight now, but she couldn't very well loosen it. She was glad she had put on the blazer because her arms looked so heavy in this blouse, but how is one supposed to diet if one is expected to entertain business people every night? Gottfried talked incessantly and the American talked hardly at all. The American was a type Frau Gesstler had met only rarely: extremely polite, extremely taciturn, somehow almost English, very tall and very thin, white hair cut close to the head, sad gray eyes and a long straight nose. He didn't seem terribly interested in Gottfried's discussion. Why had he come? What was he doing in Paris in August, all alone? When they came on board Gottfried looked like a tough little jockey beside him and Gottfried is one meter seventy-eight, not exactly a midget! Wore the strange striped wrinkled cotton suit (*sea sucker?*) one only sees on this kind of American, and a blue silk bow tie with white polka dots. Now he had changed into tennis shoes, cotton khaki trousers like the American soldiers, and a very old blue cardigan. Frau Gesstler asked if he knew her daughter who lived in Ardmore just outside of Philadelphia but he did not know her and when she was about to ask more questions a look from Gottfried stopped her. . . . Where *was* she? Here it is almost the middle of August, not so much as a telephone call to let us know. Lonesome, of course. Hurling herself around. Girls in camp this summer, so much better for them than expensive hotels all the time. Too many hotels, too many countries, too many men . . . Going on too long now! Three years? Closer to four! Why can't she settle down? Always *knew* that man would go back to his wife. Or the children: clung to the little boy. Ridiculous infatuation. Playing with her! She convinced herself because she wanted it so much, but the son of Gustaf Anders, after all! Theater pieces that betrayed his Fatherland. Shot with the Communists in Spain. Also had a rich American wife. She never listens, does what she wants. Not getting younger . . .

"To be perfectly honest, it is not only the taxes," said Gottfried Gesstler, lighting his cigar, then pointing down the coast. "You see the farthest light down there, the light that is blinking? That is Travemünde, the last port in West Germany. Then beyond the river it is the red flag all the way to the Pacific Ocean. You understand?"

Francis Hyde nodded.

"We are sitting very close to them, as you can see," said Gottfried Gesstler. "If they want to come, they will be in Hamburg in an hour. Of course you say, we have been waiting for a long time and they have not come." He shrugged. "Okay, but we still have this little feeling at the back of the neck all the time, you know. And then, perhaps more serious, we have our own young people here in the west, some are Socialist, quite a lot of them are Maoist if you can believe that, we have also extremely dangerous and crazy young people who have kidnapped and killed some of our important business leaders — well, you have read about it in the newspapers, it is not so very comfortable for people in our position, despite what you see in the immediate presence." He waved his hand, indicating the white tablecloth and the hurricane lamps and the Cognac glasses and Frau Gesstler sleepily fondling one of her gold earrings and the masts moving gently against the stars and the lights of the village waterfront behind them and Spanish tango music coming from the big Swedish sloop riding on double anchors next to them and the cooler breeze now blowing across the Baltic, blowing from the east.

"And the dollar is down-down-down this year, and D-Mark is up, the D-Mark is worth more than fifty cents for the first time in history, and also your stock market is down. Mr. Jimmy Carter does not know what to do, but we know what to do. Invest in America! This is the moment to take some of what we have built up here and move it to your country." He slapped his hand against his thigh. "I am convinced of it."

"You may be right," Francis Hyde agreed, but if he intended to say more, he was distracted by a sudden commotion amidships: the whine of an outboard motor, shouts in German, two sailors leaning down over the ship's ladder, a white canvas duffel bag landing on deck. . . . When Francis Hyde turned around, she was pulling herself up the ladder. Her hair was tied back in a black bandanna. She wore a navy blue sweater with the sleeves rolled above her elbows, faded jeans, and dirty tennis shoes. She gave the stranger on the afterdeck a dazzling prankish smile. Francis Hyde felt a sensation he had not felt in years. He could hardly believe it.

Frau Gesstler had seen this performance before. Thank you, Mutti, no dinner, she had driven straight through from Hamburg airport, she only wanted to go to the toilet, then perhaps one could get her an aquavit, a beer, some herring? She had telephoned Gottfried's secretary, who knew only that the *Möwe* was sailing east this morning, so she guessed where they would anchor the first night. Her car was at the gasoline station in the village. . . .

When she returned to the afterdeck the bandanna was gone, the golden hair was combed out, and she focused her attention upon the guest. Where did he live? What did he do? Did he know this person? Did he know that person? He seemed flattered by her examination, interested and responsive for the first time. It took very few answers to establish who he was, what he did — and that he was alone at the Paris Ritz in the middle of August. Why always so much *older* men? What does it mean? The girl can smell power like a shark smells blood. Why the lawyer, then? So stupid, so self-indulgent. Looks more like her father now, the eyes and around the nose. But not that naughty smile. That smile comes from Holland, from Frau Gesstler's brother, that laugh always put such sparks in the air, wakes everybody up, makes us feel young with that laugh. . . . Getting heavier, though. Beer. Wearing a brassiere today, thank God.

"You flew all night and drove up here from Hamburg airport? You must be exhausted."

"I took a Valium and slept on the plane. I can sleep anywhere. I'm a good traveler."

"I used to be, but I'm not anymore. I don't like taking pills, so I'm awake a lot at night. It's kind of you to stay up here with me. You should get some sleep."

"Don't worry, I'll go down when I'm ready. I wanted to ask you: are you the same family that built that castle in Chester County, that château, an exact copy of —"

"Hyde-a-Way, now Conroy House? Yeah. My grandfather built that in 1903, exact copy of some château in the Île-de-France, but I never lived in it. My cousins inherited it, and then it was sold."

"To Mr. Conroy!"

"You know Charlie Conroy?"

"No, but I know Ordway Smith, next door, and he told me the story of your place. We used to ride there."

"Did you? . . . Yeah. Ordway Smith. Started out as a steeplechaser and a playboy, but he's developed into quite a successful lawyer, I hear. How do you know Ordway?"

"He represented my husband — really my husband's father — when he bought Horizon Semiconductors. A few years ago."

"Horizon? Out in Wayne? What did you want *them* for?"

"Oh, it's a long story. Too long. And it's all over anyway. It was a mistake. I don't really want to talk about that. Tell me about *your* company."

"Well, that's a long story too. Longer than yours, I'm afraid. . . . Can I give you some more of this Cognac? . . . My grandfather organized electric railway companies, trolley companies. You know what they are? They ran electric cars on tracks around the towns and from one town to another. Before the automobile took over it was a fast, cheap way for people to get around, and it was a good business, pretty much unregulated. My grandfather and the other people like him sold stock and borrowed money to build the systems, then they set up holding companies that could control a whole pyramid of other companies, they watered the stock, they borrowed enormous amounts to buy more and more trolley companies, they did a lot of things that would be against the law today, and they got away with it for years — until people bought their own cars and stopped riding these trolleys, and then the loans went into default and everything began to crumble."

"Were you in that business?"

"No, I didn't want any part of it. My grandfather died during the Depression, my father and my uncle were running these companies, they were having all these problems but they weren't much good at it anyway, they didn't have the old man's . . . I don't know what they call it . . . toughness? Ruthlessness? Hunger? My grandfather was a farm boy from Lycoming County, ran away to the city when he was fifteen and got a job in a broker's office writing stock quotations on a blackboard with chalk. Studied accounting at night. . . . My father and my uncle mostly sat around the Union League complaining about Roosevelt. . . . Well, anyway, my grandfather died while I was in college, the trolley business was a mess, they were filing for bankruptcy, reorganizing, trying to unload the trolley companies on the cities. . . . I didn't want any part of it, I wanted to make my own way in something new. I happened to be good in chemistry in school, in college. . . . I mean I wasn't *really* good at it, but I was interested, I understood what the real chemists were talking about, and I met this German, an exchange student from Germany, and he told me how the Germans had developed all kinds of new things — synthetic substitutes for morphine, you could take them without becoming addicted . . . other things, new antibiotics, antidepressants. Of course they had these things patented in Germany, but I thought we could get a license. . . . Now I'm getting ahead of myself. . . . I had a friend at Princeton, his family had a little old drug distribution business, they supplied drugstores with prescription medicines — and he was bored with *his* family's business, didn't want to work for his family — so we switched! He went to work for my uncle and I went to work for his father. This was in the Depression, we were lucky to get jobs, of course. And I made the better deal." He paused to drink.

"Don't stop. I have my eyes closed but I'm listening to every word." She was lying flat on the deck, barefoot now, her ankles crossed, her head on a pillow and her Cognac glass between her breasts.

"Are we really going to finish this bottle?" he asked.

"Why not?"

"Indeed, why not? I don't think I've talked this much about myself in twenty years."

"Feels good?"

"Yes, I'm afraid I'm boring you."

"My dear sir, the minute you begin to bore me you will *definitely* know it!"

He laughed. The sound rang out across the silent water, and surprised him.

She prompted: "So you arranged for licenses with German companies?"

"Well, not right away. I had to learn something about this business, had to go on the road, become a traveling salesman talking to doctors about new medicines, but after a couple of years of that I persuaded them to let me look for new products, and that's when I began to negotiate with some English companies, a French company, a Belgian company — I spent a lot of time sniffing around the world, and I found us some interesting stuff."

"Which made money?"

"Made money. So I got them to let me buy into the company. Still a private company then, closely held, a couple of families. I borrowed every cent I could borrow, mortgaged my house, bought as much stock as they would sell me. These people were getting older, and to tell you the truth they had lost interest in the business, they were interested in big sailboats, like this one, and in race horses. Didn't understand the value of their company. Potential value, with me running it. I'll tell you something: the ones that *didn't* sell me their stock, I've made all of their children and grandchildren millionaires. All of them!"

"You are like your grandfather?"

"Well, I wasn't a farm boy. They sent me to St. Paul's and Princeton, and I got my job through a college classmate, so I didn't exactly make my own way."

"But you did what he did. You built something that wasn't there before."

"It was there before, but I sure as hell changed the shape of it! When I got my job we had sales of about ten million dollars a year. Last year we had sales of almost a *billion* dollars a year. When I got my job, the company was worth — well, I don't know exactly what it was worth, but the book value was under three million dollars. Today, well at yesterday's close — No, what time is it? At Friday's close, the market value of all the stock outstanding was seven hundred million dollars!"

"All yours?"

"My God, of course not, we've been public for thirty years now, we're on the New York Stock Exchange! I control only . . . well, you don't care about all this, I have just a small fraction of the stock outstanding —"

"But enough, yes?"

"Well, I certainly hope so!"

"Just like Caroline Anders."

"I beg your pardon?"

"Caroline Anders hopes she still has enough Boatwright stock to control Boatwright."

"Boatwright? What do you know about Boatwright?"

"Well, I used to hear more than I wanted to about them, I can tell you, but never mind about that. Tell me more about your company."

"Boatwright was completely turned around by a man by the name of Fleischer. He got them out of the locomotive business, as a matter of fact I think they're doing better than is generally understood —"

"Oh really, I have put the name of Boatwright and the name of Boris Fleischer far behind me! I would rather hear something new! You must have worked terribly hard to build your company. What did your wife do while you were working?"

"Well, the usual things. Ran the house . . . houses. Brought up the girls."

"And where is she tonight?"

"I don't know. She died two years ago."

"I'm so sorry. I'm asking personal questions — but I do that always! Are your girls grown up?"

"Yes. One is married to an Englishman. They live in New York. The other one was married to a tennis pro, but they're divorced. I think she's still in Santa Barbara, but I don't hear from her much."

"And now you are sitting on the deck of Herr Gesstler's *Seagull* looking across the water to the lights of Travemünde over there."

"Actually, it's not the lights of Travemünde I'm looking at."

"Well, as I have my eyes closed I can't see what you are looking at, but what I wonder is why you are on Herr Gesstler's boat this evening."

"I met him at the Paris Air Show and we had a talk, and then he wrote a letter and invited me to come up here for a sail."

"Yes, but why?"
"Wants my advice."
"About what?"
"Personal questions again?"
"Yes, always! Especially about my own family. I heard he sold one of their yards to some Arabs. Now he wants to invest his money in the States. Right?"
"That's right. At first he wanted to put it into *my* company, but I told him that was out, so now I'm supposed to suggest another idea."
"What's in it for you?"
"I beg your pardon?"
"You don't need Gottfried Gesstler and his money. You're not an investment adviser. Why did you come?"
"Maybe I'm looking for a finder's fee."
"Shit!"
Francis Hyde laughed. "My dear young woman, a finder's fee on the sum your stepfather wants to invest could amount to —"
"*Horseshit!* Men like you don't take finder's fees."
"We don't?"
"Why did you come?"
Francis Hyde swallowed the last of his Cognac. Feeling weightless, feeling that he had suddenly become somebody else, he leaned down and put his hand around her bare ankle. She didn't move. "The truth is, I don't know why I came," he said quietly.
She opened her eyes and looked at him. "But now you know, yes?"

ELEVEN

Main Line

— George? I'm sorry to do this to you on a Sunday afternoon —

— Boy, this better be important! We were just teeing off and they sent this kid out to bring me in —

— I just got some orders for you, from the Old Man.

— Well, great, but couldn't you talk to me at the Club, for Christ's sake? Did I have to drive all the way home?

— You couldn't talk about this at the Club, and we have to go over to Mary's mother's for dinner and I thought you'd like to know that you're going down to Washington on the first train tomorrow.

— I am in a pig's ass going to Washington on the first or any other train tomorrow! I've got a breakfast meeting at eight, then I've got a meeting with the trademark people —

— George, just simmer down and let me deliver this message, will you, please? I just heard from him about an hour ago, he's in some fishing port in Denmark —

— He's *where?* I thought he was in Paris getting us a new plane!

— Well, now he's on somebody's yacht sailing around the Baltic, he was talking on their radiotelephone to somebody's secretary in Hamburg, and she was repeating what he was saying to me in a *ferry Cherman ak-zent*, and here's the message: tomorrow morning George takes the first train to Washington, goes to the SEC and personally copies everything that Boatwright has filed in the last three years —

— *Who* has filed?

— Boatwright Corporation, once upon a time our good old Locomotive Works? 10-K annual reports, quarterly 10-Q reports, proxy statements — everything there is, and then you are to give all this stuff to the overnight courier service and have it in Hamburg no later than Wednesday morning at the address you're going to write down now. Got a pencil?

— Now wait a minute, just one minute, please! You are telling me that the Senior Vice President and General Counsel of Philadelphia Pharmaceutical Corporation is being sent down to the SEC to copy hundreds of pages of financial statements? My God, we have services who do that all day long, it would take one phone call tomorrow morning —

— He doesn't want anybody else in on this, George! Just thee and me.

— That is absolutely ridiculous! Hundreds of people are calling for hundreds of 10K's every day, it doesn't mean anything to anybody, but if the General Counsel of a prominent company shows up in person down there —

— You're not that famous, George!

— You never know who might turn up down there . . . and what do I tell the people at the office? I've got a breakfast meeting —

— Send Ms. What's-her-name, your gorgeous Harvard Law School acquisition.

— Very funny. She's been with us two weeks. I guess I could send Stevenson, but what do I tell him? We now have a Xerox person who gets paid a hundred and eighty thousand a year?

— Your problem, George. I'm only the messenger.

— Only the messenger, he says . . . I know! I'll call Bill Pennington and have him send one of his paralegals.

— No, George. No law firms yet.

— For Christ's sake! Some Kraut secretary in Hamburg knows all about this, and we can't tell Bill Pennington?

— You got it, George.

. . . .

— Still there, George?

— What the fuck does he want with Boatwright all of a sudden?

— Didn't say.

— I wonder what they're selling at.

— I just looked. Closed Friday at 20½, down ½.

— They're down, all right.

— So are we. Everybody's down. Jimmy Carter's stock market!

— They haven't made a locomotive since that raider took over. Fleischer. They're into all kinds of fancy Jewish real estate deals, grain exporters, trailer trucks. . . . Nothing we know anything about. I don't get it.

— Siegler?

— Oh Jesus, you're right! They picked up Siegler before we could get our act together. A Graham Anders production. Paid too much, much too much . . . but that was five-six years ago!

— He hasn't forgotten.

— Whatever became of the concept that he's *retired?* Do I remember a retirement party . . . ? We've got to get him off this medical technology kick, it's a completely different ball game, we don't know it, we're going to lose our shirts. . . .

— Best CAT scanner in the world!

— You really think he's going to try for all of Boatwright just to get Siegler?

— I have no idea, but they haven't been over 30 all year and at 20 they're cheap.

— *Cheap?* We'd have to pay close to 35 if we made a tender offer, and what if then some other people wake up and decide Boatwright's cheap, and it turns into an auction? Where do we get the cash? Even if we only borrow half of it, the interest would choke us. . . . I don't get it!

— Well, you don't have to get it this afternoon, George. All you have to do this afternoon is write down the name and address of this lady at the Hansa Nordamerika Bank, with a *k*, that is. Got your pencil?

TWELVE

Magnetic Waves

"What happened then?" asked Francis Hyde.

She blew her nose and took another drink, suddenly conscious of the maître d'hôtel and one waiter watching her all the way across the huge empty dining room of the best hotel in Hamburg. So long ago, she thought angrily. It shouldn't still hurt so much! Maybe I should buy a veil. When did they wear veils? Nineteen thirties? Quite elegant. She put her chin up and set her mouth. "Well, he moved in with me. Into my house. At first it was fun — playing house — but gradually I could feel that he was not comfortable. Maybe too old for such a change. His partners were furious. Caroline's thousand friends and relatives didn't want anything to do with us. And then came the explosion."

He had been dreaming. He stood in the silence of Germantown Friends Meeting, it was very crowded and hot and Caroline's face was wet as she looked up at him steadily, saying loud and clear: "In the presence of the Lord and this assembly I take thee Graham Anders to be my husband, promising with divine assistance to be unto thee a loving and faithful wife until death shall separate us" and hundreds of Boatwright eyes were fixed upon them but a telephone was ringing very close to his head and he smelled Karin's perfume and heard her angry voice: "*Hallo* . . . You know what time this is? . . . All right, of course," and handing him the receiver: "Your daughter."

"What's the matter? What's going on?"

"Hey, Dad?" Susan's voice was shaking. There was some noise in the background. Anders instantly woke up. "Hey, Dad, you've got to get over here right away, Boatie's gone crazy!"

"What's the matter? What's going on?"

A shriek "Oh, *Jesus Christ!*" . . . Crashing glass? "Please-please-please, Dad, get over here *right now!*" The line went dead and Anders hit the floor, grabbing for his clothes as Karin turned on the light.

"Can I help, dear? Shall I call the police?"

"No . . . I'm sorry, I'll be back as soon as I can." Down the stairs and out the door and into his car, one-two-three-four, this car is too old, a toy, an affectation, screeching around the twisting narrow lanes, then along the avenue flat out two miles, traffic lights blinking yellow this time of night, then sharp right into Rose Lane, down the hill and left into Juniper and right, into the driveway . . .

All the lights were on and all the windows were open. *No.* The windows were not open. The windows were smashed. Jagged shards hung in some of the white frames, but the flower beds, the boxwoods, and the brick walks around the house glistened under a layer of broken glass. . . .

When he turned the engine off he heard the screaming. The front door was open and the baseball bat lay at the foot of the stairs. Anders went up two at a time and found himself face to face with Caroline, who was lying on top of the screaming boy, trying to hold his arms down while Susan held his ankles as he tried to kick her.

All three of them saw Anders at the same instant. The screaming stopped. Everything stopped. Anders knew that for the rest of his life he would remember the agony in his son's eyes.

Caroline said: "Look what you've done to the person who loves you more than anything in the world, Graham. Is she really *that* terrific?"

Anders felt his heart break.

"You mean to tell me he went back to his wife just because the boy was upset?"

"Not right away, but it made him so guilty, it gave him a depression. He couldn't sleep, he couldn't concentrate on his work and he couldn't . . . function in other ways." She examined her fingernails.

"What other ways?"

She put her hand on top of his hand. "Didn't I show you it is all in your head?"

"Jesus, yes!" Francis Hyde could not remember the last time a woman had put her hand on his hand that way. Maybe no woman had ever done it. . . .

"Well, for him it was the other way around," said Karin. "The great lover, adored by women all his life, and now it suddenly doesn't work anymore. And you can guess who he blamed for that."

"So he didn't go back?"

"Not to Caroline, at first. He started seeing the other one again, I haven't told you about her, a girl who was his secretary once, a bathing beauty queen from New Jersey, by this time she was a stockbroker or something, and she was married, too, but of course that didn't matter. . . . I don't know exactly what she did, but I think it worked again with her and then of course everything was okay, she even made some arrangement with the boy —"

"This other girl made some arrangement with his son? I don't understand —"

"I don't understand it either, what difference does it make, I think she persuaded the boy to come somewhere to meet his father, and the next thing he took Caroline to the movies and then he spent the night out there —"

"But why would the other girl —"

"*Why? Why? Why?* How do I know why! Could we talk about something else now, my dear sir?"

Francis Hyde watched her swallow half a glass of white wine. "I'm sorry, but I'd like to know how you feel about him now."

"How do I feel about him now?" Karin turned her head and looked out of the window at the passing cars and the trees along the river front. "What is the story in the Bible, where the girl dances for the king, and the king tells her she can have whatever she wants?"

"Are you talking about John the Baptist?"

"Yes, well, Mr. Anders is not exactly John the Baptist." She turned to face him again and smiled. "Mr. Anders is not John the Baptist, but would you like to bring me his head on a silver platter?"

"Are you serious?"

Looking down, she shook her head. Francis Hyde reached out and gently tipped her chin up with his index finger so that she had to look into his questioning eyes and this time she did not smile. "It was years ago," she said. "It's over."

He sat back in his chair with a grunt. "As a matter of fact, I have a bone to pick with your friend Anders."

"You know him?"

"No, I don't know him personally, although I knew his grandfather, of course, but he and that Rumanian Jew of his grabbed a company for Boatwright that I'd had my eye on for a while and I don't like it when people do that to me!"

"Is this the thing you are talking about with Gottfried Gesstler?"

"Yes. I've given him some information about Boatwright. I must say I was surprised when I examined it. Fleischer seems to have changed. When he was younger he took big risks, borrowed lots of money, worked on leverage, stuck his neck out. . . . That doesn't seem to be the picture today. Very little debt, lots of cash. Mr. Fleischer seems to have lost his taste for raiding other people's companies."

"I thought you said he took something away from you. He and Graham —"

"Well, in the first place that was several years ago, and in the second place it wasn't a raid. They just moved faster than my people, and they paid top dollar so they got the company. My own fault, but I'd like to get my hands on it now."

"You mean together with Gottfried Gesstler? Whatever it was you suggested has certainly excited him. My mother says he is meeting with his technical people night and day. What kind of company is it?"

"You're not interested in this sort of thing, are you?"

"You think I ask men about their business to flatter them? If I was not interested I would not ask, you can believe me! And will you please tell them to bring another bottle?"

Francis Hyde looked at his watch. Another bottle? Now? Was he really ready for a new life? He signaled the waiter and turned back to her. "All right, if you really want to hear this story I'll tell it to you. I guess you could say it began when Dr. Walther Siegler had to flee from Vienna in 1938, because he was Jewish. He got to England, but he wasn't allowed to practice medicine there so he went into technical X-ray research, worked together with English doctors who later developed the first CAT scanner. *Computerized Axial Tomography*. What is it? Essentially it is an X-ray camera that moves around the body taking hundreds of pictures from different angles, and a computer that figures out what the pictures mean. At first they used it on the head, to look for brain tumors without opening the skull, but now they can go over the whole body with the thing. . . .

"Well anyway, Dr. Siegler eventually got to the United States and interested some people with money to invest. More years of research and testing. They started to build these machines. CAT scanners. They cost over seven hundred thousand dollars apiece, and gradually every hospital decided it had to have one. Oh, Siegler didn't have a patent or anything like that, a lot of people make these things now, General Electric makes them, your German Siemens company makes them . . . but Siegler makes a very good one, and makes a lot of money doing it, and it would have made a good fit for us . . . but Boris Fleischer sent your friend Anders to talk German to Walther Siegler, or something, I don't know exactly what happened but it happened pretty damn fast. My people were still doing their homework when we read in *The Wall Street Journal* that Boris Fleischer — I mean Boatwright, of course — has bought all of Siegler's stock for cash, one hell of a lot of cash. Closed the deal in the morning and announced it in the afternoon!

"But that's not the end of the story. It seems that there are problems with these CAT scanner machines. They shoot the patient full of X rays, and X rays are dangerous, and there have to be controls that measure how much radiation the patient is getting to make sure he doesn't get too much, and these controls have broken down once in a while. Even Siegler's. So these seven-hundred-thousand-dollar machines are not foolproof, and there's been trouble. Law suits. Now they've come up with another scanner, a completely different principle. *No X rays!* This thing is called NMR, which means *Nuclear Magnetic Resonance*. What they do is, they throw a magnetic field into the patient, magnetic waves and radio waves. Harmless. Can't burn the patient. As I understand it — and I really don't completely understand it myself — these magnetic waves make the atoms in the patient's body line up in some way, and when they turn the magnet off, the atoms move back to where they were in the first place, and by the speed with which these atoms move back, the doctors can tell exactly what kind of tissue they are moving *through*, and again they have a computer that keeps track of every magnetic wave they shoot through the body. . . . There's no point in trying to explain all this technical stuff, especially as I don't completely understand it myself, but take it from me, this is *the* hot product right now, and Siegler is on the ground floor, actually making the NMR machines, installing them in hospitals! Again, they don't have a patent, they're not the only one, but they are one of the first, they are real pioneers in the commercial application of this technique. They have different kinds of magnets: the smallest one weighs four tons and the biggest one weighs a hundred tons. And they cost up to three million dollars a piece!"

Francis Hyde was out of breath. His eyes were shining.

THIRTEEN

Prenuptials

By Christmas, 1977, all the other big law firms had either discontinued their traditional parties or they were giving them in the ballrooms of downtown hotels. Conyers & Dean refused to budge. As always, a quartet played in the thirty-first-floor reception lobby, waiters passed drinks through the crowd, lawyers wearing white carnations greeted guests crowding off the elevators, secretaries wearing mistletoe corsages hung together in giggling groups, drinking gin and tonic until some of them were asked to dance. The Turkish carpets were rolled off the parquet. . . .

It had been easier in the old days, when all the men were lawyers, all the women were secretaries, and everybody knew everybody else. Today, a lot of the young women were lawyers, a lot of the young women were paralegal assistants, and some of the men were paralegals, too. The older lawyers didn't know exactly who all of the younger people were, so they and their clients drifted away from the music and the dancing. In some offices potential new deals were tried out over plates of lobster salad. In other offices, people put their feet on the tables and discussed the stock market, waving highballs at each other.

"Graham, I see that Boatwright's down to 18. Something going on there?" Pin-striped red-faced Mo Patterson settled himself into Ordway Smith's black leather sofa.

"The whole market is going to hell," Anders replied. "Boatwright's doing fine."

"Lot of cash there, Graham. What's happened to Fleischer's lean and hungry look?"

"Perhaps we all get more conservative as we get older," suggested Ordway Smith.

"He hasn't made an acquisition since — jeez, what *was* his last acquisition, anyway?"

"Siegler," said Anders.

"That was *years* ago!"

"Five years ago, and you don't make acquisitions just to make acquisitions, Mo. Sometimes you consolidate and digest. Earnings have increased steadily every year. He's paid dividends every year. You guys focus on the razzle-dazzle too much. Yeah, do you want me?"

A secretary had put her head in the door. "They've got a call for you up front, Mr. Anders. Do you want them to put it into your room?"

He closed his door against the music and the voices and then he picked up the telephone. "Graham Anders."

"Ja, Fröhliche Weinachten!"

The voice went through him like an electric current. Still. "Where are you?" It didn't sound right. His mouth was dry.

"Right here, at home. I just put the girls into the limousine for the airport, they will visit Bob in Berkeley, then I'm off myself in the other direction, I just wanted to wish you Merry Christmas, dear."

"I read about your father-in-law. I'm terribly sorry, I wrote Mrs. Bromberg a note —"

"Yes, it was sad, but it happened quickly, the best way, I think. I was still in Europe and I couldn't even get back for the funeral. . . . Graham, will you see me for a few minutes? Please?"

"When?"

"Tonight. I mean, this afternoon. We are taking off from Kennedy in the morning."

"Who's *we?*"

"Francis Hyde. We are spending Christmas in Paris and then we go skiing in Klosters —"

"*Francis Hyde?* . . . Isn't he a little old for skiing?"

"No, he is quite well preserved, as a matter of fact, and he wants to marry me! What do you think of that?"

. . . .

"Graham?"

"What do *you* think of it?"

A sigh. "Well . . . that is what I want to see you about. You know, of course, that he has a lot of money. And he has two daughters, horrible fat women, much older than I am, one of them is married to an English lord, they will not even meet me, but they are making a terrible fuss with their father, about the money, of course —"

"Well, you can hardly blame them, can you?"

"My God, it's not *their* money!"

"Come on, now! They've spent their lives expecting to inherit a great deal of money, and all of a sudden dear old Dad finds himself somebody younger than they are, somebody who can walk off with maybe a third of his estate? Where did you run into Francis Hyde, if I may ask?"

"You have a Christmas drink with me, please, dear? I will tell you all about it."

"I have to be home at seven, we're going out to dinner —"

"I will drive into town right now and pick you up on the same old corner and we come here and have a drink and then I will drive you to your car. I see it is still in the same spot."

"Just don't put any flowers on it!"

She giggled. "Four o'clock on that corner?"

Her hair was pinned up with a golden barrette. She looked a little rounder in the face. She smiled, but it was not a happy smile. She kissed him on the mouth with her eyes wide open, put the car in gear, and drove off into the stream of traffic without a word. She wore a black cashmere sweater and black wool slacks and velvet boots with zippers down the sides. She drove as fast as she could, but she didn't say anything, and Anders was damned if he would make conversation, but then she smiled at him again: "We don't have to talk, do we?" and she was right.

Finally, as they came off the Expressway ramp and turned under the little railroad bridge, she asked about his children.

"Suzie's quite happily married, but the boy flies jet fighters off an aircraft carrier, not the safest job in the world. She's out at Pearl Harbor, playing bridge and tennis every day, apparently the right life for her — she could go to college out there, of course, but she doesn't —"

"And Boatie? Will he apply to Harvard?"

"He's in! Early admission, we just heard last week, but he's really too young, I want him to take a year off —"

"Oh, *Graham!*" She wrenched the Porsche off the road and jerked back the hand brake, and as she turned to him, Anders was startled to see tears in her eyes. She threw herself against his chest. "Oh dear, that is the most important thing in the world for you!"

"Well, I guess it's not the most important thing in the world, but it feels pretty nice, yes."

"And Caroline is ecstatic?"

"Caroline is very happy, yes, but I want to hear about you. Where is Mr. Hyde?"

She kept her face against his overcoat lapel for a moment. Then she sat up, found a handkerchief, blew her nose, glanced over her shoulder, released the brake and drove onto the road. "He's in New York. We are meeting at Kennedy in the morning."

"Where did you meet him in the first place?"

"On the *Möwe*, in August."

"*Möwe? Seagull?* Oh, that's your stepfather's boat."

"Yes, they asked him to go sailing, Gottfried wants to do some business with him and I was visiting friends in Cuernavaca but I decided to fly home for a few days' sailing and some sea air, and there he was. . . . Well —"

"Well, tell me about it."

She shook her head. "I don't tell you what I do with other men."

There was more snow on these twisting suburban lanes, and as she watched the road, Anders watched her. When she called him at the office she said she was home — in Ardmore. Just now she had gone home — to Hamburg. She couldn't go back to Berkeley, nor to that ranch in Sonoma. She didn't have a home. Whose fault was that? All these years of rattling around different countries with different men . . . Francis Hyde? Exactly what she needs — but still it hurt. After all this time, it hurt.

It was a handsome document, produced on a word processor, bound together like a slim book with a sky-blue cover bearing the name and address of Openshaw, Prescott, Pennington & Lee, Attorneys and Counsellors at Law.

    This Agreement made between Karin Müller

Bromberg, a divorced woman, residing at . . . (herein called Mrs. Bromberg) and Francis Hyde, a widower, residing at . . . (herein called Mr. Hyde) WITNESSETH:

The parties are about to marry. In anticipation thereof, they desire to settle by prenuptial agreement the rights and claims that will accrue to each of them in the estate and property of the other by reason of the marriage, and to accept the provisions of this Agreement in lieu of and in full discharge and settlement . . .

Anders sat slumped back in the familiar glove leather sofa, his feet toward the fire, and she sat directly beside him, reading with him as he turned the pages. He could feel her arm against his arm, he could smell her, and he could feel his heart beating.

He put the agreement face-down on the coffee table and picked up his drink. "Listen, this is ridiculous. This isn't my field of law, there are dozens of people in this town who can advise you about this thing —"

"But I don't want them!"

"Didn't Pennington explain this to you?"

"Bill Pennington is *his* lawyer. Yes, he explained it. He also said I should have my own lawyer look at it — so please read it for me, Graham!"

"Let me ask you this: what's your agreement with Bob? We didn't represent either of you in the divorce, so I don't have any idea —"

"I got this house, but my income stops if I remarry. You may remember why I was not in a very strong bargaining position at that time!"

"But what about your father-in-law? I thought he was going to take care of everything."

"He took very good care of the girls. They have a trust, the Wells Fargo Bank is trustee, they are quite rich little girls."

"What did he leave you?"

"This house, and another trust with enough money for the taxes and groceries and a couple of dresses every year . . ."

"Does that stop if you remarry?"

"No."

"So he did leave you enough to live on?"

She shrugged. "Just enough." She took the agreement off the table and put it on his lap. "Please read it, dear."

NOW, THEREFORE, in consideration of the premises and of the marriage and in further consideration of the mutual promises and understandings hereinafter set forth, the parties agree as follows:

Section 1. By deed executed and delivered upon the effective date of this Agreement, Mr. Hyde will grant and convey (or cause the present owner to grant and convey) to Mrs. Bromberg the real property consisting of approximately 300 acres and improvements thereon in the Township of Tredyffrin, Chester County, Pennsylvania, variously known as *Hyde-a-Way* and *Conroy House*. Mr. Hyde agrees to pay all taxes, operating and maintenance costs upon the said premises . . .

"Now what the hell is *this?* He's giving you the Hyde Place? He doesn't even own it! Charlie Conroy owns the Hydes' Place —"

Karin looked down at the agreement. "As you know, Charlie Conroy has never been happy with that house, Charlie Conroy is now in very serious difficulties, Charlie Conroy has agreed to sell the place to us —"

"My God, what do you want it for?"

Now she looked up angrily. "What do I want it for? I want it to ride my horse on. I don't want Mr. Ordway Smith telling me where I can and cannot ride my horse, that's what I want it for!"

"Karin, that was *years* ago!"

Her eyes flashed. "I remember it!"

Anders shook his head and continued to read. Section 2: Subject to the conditions set forth in Section 4, Mrs. Bromberg was to receive and accept from Mr. Hyde's estate the sum of Five Million Dollars ($5,000,000) free and clear of all inheritance taxes. . . . Section 3 explained exactly how soon after Mr. Hyde's death Mrs. Bromberg would receive her Five Million Dollars. . . .

Section 4 contained the hook: Mrs. Bromberg would get *nothing* from Mr. Hyde's estate unless (a) she survived him, (b) they were living together as man and wife at the time of Mr. Hyde's death, and

(c) they had been living together as man and wife continuously from their marriage until Mr. Hyde's death.

In Section 5 Mrs. Bromberg waives and releases all rights and claims that she might acquire as Mr. Hyde's surviving spouse in his estate, including any and all rights of intestacy and all rights to take against Mr. Hyde's will . . .

"You're going to be a rich widow," said Anders.

"Rich enough?"

"Rich enough for what?"

"Keep reading."

In Section 6 Mr. Hyde waives all his rights and claims to Mrs. Bromberg's property, should he survive her . . .

In Section 7 Mrs. Bromberg acknowledges that Mr. Hyde has fully disclosed his financial situation to her and has furnished her with his personal balance sheet as of September 30, 1977, which is attached as Exhibit A, and a copy of his federal income tax return for the calendar year ended December 31, 1976, which is attached as Exhibit B . . .

Anders stopped and turned to her. "Karin, you really want me to look at Francis Hyde's balance sheet? At his income tax return?"

She frowned. "Of course. It's the whole point." So Anders reached for his glass, drank some iced vodka, leaned back again, and paged through the Exhibits. Then he put the booklet back on the coffee table and looked into the fire.

"Well? What do you think now?" she asked.

"Kind of takes your breath away, doesn't it, but I can't say I'm surprised. That's a terrific company — and they certainly laid it right out for you. Nobody's going to break this agreement on the ground that you weren't told what he was worth!"

"They laid it out for me, all right. He is worth over a hundred million dollars, and if I sign nothing and then I take, as you lawyers say 'against the will,' I can get about a third of that, but I am supposed to sign this thing and settle for *five?*"

Anders grinned. "Plus the Hyde Place."

"You find this funny?"

"Well now really! Your girls are taken care of, you wind up with two houses, five million bucks — and Bernard Bromberg's trust. I don't think most people would consider this exactly a tragedy. You don't want the man to think you're marrying him for his money, do you?"

She sat up straight and filled her lungs. Her face darkened. "You want to hear what he said, a joke he told to me? A man sits next to a very beautiful girl at a dinner party, yes? And as the dinner ends he whispers to her, 'I would love to go to bed with you!' and of course she just laughs. Then the man says, 'If I pay you a million dollars right now, will you go to bed with me just once?' and of course she doesn't believe he is serious, but he really convinces her that he has that much money and will really pay in advance, so she says okay, for a million dollars she will do it, so then the man takes out his wallet and puts a hundred-dollar bill in her hand and says, 'Let's go upstairs,' and the girl says, 'What do you think I am?' and the man says, 'We've already established what you are. We are now negotiating the price!' "

"Old story," said Anders, but he was embarrassed.

"He told *me* this story!" She said it through clenched teeth. "Big joke! I don't think it is so funny! We have already established what I am, you see. We are now negotiating the price," and she put her head on his shoulder. "Oh, Graham, what am I going to do? You're not going to let me do this, are you?"

Suddenly Anders was furious: "What do you mean, don't let you do this? Do you want to marry this man or don't you? What's this got to do with me?"

"Everything, and you know it!"

"Why?"

"Because I still want you so much but I can't have you, and now this old man wants me, he really needs me, you know, the man has not loved a woman in ten years! Can you imagine that? And why shouldn't I have a nice life with a man who is crazy about me, who likes to travel with me and take me to the theater and to the races in France and to the best skiing places —"

"Well then, what's the problem?"

"*This!*" She picked up the sky blue agreement and hurled it across the room — a flutter of pages and a splat as it landed on the beautiful carpet in front of the bookshelves. "I'm being paid off like a little whore *if* we are living together as man and wife when he dies! And he didn't even have the courage to explain it to me. Bill Pennington will explain. Fat, bald little man! Smiling! Horrible necktie! We have drawn up this little agreement so that everything is perfectly clear at the outset and everybody knows where they stand —"

"I don't see where signing this kind of an agreement makes you a whore. This is a marriage settlement. No king or queen or prince or princess ever got married without some kind of marriage settlement; you know that. You can bet your life that the Lord St. Eustace didn't marry Fanny Hyde without some very generous marriage settlement from her father. Got nothing to do with love, it's just a question of who gets how much money —"

"Well, he makes me feel like a whore with this thing, I can tell you that. 'Bill Pennington will explain it all'!"

"Francis Hyde didn't discuss the numbers with you? You must have talked about the Hyde Place, if you've persuaded him to buy it from Charlie Conroy."

"Yes, we talked about the Hyde Place; he asked the same thing you asked: what am I going to do with it? And I said I want a home, my own home where I can ride my own horse on my own land — and where they won't see your car in the driveway —"

"Jesus Christ, Karin, you didn't say *that!*"

"No, of course I didn't say that, but the man is sixty-eight years old; he isn't going to live forever."

Anders took her hand off his arm and stood up. "Look, I don't want to *ever* hear you say things like that, I think you must be crazy to say things like that!"

She leaned back into the sofa and looked up at him. "You have been thinking it, too."

"No, I have not been thinking any such thing," he said, but it wasn't true.

"You want to make love now?" She took his hand.

"I want to, but I don't think I could."

"Oh, I think you could. How *is* Miss Cranberries? Or Mrs. Cranberries now?"

"She's fine. She's having a baby."

"A baby! *Your* baby?"

"Karin, she's been married for years —"

"Married for years, a little older than I am, and *now* she can suddenly have a baby? . . . A boy into Harvard and a new baby to be born . . . Oh dear, what a successful man at middle age! You have no reason to miss me, have you?"

"I wish I didn't miss you, but I do."

She pressed his hand against her cheek for a moment. Then she whispered: "Please tell me what to do about this disgusting contract."

"I've told you I don't see what's so disgusting about it; I think it is a fairly generous marriage settlement, it clears the air with his daughters, and you don't need any more money than that. But if you really don't want to sign it, he can't make you. The only thing he can do is not marry you."

She let go of his hand and stared into the fire. "That's right. If he really loves me, he doesn't make me sign something like this, because it isn't fair. He has two daughters, and he has me. So at best, I would get a third, and they would each get a third. What's wrong with that? Why should I get less than they do?"

"Why indeed?" said Anders. "Are you going to take me to my car now?"

She looked at her watch and then back at him, stretched her arms, and yawned. "It's not even six o'clock yet."

BOOK III

FOURTEEN

Isn't That Illegal?

"Did she sign the agreement?" asked Boris Fleischer, who had been listening to the story with his chin in his hand.

"Apparently not," said Anders. "At least, at lunch today Ordway Smith was telling me that one of Hyde's daughters is worried about her financial situation. . . . This day seems to have gone full circle for me."

Fleischer was turning the pages of the Schedule 13D. "This Gesstler with his Hansa Nordamerika Bank, this is her stepfather?"

"Yes, he is. *His* father was one of these guys who gave money to Hitler way back in the beginning. A real, original Nazi. During the war he had prisoners from the concentration camps working in his factories. The British military government put him in jail and dismantled his empire — coal mines, chemical plants, shipyards — and then this son, this Gottfried who owns this schooner *Möwe* now, he came back from the war and he gradually put the family business back together — with some help from the Marshall Plan, of course."

"You know him?" asked Fleischer.

"No, I don't know him, but she's told me about him. He's a little younger than her mother. He was eighteen or nineteen in 1944, he served in the Waffen-SS; you know what that was? The SS combat formations?"

"I know what the Waffen-SS was," said Fleischer quietly.

"Well, of course he was taken prisoner, but after the war was over, he went back to Hamburg and married Karin's mother and somehow reestablished himself — and he's built up quite an empire now —"

"Graham, what is going on here?"

Anders shook his head. "I don't understand it. Apparently Gesstler and Hyde met someplace by accident, but what they want with us . . . Well, looking at it objectively, our stock is down to 17, been down below 17 this winter, we have a very strong balance sheet. . . . Boris, I don't have to tell you this, Boatwright is *cheap!*"

"And the German mark is very strong," said Fleischer. "As strong as it has ever been, so clearly this is a good time for Germans to buy American investments. But Francis Hyde is not a German. Philadelphia Pharmaceuticals and Boatwright?" and then, as they looked at each other across the beautiful marquetry library table that may have belonged to Madame de Pompadour, they had the answer in the same instant, and each could see that the other had it.

Fleischer's eyebrows rose and the corners of his mouth went down. "Walther Siegler with the SS?"

"Boris Fleischer with the SS?" asked Anders.

Fleischer shook his head. "Something missing here. Is it possible that Hyde doesn't know what you know? This SS business? Would it be possible that nobody has told him?"

"Anything is possible."

"If she told you, why wouldn't she tell him?"

"I don't know, but she didn't tell me that they were coming after Boatwright."

"If she knew."

"She knew," said Anders grimly.

Fleischer looked sad, and much older. It was getting very late.

Anders began thinking out loud. "Of course the most likely possibility is that Hyde knows all about Gesstler's background, and that he doesn't give a damn. After all it was — what, over thirty years ago? The man was a nineteen-year-old cadet, I think a tank gunner; does that really make any difference now?"

Fleischer nodded, but he did not say anything.

"This is a political issue in Germany," said Anders. "The Waffen-SS claim they were soldiers like any others, they were soldiers like the Wehrmacht, like the German army. They want to have their own veterans' associations and war memorials and reunions."

"Then there is the other matter." Fleischer interrupted, surprising

Anders, because Fleischer never interrupted. "They must know how much Boatwright stock I have, and how much your wife has. Does one try to take over a public company of which two people own twenty percent — unless one has made a deal with them?" The light reflected on Fleischer's glasses so that Anders could not see his eyes. "Or at least with one of them?"

To Anders, the library seemed to turn yellow, as if he were looking through a filter, and he felt a sudden nausea, like seasickness. In all the years of working with Boris Fleischer, all the years since the summer of 1961 when they made their armistice in the Salzburg airport, Anders had felt that Fleischer trusted him: the Third Trustee.

"Boris, I'm not sure what you mean." It came out in a whisper.

"I mean, have you discussed this with your wife?"

"With my wife? That 13D you have there? How could I have —"

"You think perhaps Mr. Hyde, or Mrs. Bromberg, or some emissary, has been in touch with your wife?"

"About what, Boris?"

"About selling them her Boatwright stock."

"Boris, Caroline would *never* sell her Boatwright stock. Not for a hundred dollars a share. You know that!"

Fleischer took off his glasses and rubbed his eyes. "Never is a long time."

"Boris, they would be required to disclose such a deal in that 13D you have there."

"Yes, if they have actually made such a deal, but if they have only discussed it, have not yet made a deal, when would they have to disclose it?"

Silence in the room. Then Anders said: "Boris, I told you *first thing* that you had better talk to another law firm about this. There are two firms here in New York who are on one side or the other of almost every big tender offer —"

Fleischer sighed. "I know, I know, but once you get into that, you are in a war, and there must be some way to avoid this war."

"I don't understand what you mean, Boris."

"I mean these tender offer battles we have in this country now, they are terrible things. They destroy companies who fight them! The only people who make money are the lawyers and the investment bankers!"

"Well Boris, forgive me, but Boatwright as it exists today is the product of some pretty aggressive takeovers dreamed up by Boris Fleischer —"

Suddenly a hunted look: "So this now is — what do you say, poetic justice?"

"Boris!" Anders took a deep breath, praying that his voice would not shake. "Boris, we have got to get something straight right here and now, and it's got nothing to do with whether tender offers are a good idea, or whether you use Conyers & Dean or one of the tender offer law firms, or both." Anders swallowed. "I have to know whether you trust me or not."

"Graham, of course I trust you."

"Well, you're beginning to sound a little different, Boris, when you ask if I've discussed this with Caroline —"

Fleischer shook his head. "Nothing to do with trust. No, no, no, not with trust. With what, then? How do I explain this? Look, ever since I have known you, you have been — what shall we say? Very fortunate with the ladies? Not so many, just a few, but perhaps more than is expected of a man in your position, and I have never talked about it with you because it was none of my business and it had no effect whatever on your work — or on my company. . . . But now, I begin to wonder."

"Boris —"

"Please, let me finish. This story that is developing now, this story about a woman in her thirties who thinks to marry a man of sixty-eight for his money, who apparently still wants to end up with you, this man who still wants to get Walther Siegler's NMR technology five years later and maybe has found in Germany the money to do this with, found this money with the family of this woman, and you wonder that I ask if you have discussed this with your wife? Your wife with some ten percent of Boatwright stock?"

"Well, of course I'm going to have to discuss this with Caroline immediately," said Anders.

"What will you tell her?"

"Exactly what happened."

"*Exactly?*"

"Boris . . ." Anders felt terribly tired now, and he had to search for the right words. "Of course you're right, I've involved myself with too many people, but in really important things . . . Boatwright — I really think of Boatwright as Caroline's inheritance — in really important things I trust her. Not only her judgment, Boris. I would trust her with my life."

Boris Fleischer nodded.

* * *

— Hello?

— Hi, this is me. I'm sorry to wake you up —

— Graham! Are you all right? What time is it?

— It's about one o'clock. . . . Caroline, there's a problem with Boatwright, I've got to fly to Germany tomorrow and there may be something in *The Wall Street Journal* and I want you to hear about it first from me.

— Just a minute, Graham, I want to turn the light on, I want to sit up. . . . Okay now. Are you with Boris?

— No, I'm down in my own room now. . . . Look, you know who Francis Hyde is, don't you? Philadelphia Pharma? I think your father used to know him —

— Sure, he has two daughters. Fanny, and I forget the other one — What about him?

— Well, he's been buying Boatwright stock together with a syndicate of Germans. They're over five percent now, so they had to file a report with the SEC, and send the Company a copy.

— And why is that a problem?

— Because we don't think they'll stop at where they are, we think they may want to take over the whole Company. We don't know about the Germans, but we think Hyde is mainly interested in Siegler: you know, the scanner people up in Cambridge. Remember we bought Siegler very quickly when Philadelphia Pharma was looking at them too.

— Isn't Mr. Hyde getting a little old for these things? I mean, he was a friend of Dad's —

— Apparently not, in fact he's about to get married again. . . . Listen, there is another angle to this thing I have to tell you about, I just promised Boris I would tell you about —

— I see.

— It has to do with the Germans, who appear to be putting up the money, who want to buy Boatwright, maybe even take over Boatwright. . . .

— What about them?

— Well, the main German is a man called Gesstler, Gottfried Gesstler, a big industrialist in Hamburg, and I think he was a Nazi, at any rate he served in the SS —

— He served in what?

— You know what the SS was? Hitler's *Schutzstaffeln*, the ones in black uniforms?

— Yes, of course I know. . . . Graham, is this something you found out about when you were in the army? You found out about this man when you were eighteen? You've known him all this time?

— No, not this particular man!

— Well, how do you know about this particular man, Graham?

— That's what I'm trying to tell you. . . .

— Well, go ahead and tell me.

— He's Karin's stepfather. Her mother married him when he came back from the war. Karin didn't like him and she never had much to do with him, but he is her stepfather, and that's how I've heard about him. So there you are!

— How charming. I take it, then, you know this gentleman.

— No, I don't know him. I've never met the man.

— But she's told you about this SS business?

— A long time ago she told me something about it, yes.

— A long time ago?

— That's right. The reason I'm telling you all this is that Boris thinks they might have approached you.

— Who might have approached me?

— Hyde, or the Germans.

— About what, Graham?

— Making a deal to sell them your Boatwright stock. That would give them a tremendous advantage in any takeover.

— Boris thinks I'd sell my Boatwright stock to Karin Bromberg's stepfather, who was in Hitler's SS? I just don't believe that, Graham. That doesn't make one bit of sense to me, and it doesn't sound like Boris Fleischer.

— He wanted me to ask you, so I've done that. I told him you'd never sell your stock, and he said, "Never is a long time."

— That's true enough. Never *is* a long time. . . . But this story still doesn't make sense to me . . . especially as this is the second time today that I'm talking about Mr. Francis Hyde, when I haven't heard a word about him for years and years. . . .

— The second time today?

— Marion Smith called me at the office to ask if I heard anything about Mr. Hyde trying to buy the old Hyde Place from Charlie Conroy. It's right next door to them, you know.

— Marion Smith? I had lunch with Ordway today, and he didn't say a word about it.

— Well, maybe he didn't hear about it, since you all don't represent Charlie anymore —

— Well then, where did Marion —

— She didn't want to say and I didn't want to press her, but I suspect that somebody in Bill Pennington's law firm talked to his wife, who talked to Patsy Paul, who plays tennis with Marion —

— Is that all the news Marion Smith had from Pennington's law firm?

. . . .

— You there, Caroline?

— Yes, I am, Graham. I'm still right here. Twelve Juniper Lane, Haverford, Pennsylvania. . . . I understood you to say something about wanting to hear it first from you.

— Now you're playing games with me, Miss Boatwright.

— Oh no, Graham I'm not good at games like this, because I hate them so. . . . It seems that Ordway once years ago told her that she couldn't ride on Charlie Conroy's land, so now it's going to be *her* land! But if you're thinking to find her in Germany, I'm afraid you'll be disappointed, because she nearly ran me down driving her Porsche out of the Acme this afternoon!

— You've got it wrong, Caroline. I'm going to Hamburg to see an old friend of Boris's, an old man called Otto Waldstein, whose family has run a private bank in Hamburg for two hundred years and he's supposed to tell me all about Gesstler.

— I see. . . . No, I *don't* see. Why doesn't Boris just call his friend on the telephone?

— Well, of course he is going to call first thing in the morning, but these old guys don't do business that way, they want to see you face-to-face, to get a look at you, so that's why he's sending me over. But to tell you the truth, I'm getting a little worried about Boris. He got that SEC report in the morning mail and he made me come to New York without saying a word about it, spent the whole time at dinner worried sick about a revolution he thinks we're going to have in this country and then after dinner he suddenly pulls this Schedule 13-D, this SEC form, out of his drawer! Boris isn't getting any younger.

— Yes. And what happens to Boatwright when Boris dies?

— What's that?

— I said, Graham, what happens to Boatwright when Boris Fleischer dies? What happens to his Boatwright stock, for example?

— Caroline, we talked about this before —

— Yeah, but now we're really faced with it, aren't we? Those Jewish charities aren't going to hold his Boatwright stock. They're going to sell it. And they're supposed to offer it to me first. But what am I going to use for money to buy it with?

— I don't think it will be a problem; we'll be able to borrow —

— But what's the point of it all, Graham? By that time you'll be out in the Hyde Place, exact copy of the Château de Monmort, with that crazy Lorelei of yours —

— Caroline, for Christ's sake!

— And I'll be up to my ears in debt just to keep control of my great-grandfather's company! I mean, what *is* the point?

— Caroline . . . If you're in this kind of state, perhaps I better put off this trip for a day and come home. . . . Don't you believe that if I wanted to be with her I'd *be* with her? Haven't we been around this whole course before?

— She isn't giving up.

— Caroline, she is getting married to another man!

— Lot of difference that made to her the last time! And besides, she's not married to him yet; she won't sign the marriage settlement or something, I understand.

— Well, Ordway did mention that at lunch.

— But you didn't know that before? She hasn't discussed all this with you? Here Ordway is representing Fanny Hyde and you are representing Karin Bromberg! Isn't that illegal?

— I am *not* representing Karin Bromberg! Look, I'm coming home tomorrow morning, I'm not going to leave you in this kind of —

— No, no, it's all right, I'm all right now, it's just that for a minute I felt that I was all alone on the edge of a cliff — Don't you need some clothes? What's happening tomorrow?

— Well, we're meeting with investment bankers. Boris doesn't want to, but if you get into this kind of a fight, you've got to have investment bankers, there's no way out of it. I guess I'll just have to go out and buy some shirts and underwear. . . . They'll have to send my passport over with an office messenger —

— Tell them to have the messenger wait; I'll pack you a bag and bring it to your office. How long will you be gone?

— You don't need to do that, Caroline.

— No, that's all right, it's silly to buy all new stuff and you won't have time. . . . What was the name of the man you're going to see in Hamburg?

— Otto Waldstein, Waldstein and somebody, they are an old Jewish banking house, they were driven out by the Nazis but they went back after the war, they've done a lot of business with Boris —

— How long do you think you'll be gone?

— Just a couple of days, I hope. A week, maybe. Just long enough to find out what the hell is going on.

— Well, if you decide to fly directly to Philadelphia, give me a call and I'll meet your plane.

— That would be terrific.

— Graham?

— Yeah?

— Never mind. Have a good trip. Good night.

FIFTEEN

WALDSTEIN, HAMMERBROOK & CO.
BALLINDAMM 175
2000 HAMBURG 1

It was a high-ceilinged corner office, but it felt more like a museum. One of the tall windows looked out across the Binnenalster, the smaller of the two lakes at the center of the city. Through the other window, Anders could see slim church spires rising against the gray winter sky. The paneled walls were covered with pictures, and the pictures were being explained.

There was the family: the Hamburg bankers of 1785 and the Hamburg bankers of 1885, the buildings in which they had worked, and the uncles and cousins in Berlin and London and New York. There were groups: a training company of Infantry Regiment 76 (Hamburg Volunteers) — very young men with rifles and German helmets, posing together in some forest on September 12, 1918; the Directors of the Hamburg-Amerika line, sitting around their board table and glowering into the camera on April 15, 1931; another training company — ski troops of the Tenth U.S. Mountain Division, white smiles on sunburned faces at Camp Carson, Colorado, September, 1942. There was a picture of two British officers showing the ruins of Hamburg to Lieutenant Colonel Waldstein, who is wearing the flaming sword patch of General Eisenhower's Supreme Headquarters. There were inscribed portraits: General Mark W. Clark, General Walter Bedell Smith, General George S. Patton, Jr., General Lucius D. Clay, Allen W. Dulles, Konrad Adenauer, John F. Kennedy. . . .

If Boris Fleischer looked like a small parrot, Otto Waldstein looked like a tiny eagle: a bald, double-breasted gray flannel eagle, with white brows bristling over ice-blue eyes. If Boris Fleischer was given to long, reflective silences, Otto Waldstein rarely paused between the stories about himself and the people on the walls — and yet Anders sensed that he was being carefully studied. He had not expected so much charm and good humor. "Otto Waldstein knows everybody," Fleischer had said. "He has agreed to see you, but he wants to hear the whole story before he'll tell us anything."

Anders was eager to tell the whole story, but Otto Waldstein seemed in no hurry to hear it.

Anders had been drinking coffee and Cognac all night, flying from New York to Frankfurt. Waiting at Kennedy, he had browsed in a bookstore. Shiny jackets. Paperback covers. A recurring theme seemed to be the swastika. Why does the swastika sell books? He bought *The New Yorker* to read on the plane, but then he didn't read it, he only paged through the expensive glasses and the dressy women and the cars and the jewelry and the cartoons. . . . Peter Arno is dead. Anders drank coffee, drank Cognac, and tried to remember what he knew about the SS . . . besides the photograph of Gustaf Anders in Dachau.

He had read some of those books, a long time ago, and he knew some of the story: Adolf Hitler's personal bodyguards, Heinrich Himmler's Order of the Death's Head, the Black Corps that first attracted international attention one summer night in 1934 when they murdered some eighty of their comrades, leaders of the other Nazi storm troop, the SA, demonstrating that they were beyond any law, that they had power to kill anybody at all. (German generals smiled and said, "They're killing each other." Ten years later the SS was hanging the same generals from meat hooks.) They developed their concentration camps into death camps, they organized a hell on earth, and in twelve years they killed so many people that the world lost count, but when the killing stopped, it was hard to tie specific men to specific piles of corpses. Only a few of the most conspicuous killers were brought to trial, and even fewer were executed. What happened to all the others?

When Anders was stationed in Austria, the SS was nowhere to be seen — except for an occasional hungry man in ragged clothes brought in by the Austrian border patrols. They filtered out of the forests of the Salzkammergut, having escaped from Russian camps in Hungary, in Poland, in the Ukraine. By that time nobody was being returned to the Russians, so they were shipped to stockades in Western Germany where they were not held long, and now the bookstores are full of swastikas. Terror attracts, absolute terror attracts absolutely, and who won the war? — and smiling German girls woke him up with orange juice and coffee and rolls, he saw the pine trees racing by, he saw the tarmac, he wished that he had known his father, he wished that he could talk about these things with his father, thank you for flying Lufthansa in both languages, and then he wandered dazedly among the jewelry shops and bookshops and camera shops and luggage shops and liquor shops and delicatessens and sleeping people from Argentina and India and Turkey and Japan — remembering another time when there was nothing in this airport between the rivers Rhine and Main except the freezing wind blowing through cement halls constructed for the Luftwaffe, and American officers lugging their duffel bags from one propeller-driven C-54 to another. In those days it took fourteen hours to get across the Atlantic, but that was better than a week on a troop ship, and one didn't arrive light-headed from jet lag. . . .

The connecting flight put Anders into Hamburg in the middle of the afternoon, and by the time he had checked into the pompous, comfortable silence of the Hotel Vier Jahreszeiten, Otto Waldstein's secretary reported in perfect English English: Herr Waldstein had gone home, had expressed the hope that Mr. Anders would get a good night's sleep, regretted that he had a meeting first thing in the morning and another meeting after that, would be delighted to receive Mr. Anders at eleven o'clock — and he hoped to have Mr. Anders for lunch, alone, at the bank.

It was dark outside. Anders walked through the wet foggy streets, looked into the store windows, sat alone drinking Polish vodka among the loud German conversations in the hotel bar, retreated to his room, consumed a mushroom omelet with a half-bottle of Riesling, and fell asleep watching a movie in which Elizabeth Taylor and Richard Burton screamed at each other in German.

"Mr. Waldstein, the reason I've come —"

"Call me Otto, if you please, old man! On and off, I've spent over twenty years in the States, and I much prefer the way you use first names. You are Boris's lawyer, and Boris's lawyer must call me Otto!"

"Okay, Otto, that's very nice of you, and you call me Graham. Now, as Boris has told you —"

"Boris has told me you are the son of Gustaf Anders."

"Yes, I am, but —"

"But that is *extremely* interesting!" Another direction: in 1923, Otto Waldstein had attended a performance of the hit *Trompeten* in Berlin. The audience had stood up, had roared along with the actors on the stage, and why had the Nazis forbidden the plays of Gustaf Anders? Why had Gustaf Anders gone to Spain in 1936, when he could have remained in England with his American wife and his little son — questions Graham Anders had been asked all his life, questions that did not seem relevant to this mission . . . and then it was time for lunch. Otto Waldstein led the way to a tiny elevator, which brought them up to the private dining rooms: more pictures, beautiful models of clipper ships and steamers the firm had financed, even better views of the spires, the lakes, the cranes and smokestacks of the harbor, the river Elbe flowing across the flatlands to the sea. . . .

Sherry? Red wine or white? What are we eating? You can have veal or sole. . . . White wine then? Otto Waldstein himself drank Apollinaris water, with a twist.

After the second attempt, Anders gave up trying to question the old man. He knows why I've come; if he doesn't want to tell me anything, he won't, and if he does, he'll do it in his own time.

The time came when the coffee had been poured, when all the dishes except the blue-and-white onion pattern Meissen coffee pot and the cups had been removed, when the door had been closed from the outside in a way that suggested it would not be opened again.

Otto Waldstein sighed. "You wish to know about the Hansa Nordamerika Bank, Ferdinandstrasse 27, just in the next street."

Anders leaned forward. "Particularly about Herr Gottfried Gesstler."

"Yes, it's the same thing. They call it a bank, but it is really more of what in America we call an investment company, to invest the money of the Gesstlers and their friends — particularly to invest their money outside Germany. Perfectly normal arrangement here. You have heard about Herr Gesstler's father?"

Anders told him what he knew: early support of Hitler, military contracts, slave laborers, imprisonment by the British military government.

Otto Waldstein nodded. "All that is correct, but you should know it was not such an unusual history in this country, in those years. There were lots of powerful men who saw in Adolf Hitler the leader who would restore Germany's position in the world, the leader who would prevent a communist revolution here. And then, during the war, the Nazi government put prisoners from the concentration camps into everybody's mines, everybody's factories: the work had to be done, it was a question of whether these people would die in gas chambers or live as slave workers. From that point of view, the people who were strong enough to work were lucky ones, if they didn't collapse from overwork and nothing to eat — so Herr Gesstler saved thousands of Jews and Poles and Russians — as he tried to explain to the British court in 1946! But that gentleman is dead now, and you are interested in his son. All right, the son."

Otto Waldstein paused to drink some coffee, perhaps to catch his breath. "All right, the son! Just imagine: a boy in a Nazi family, at the height of Nazi power. Ten years old when the Olympics are held in Berlin. The eyes of the world on Germany again. Fourteen years old when German armies sweep through Denmark and Norway and Holland and Belgium and France! Hitler Youth! SS Cadet School Braunschweig! Then the Leibstandarte SS Adolf Hitler . . . black uniforms, military bands, parades, this was the lifeguard regiment of Adolf Hitler. For this young man at this time, it must have been something like the Prussian Guards for us, the greatest honor to be allowed to join. . . . But by the time he was old enough to join, it was an armored division. And the war had turned. Must have been about 1944. In Russia, the Germans were in retreat, they had enormous casualties, they had lost an entire army at Stalingrad, in the west the Allies had landed, these special SS Panzer divisions were rushed by train from one front to another. No more parades! Just mud and snow and burning tanks and burning people. These units took the heaviest losses because their officers paid no attention at all to human cost — whether it was the enemy, or civilians, or prisoners, or their own men!" Otto Waldstein stopped again. "Perhaps you know all this? Boris told me you were in the U.S. Army."

"Yes," said Anders. "In general I know about the SS, I mean I know what they did in the war, but what I don't know is what's happened to those people *now*. The war's been over — what, thirty-five years? What about Gottfried Gesstler now? Do you know him?"

Otto Waldstein suddenly stood up, put his hands in his pockets, walked over to the window and looked out across the town. "Well, how do I explain this to you? I made the decision to return to Germany, to return to this city where my family has lived and worked for hundreds of years. Despite what happened. I felt that this is the place where I belonged. Hard to explain, but that is how I felt, how I still feel. We can never forget what happened. On the other hand, one cannot live here, one cannot work here, if one is obsessed with this subject, if one worries every minute what was this man or that man doing in the time of Adolf Hitler. In a town like this, of course Mr. Gottfried Gesstler knows who I am, and I know who Mr. Gottfried Gesstler is, and sometimes we must be in the same room at the same time, but we manage to stay out of each other's way. Of course he doesn't want to look back, to be reminded. . . . Well, as a matter of fact, I was on a committee to provide financial help for the people who worked in the factories during the war, the slave laborers we were talking about, and we asked these big industrialists for contributions, and most of them did it, were glad to do it. Some refused. Gesstler did not refuse, he gave what we asked. This was a voluntary thing, you understand, not a restitution lawsuit. He gave despite the fact that Americans kept him in custody for quite a while after the war was over. Down in Bavaria, the American zone. Then he came back here to Hamburg, found his father in prison, found the shipyards and the plants destroyed, found the whole family enterprise sequestered by the British. . . . Well, I must say, over a generation he has built it back, bigger than it was before, a soldier with no business training whatever. I think he found good people to advise him, I think he drove his people unmercifully, I think he benefited — as we all did — from American financial aid, from the Marshall Plan. I know he did well with shipbuilding contracts from American oil companies — and I think perhaps he is quite smart! For example, last year he sold his biggest shipyard to some Arabs, just at the time the Koreans are beginning to take the tanker-building business away from Hamburg! Perhaps the Arabs didn't know that, or perhaps the Arabs knew something we don't know, but in any event, the Arabs have Herr Gesstler's empty shipyard over there on the river and Herr Gesstler has their money — with which I understand he wants to buy your company, Boris Fleischer's company?"

"Well, that's what we're afraid of," said Anders. "He and an American partner have bought about six percent so far, and we think they might buy more. . . . Let me ask you this, Otto: what would you do if Gottfried Gesstler were trying to buy your company?"

Otto Waldstein began to pace around the little dining room, hands still in his trouser pockets. "What would I do? What would I do? We don't have this over here, you know. We read about this in *The Wall Street Journal*, this new American sport, the hostile tender offer. It is not something we like to do. Buy a company where they don't want us? A company is the people who run it, we think. If the people who run the company get up and leave, why are we buying the company?"

"I'm afraid that's not the attitude where I come from," said Anders. "A company is a balance sheet, a company is factories and machinery, a company is money, and if you've got enough money you can always go out and get new people — but basically you're perfectly right, these takeover fights are unbelievably expensive, the stakes are so high, everybody is fighting for his life, I've seen situations where they have practically destroyed the company that they were fighting over, that's called a scorched earth defense —"

"You know, there is something wrong with this whole story," said Otto Waldstein, interrupting, thinking along his own train of thought. "German investors have *never* made a hostile tender offer in the United States. Never! Why not? Well, for some residual feeling from the past, they don't want to be seen as invading Huns, the invading Nazis — I'm sure you know what I mean — and for somebody with Gottfried Gesstler's background . . ." He paused, shaking his head.

"Of course he's in this with Francis Hyde," said Anders. "And Francis Hyde wouldn't have the slightest problem about that kind of thing, and this whole deal could be presented as a Philadelphia Pharma operation, with the Germans in a minority position. Passive investors."

"Hmm" was the only response this time. Otto Waldstein was looking out of the window again. Then he glanced at his watch and turned around. "Look here, old man, after three o'clock you will want to telephone with your office, won't you? Nine o'clock at home? We will give you a room where you can do that, and also speak with Boris of course, anyone you like, and in the meantime I will consult one of my partners about this story, because there is really something a little strange about this whole thing, and I want to find out what he thinks. I want you to meet him. His name is Alexander Hammerbrook. He belongs to a very ancient family here. His uncle was Lord Mayor of Hamburg during the Weimar Republic. He and his father held this bank together in the Nazi time, as Hammerbrook & Co., when my family had to leave Germany, and when I decided to return, they gave back my share and we rebuilt the business together. During the war, he was an officer in the German army. He is a very decent honorable man, one of my best friends, although he is much younger than I am, he knows a lot of things I don't know, he knows a lot of people I don't know, and I think we should find out what he thinks. One more thing you should perhaps know about him: in the last days of the war, the SS shot his brother. Shall we go downstairs now?"

*   *   *

Anders sat alone in a small white conference room and listened to echoing voices from home. Boris Fleischer was still depressed. There had been a story in *The Wall Street Journal*. Boatwright stock was up two dollars on heavy volume. No new law firm and no investment bankers had been hired. No new Schedule 13-D had been received from Seagull — meaning that up to ten days ago they had not bought more stock. Fleischer had telephoned with Walther Siegler. Walther Siegler became very agitated, wanted Fleischer to come up to Boston immediately to meet with Siegler's sons, who are running the operation now, but Fleischer persuaded him to wait for Graham Anders's report, and you might consider flying directly into Boston on your way home so that you can give them your report in person, Graham. Siegler says he doesn't need something like this at the end of his life. He reminds me that none of his technical people have noncompetition agreements, and neither do his sons have them, they can all go to General Electric tomorrow morning if they want. Boris Fleischer really wonders what Francis Hyde is thinking of. Anders is to go ahead with what he is doing, report again tomorrow. Good-bye. Boris Fleischer dislikes the telephone.

At Conyers & Dean, Anders's secretary read off nine telephone slips, seven of them obviously about Boatwright. There had been a story in *The Wall Street Journal*. One of the calls was from Ordway Smith, so Anders asked to be switched over. What's happening? Ordway wanted to know. Anders gave him a brief outline. Don't Fleischer and Caroline control a very big block? Yes, said Anders, but not a majority. Well, even so, Graham, does this make any sense? Several aspects don't make any sense, that's what I'm looking into over here. How long do you think you'll be? Don't know, just a couple of days, I hope. Want anybody to cover for you? Your other clients? Departmental administration? Other clients are covered by younger people. Departmental administration can wait, will have to wait. We have to free-up a team for this thing, though. SEC people, litigators . . . and there won't be time to teach anybody anything. Boris isn't eager to bring in one of the New York firms, and I told him we could do it. Well, of course we can do it, I'll get on that right away. Good luck, Graham, keep us posted!

Anders did nothing about the call from Mrs. Bromberg.

Alexander Hammerbrook was a busy man, and Anders did not get in to see him until late that afternoon. Otto Waldstein was tired. He sat deep into Hammerbrook's black leather sofa, stretched out his legs, folded his hands, closed his eyes, and allowed his glasses to slip down his nose — but he was not asleep. He had explained the basic story, and now he threw in questions and answers whenever he wanted.

Alexander Hammerbrook was a round, square-shouldered giant with a round, pink face and clear blue eyes and a fine head of white hair that had once been blond. He wore a starched white collar, a navy blue necktie with little silver anchors on it, a navy blue suit with a well-filled vest, and a gold watch chain. He was a clean-desk man, and the white walls of his office were bare except for one big photograph of a beautiful sloop under sail. He was smoking a cigar and he offered one to Anders, who declined it.

Well, well, well, so Gottfried Gesstler wants to go on to an American adventure, eh? A Hamburger on Wall Street, eh?

"A Hamburger on Wall Street!" Alexander Hammerbrook leaned back in his chair and slapped his thigh with delight. "You know that there is in Hamburg now a McDonald's, to sell hamburgers to Hamburgers?" This time he took the cigar out of his mouth and roared with laughter. "*Hamburgers!* Can you tell me why you call them hamburgers? I am asking every American I meet, but none of them can tell me."

Taken aback, Anders confessed that he didn't know either.

"Gottfried Gesstler," said Otto Waldstein. His eyes were still shut.

"Yes yes yes yes yes, our learned senior partner has told me your story. Interesting story. Curious story. Holes in it. Isn't that what you say, holes in the story? But I can explain one thing: Gesstler has a tax problem. He last summer sold one of his yards to some gentlemen from Riyadh, and he would have to pay an enormous tax unless he reinvests the proceeds in accordance with German tax laws. Now, some people have been allowed to make such investments outside of Germany if they can show that the German economy will be helped, perhaps by bringing new products or new jobs technical or scientific know-how to Germany. . . . You have something like that in your company?"

Anders told them about Walther Siegler, about CAT scanners, about nuclear magnetic resonance, and about Francis Hyde's fascination with the subject. Anders told them about Francis Hyde.

Alexander Hammerbrook puffed happily on his cigar. Yes yes yes yes, that fits together very well, Gesstler has also a pharmaceutical plant down in Leverkusen, this sophisticated medical technology could help the German economy, a man like Hyde would be exactly the right partner for a new adventure in America, a man with such a company and such a background is exactly what Gesstler needs for such a project. . . .

"Boris Fleischer lost his entire family in the concentration camps," said Otto Waldstein. "Dr. Siegler was driven from Vienna in 1938. It does not seem to me that this fits together all that well."

Yes yes yes yes, of course not! Now a question: how is it that Herr Gesstler's membership in the SS over thirty years ago is so well known in the United States?

"It's not so well known," said Anders.

Otto Waldstein opened his eyes and looked at him over the tops of his glasses. Alexander Hammerbrook looked at him through a cloud of cigar smoke. Neither of them said anything.

"So far as I know, only Boris Fleischer and I know about it — no, I'm sorry, he's already discussed it with Dr. Siegler; he just told me that on the telephone —"

"But how did Boris find out about it?" asked Otto Waldstein.

"I told him about it."

Another silence.

Anders cleared his throat. "The reason I know about it . . . a woman I know, a friend of mine . . . after her mother was divorced from her father, the mother then married Gottfried Gesstler, so this woman, this friend of mine, actually spent part of her childhood in Gesstler's house, and she is the one who told me about the SS. Long ago. I only made the connection when I saw his name on the papers they had to file with the SEC."

They still did not say anything.

"This same lady, the one who told me about Gesstler, is now supposedly going to marry Francis Hyde, whom she met on Gesstler's boat. He's got a boat around here somewhere?"

"Yes," said Waldstein and Hammerbrook in unison.

"Well, they were all together on the boat last year. I don't know how Hyde and Gesstler met each other in the first place, but I suppose whatever plan they have for Boatwright was hatched at that time."

Waldstein and Hammerbrook looked at each other. Otto Waldstein turned to Anders. "If she told you Gesstler was in the SS, may we assume that she has told her future husband?"

"I suppose so."

"But you don't know?"

"No, I have no idea if it even came up."

"All right, suppose she did tell him. Suppose she did tell Mr. Hyde that in 1944 and 1945 Mr. Gesstler served with the tanks of the Panzer Division Leibstandarte SS Adolf Hitler. What would Mr. Hyde's reaction be?"

Anders shook his head. "I don't know. I really don't. It was so long ago, and I wouldn't think that Francis Hyde would give a damn one way or the other —"

"But he knows about Fleischer's background?" Otto Waldstein was incredulous. "He knows that Siegler had to leave Vienna when the Nazis invaded? He knows what the SS was?"

"Yeah, well, I suppose he knows about all that, in a general way, but I'm not convinced he put it all together the way you're doing; I think it's conceivable that he just plain didn't give it a thought."

"Yes yes yes yes yes," said Alexander Hammerbrook, slamming a large palm down upon his desk. "And on the other side too! How much about Mr. Fleischer and about Dr. Siegler did they tell to Gottfried Gesstler? Do we know that? No, we do *not* know that! Such people, we find, are very much interested in financial statements, balance sheets, earnings, dividends — maybe not so much interested in people. You would think that with all the lawyers and accountants and financial analysts they bring into such deals, somebody working for Hyde would examine Mr. Gesstler's history, and the somebody working for Gesstler would find out all about Boris Fleischer and Dr. Siegler. You would think that, but you might be wrong!"

The telephone buzzed. Alexander Hammerbrook frowned for the first time, then picked up the receiver, listened, said "Okay, *vielen dank*," and hung up. "Herr Waldstein's driver is in front."

Otto Waldstein was on his feet. "I'm sorry, Graham, I must ask to be excused, we must get ready for a dinner party —"

"Perfectly all right —" As they all rose, Alexander Hammerbrook announced that he would show Anders around the town. "But first, of course, we will have a few drinks. And then — an excellent dinner. And tomorrow I will make a few telephone calls."

It was after midnight when Anders climbed out of Hammerbrook's black Mercedes and ascended the steps into the dignified silence of the lobby. The concierge smiled an exceedingly friendly smile as he gave Anders the heavy key. Anders rode up in the slow, empty automatic elevator, walked down the long corridor, and unlocked the door. The room was dark, but with his first breath he smelled why the concierge had smiled like that.

SIXTEEN

What Difference Does It Make?

They didn't say a word until they were finished. Her skin was scalding. He always forgot how big and soft she was, and how strong. She wrapped herself around him and put her tongue into his ear and raked her nails down his back and squeezed his testicles, but she didn't say a word until the wild gallop was over, until they were both gasping for breath.

"Oh *dear* . . . That's a nice way to wake up. . . . Really worth the trip!"

Anders didn't say anything.

"I thought perhaps you would kick me out," she said.

"No you didn't."

"Well, you should, you know. I'm a bad woman." She rolled sideways, fitted his hands over her breasts, pressed her rump against his stomach, and fell asleep.

You're hooked, he told himself. It doesn't matter what she does. She's your own special addiction, and you might as well learn to live with it — not with her.

He woke up because his bladder was full. He went into the bathroom, urinated, brushed his teeth, then walked back into the living room and parted the curtains. It was still dark. Streetlights, an occasional car. The fog had lifted. On the other side of the Alster — which he had learned was a dammed-up river and not a lake — he could make out the handsome white facade of Waldstein, Hammerbrook & Co. He liked the look of it. The sight of it made him feel better. Somehow, perhaps, an answer was in that building. When he slid back into the bed she put her head on his chest. "It's *so* nice to be with you."

"What's the occasion for this visit?"

"Just to be with you alone?"

"Where's your fiancé?"

"In the hospital."

"Here in Hamburg?"

"God, no! In Bryn Mawr."

"Well then, what are you doing here? What's wrong with him?"

"He has . . . how do you call this?" She inserted a finger into Anders, who jumped. "A prostrate operation?"

"Stop that! Pros*tate*. You've worn him out already. Shouldn't you be with him?"

"No, his two horrible fat daughters are with him, *both* of them! One of them he hasn't seen in five years, but *now* of course, if dear Daddy is sick, his middle-aged little girls come from Santa Barbara and from New York to sit in his room and talk to him all day and order tons of flowers, and there isn't even space for me to be there, so I thought I could come home for a few days and also talk to you, dear, because I know that you must be angry with me."

Could have called me on the telephone any day of the week, thought Anders. Didn't have to wait until the cat's out of the bag, *then* jump on a plane, fly to Hamburg, and fall asleep in my bed. But he didn't say any of that. What is she doing here?

"You think I should have told you that Francis and Herr Gesstler have joined together to buy Boatwright stock? You think that, don't you?"

"That would have been helpful, yes."

"Helpful to you, but disloyal to Francis."

"*Disloyal to Francis?* Christ Almighty, are you being loyal to Francis right now?"

"Oh, this is different."

"What's different about it?"

"Because this is pleasure and that is business."

Anders laughed despite himself. "All right, I give up, I can't argue with a philosopher, but I know you didn't fly over here to go to bed with me — so what's on your mind?"

"I want to be alone with you. . . . I want you to tell me what to do."

"About what?"

"About Francis. You just called him my fiancé, but I'm not sure he is that anymore. He won't marry me unless I sign that contract I showed you, and I won't sign it. *I won't!* Everybody says that makes me a gold digger, that makes me a whore, but I think just the opposite — to sign a contract like that is what makes me a whore. But his lawyers and his daughters and the people in his company are all telling him about what a terrible person I am, about how I am still Anders's girl —"

"So you prove it by coming over here to see me?"

"Francis doesn't worry about me being Anders's girl. I told him you were impotent."

Anders went up on his elbow. "You told him *what?*"

"Well, dear, you did have some trouble, you know, when you were feeling guilty about me, when you first went back to Miss Cranberries, then back to your wife —"

"You told all that to Francis Hyde?"

"My God, what do you care what Francis Hyde thinks about your sex life? An old man, this makes him feel better, this makes him feel perhaps that I am not only after his money, but we both still know that I am Anders's girl, I will always be Anders's girl, and maybe what I just said is wrong, maybe underneath he understands it too, maybe this stupid contract is just an excuse now, he really doesn't want to marry me at all?"

"Are you asking me? How would I know?"

"Darling, *tell* me what to do!"

"I already told you the wisest thing would be to sign the agreement, assuming you really want to marry the guy. I'm beginning to think you're the one who is using his contract as an excuse, but I don't see why you have to do anything you don't want to do. What you *could* do is help me deal with this attack on Boatwright. What the hell are these people thinking of? Doesn't Francis Hyde know that Gesstler was in the SS?"

He felt her shrug. "Don't know."

"What do you mean you don't know? Did you tell him or didn't you tell him?"

"Ach, Mensch, I don't remember everything I told him, what difference does it make?"

"*What difference?*" Anders sat up again and turned on the light and Karin buried her face in the pillow. "How could you not remember something like that, for Christ's sake? In that first letter you ever sent me, that letter from California, you told me how the Brombergs wouldn't meet your mother and Gesstler, because Gesstler was a Nazi. And then later you told me Gesstler went to an SS cadet school, then he was put into that armored division, and you couldn't tell the Brombergs. . . . Remember?"

She nodded, her face still in the pillow.

"Well then, what about it? Did you tell him? Did somebody else tell him?"

She only shook her head, and suddenly a fury seized him, a rage that was almost sexual, and he grabbed her wrist and twisted until, biting her lips, she had to roll over. The pillow fell to the floor. With the open palm of his right hand he slapped her face to the left and with the back of the hand he slapped her face to the right, and panting for breath they stared into each other's eyes.

"You never did that before," she whispered. Her cheeks blazed.

"Well, you know how to drive a person crazy. You *did* tell him about Gesstler. You must have!"

She nodded, biting her lip. "Yes, but it didn't interest him much. Graham, it was over thirty years ago, and what does he care about SS? Means nothing to him. He's not a Jew, he hardly *knows* any Jews, and you know something else? I don't mind that at all, I find it refreshing, I'm quite tired of Jewish hangups — and a Jewish name. . . . Don't look at me like that, you hypocrite, you know what I mean!"

"I guess you'd better sign Hyde's agreement and get rid of that name!"

"That's your advice?"

"I told you the same thing at Christmas. But I still can hardly believe what you're telling me now: he knows about Fleischer, doesn't he? He knows about Siegler? I *know* he knows about Siegler —"

"My God, must we talk about this until breakfast? He knows about Siegler fleeing from Vienna, because he told me about it."

"And he thinks that Siegler will work for the SS?"

"Dr. Siegler will *not* be working for the SS, Graham! I believe that Dr. Siegler is over eighty years old and retired, another millionaire.

I believe there is a huge company with the name of your wife. I believe that Dr. Siegler's company — now being run by other people — is only a part of the huge company with the name of your wife. And Gottfried Gesstler, who was an eighteen-year-old officer-cadet in a Waffen-SS Panzer division thirty years ago — more than thirty years ago — is only *one* investor in a group that has made what they think is a good investment in an American company, an American company with the name of your virtuous little Quaker wife. Would you like to hit me again, my dear sir?" and as she said that, staring into his eyes, Anders felt in his heart why she had come.

He didn't hit her again. He let go of her wrist, switched off the light, and lay down with his back to her.

"What's the matter?" she asked. "I'm not even allowed to mention her?"

Anders said nothing.

"Oh dear, what is it now?" She put her hand on his shoulder, but he brushed it away.

"You're setting me up," he said through his teeth.

"What does that mean?"

"You want Caroline to find out about this! Gesstler and Hyde arranged this date!"

She gasped. "Graham! You really believe that? Of me? Oh dear, I would much rather you beat the shit out of me than have you think something like that. . . . I know I'm bad, but I'm not *that* bad!" She was crying now. She got out of bed and stumbled heavily around the room until she found the floor lamp. She turned it on and began to dress. "I come to you for love and for advice . . ." She was crying hard. "I come to you because I miss you . . . I want to be with you . . . I want to talk with you about my problems . . . and all the time you think I set a trap for you?"

He had shut his eyes against the light and the sight of her face, but he could hear the furious swishing and snapping and zipping, and then her heels on the bathroom floor.

"Where can you go this time of night?" he asked. "It's almost morning."

From the bathroom, water running: "I grew up in this town, remember? You don't worry about me, my dear sir, I don't stay with a man who thinks I am betraying him!"

Anders lay on his side. He could still feel her fingernails across his back.

Has she ever lied to you?

She lies to everybody.

Has she ever lied to *you?*

These are smart and ruthless people, and they've found the bait you go for.

Nonsense.

Can't resist the smell of their bait.

Wrong.

This is somebody's sophisticated plan.

This is paranoia.

The toilet flushed and she stepped out of the bathroom. He opened his eyes. They looked at each other as she put on her raincoat. Her face was washed defiantly clean. She slung a red canvas carry-on bag over her shoulder, turned her back, and without another word she slammed out of the room.

He had to get out of bed to turn off the floor lamp, but he didn't think he could fall asleep again.

Telephone?

Anders was so deep down, so passionately involved in the dream, that it took him forever to swim to the surface, but by the time he found the receiver in the darkness he could not remember what the dream was about.

"Mr. Anders? We are sorry to wake you, sir, but we have a call from the States. . . ." and then Walther Siegler was talking to him in German. Walther Siegler was home in Concord, Massachusetts, where it was still midnight, but Walther Siegler was so disturbed by his conversation with Boris Fleischer that Walther Siegler could not go to sleep and he wanted to know right now exactly what was being done about this quite impossible situation. . . .

Anders moved his arm. Anders stretched out his leg. Where the hell was she? Then he remembered, cringing. Could he have dreamed the whole thing? No, he was naked, and everything smelled of her.

Walther Siegler spoke very slowly and very softly, with an Austrian accent. Walther Siegler could not understand how Boris Fleischer — who had spent the war with false papers and in mortal danger right under the noses of the SS, whose entire family had been murdered in Hitler's camps — how Boris Fleischer could react to this quite impossible situation with such apparent calm, with such — one was almost tempted to say *Viennese* fatalism — whereas Walther Siegler himself was so worried that he could not sleep! Of course, he never slept well anymore. The older he got, the more things he remembered. One thing he remembered this evening was a play by Gustaf Anders that he saw in 1925? 1926? That play that infuriated the Nazis, infuriated Hermann Göring so much, what was that play about the Reichswehr officers secretly training their troops in Soviet Russia? German officers secretly training German pilots, German tank crews, in violation of the Versailles Treaty, training their troops far out across the Russian steppes where the British and the French could not see them . . . Gustaf Anders knew about that, Gustaf Anders wrote a play about it. Treason, they screamed! Of course, it was before they came to power, but the Nazis later put him into Dachau, did you know that? . . . It was in Malachowski's biography? Walther Siegler had not read that book, because in 1950 he was working eighteen hours each day to survive in this new country, to find money to continue his work, to find money to build his instruments. Walther Siegler had quite literally devoted his life to the development of diagnostic imaging techniques, and when his life's work was finally — *finally* — beginning to yield financial rewards, then the inheritance tax laws and the constantly increasing demands for capital had forced him to sell his company. . . .

Anders listened with his eyes shut. This was billable time. Under the present system of practicing law, Anders would have to charge the Boatwright Corporation for the time he was lying here naked in bed, listening to another old man talk. Where had she gone?

Walther Siegler had sold out to Boatwright because Anders, speaking for Fleischer, had promised him both security and independence. Many people had warned him about Boris Fleischer, but when the son of Gustaf Anders came up to Cambridge and explained how Fleischer ran his companies, Walther Siegler had believed him — and so far, Fleischer had kept his promise. Walther Siegler's sons were carrying on their father's work, the magnetic resonance devices were doing well. . . . But what has been discovered about this man Gesstler? . . .

Unbelievable! It's not enough the man is the son of a war criminal, it's not enough the man was in the SS, this man was in Adolf Hitler's lifeguards? The Sieglers are not going to do it, is that absolutely crystal clear? *Absolutely crystal clear?*

Another thing: Walther Siegler's sons are not satisfied that Fleischer is moving fast enough, these takeovers are sometimes done in a matter of hours, Walther Siegler's sons have consulted their law firm in Boston, which has recommended a law firm in New York that specializes in defending against such takeovers and that is no reflection upon Anders and *his* law firm, but there are a number of legal tactics that must be undertaken immediately and some of the people at the Boatwright headquarters in New York are also not satisfied that everything must stand still while Graham Anders makes his own investigations in Hamburg, there are a lot of things that can be done — *must* be done — immediately.

Another thing: it seems that nobody at Boatwright headquarters in New York understands why this man Gesstler and Philadelphia Pharma have made this move when such a large part of Boatwright's stock is owned by Mrs. Graham Anders. Apparently it is unusual to attempt a takeover without having a considerable block, as they put it, "locked up" and some people heard that Graham Anders was separated from his wife at one time. . . . Yes, but Walther Siegler wanted to hear that personally from Graham Anders. If Graham Anders tells him that, then Walther Siegler believes him. . . . At the moment, his sons will do what he tells them. . . . But how long, please? They could be buying all this week, the volume is up sharply, and what if we wake up one morning and the game is over? . . . Who? Waldstein, yes, of course, a well-known house there in Hamburg, the one son went back after the war, personally Walther Siegler cannot imagine doing that, but of course people are different. . . . Who? Hammerbrook? Yes, Walther Siegler has heard the name, what does he propose to do? . . . Hmm . . . How long would that take? What does Fleischer think? Tomorrow? It is tomorrow over there, isn't it? Long pauses. Sound of breathing. Walther Siegler seemed to be dozing. . . .

All these old men! Anders remembered when he thought fifty was over the hill, one foot in the grave. Told him she told Hyde: was that what exploded such a lightning bolt of suspicion?

Walther Siegler thought he could sleep now, was glad as always to speak with Anders, expected a full report from either Fleischer or Anders within twenty-four hours, otherwise Walther Siegler and his sons must take steps to protect themselves. *Servus*, Anders. Walther Siegler hung up.

The name of the play was *Hinter dem Morgenrot* or *Behind the Dawn* in English, but it had never been translated into English. According to Professor Malachowski's biography (published in Frankfurt in 1950, also never translated) Gustaf Anders and the play's producer had almost gone to jail, because the play revealed the fact that the German General Staff had made a secret deal with the Bolsheviks, a deal that permitted the Germans to train their troops deep inside Russia, in violation of the Versailles Treaty. Dive-bombers, tanks, and motorized infantry working together. Gustaf Anders had been a German officer, wounded twice on the Western Front, Fusilier Regiment Grossherzogin von Hessen-Darmstadt. Iron Cross, first class. Can you prevent history from repeating itself with plays?

It was still dark outside.

A company is people. If Siegler's people quit and go to General Electric, what is Francis Hyde paying for? Patents? Inventory? Two factories? What good are they without the people who know how to build and sell nuclear magnetic resonance machines that cost a million dollars apiece? What is Hyde thinking of? Call him up in Bryn Mawr Hospital and ask him? No way. *Prostrate*, she said. Prostrate is right. She doesn't want to marry him; the agreement's an excuse so she doesn't have to marry him. Is that true?

Anders didn't want to answer his own question.

Anders fell asleep.

SEVENTEEN

Villa Gesstler

Frau Gesstler knew there was going to be trouble when Gottfried came home from the office. The trouble had already started yesterday: first that strange telephone call from Mr. Hyde, who seemed to think that Karin was here, and then an equally strange telephone call from Alexander Hammerbrook, of all people, who wanted an appointment with Gottfried today. Alexander Hammerbrook had never called Gottfried in his life, so far as she knew no member of that extremely arrogant family had ever called any Gesstler for any reason, but now Alexander Hammerbrook has something so important that he calls Gottfried in the evening at home? And why would Mr. Hyde expect Karin to be here in Hamburg when they have not heard one word from her and hardly know what they are supposed to say to Mr. Hyde, who explains he is in the hospital but will not say why he is in the hospital? This morning after Gottfried is driven to the office, Karin arrives in a taxi, looking angry and not quite put together, with a story about a delayed airplane, she missed her connection and had to spend the night in London. Why hadn't she called anybody from London? If Mr. Hyde is sick in the hospital, should she not be with him? What if his daughters *are* with him, that sort of operation is always unpleasant for a man, one should be especially considerate at a time like that. Was this still an argument about the marriage settlement? Frau Gesstler simply could not understand how Karin could put herself into such a position! What are people supposed to think? But as usual Karin did not hear a word that Frau Gesstler was trying to tell her. No breakfast either? She had eaten on the flight from London, she said, but she had slept badly there, and now she only wanted to go up to her room and go to bed. No, she would *not* call Francis now, Mutti, it's the middle of the night over there, she would call him later, he won't go away!

She did sit down at the breakfast table, however; she did drink a cup of coffee; she did eat a roll with butter and honey and she did show Frau Gesstler some new photographs of the girls. Dolly was twelve now, and Frau Gesstler was startled, once again, to see the long aristocratic face of her first husband developing amid the white-blonde hair. . . . A beautiful man, but cold as ice, his seed felt cold as rocket fuel. . . .

Should she have called Gottfried to tell him Karin had arrived? Later it turned out that she should have, because Gottfried should have called Mr. Hyde immediately after he saw Dr. Hammerbrook, but he did not want to call when he did not know what to say to Mr. Hyde about Karin, but how was she to know that? Gottfried hated to be disturbed at the office, and how should she know that on this particular day . . .

In any case, by the time Karin had gone upstairs Gudrun Borgward was there to pick Frau Gesstler up for tennis, but Frau Gesstler worried about it all day: at tennis, at lunch where everybody talked about their trips to Rio or their new houses at Hilton Head when Gottfried had been too busy this winter even for Greece. The shopping did not distract her mind today, although she did find a nice silk navy blue bathrobe for Karin, who as usual arrived with just one tiny canvas carry-on bag, although of course she still had plenty of clothes here if she could still fit into them, and then Frau Gesstler tried to remember what she had ordered for dinner, but of course Phitak would know Karin was there and would take care of it, it happened all the time that Gottfried would call at the last minute and say I have to bring three people for dinner, and when she was having her tea and a piece of cake inside the Alsterpavillon with Gisela she wished she had the courage to tell Gisela right to her face what she thought of Gisela (and Horst, too, of course) for sending a message through the servants that Gisela and Horst would pay Phitak a thousand (!) marks a month more than he was getting — and Gottfried had brought him all the way from Bangkok! It was really *sad* when you could not trust your oldest friends, but then Fritz, who was Gottfried's chauffeur, was suddenly standing beside their table, pardon, Gnädige Frau, Herr Generaldirektor came home early today. . . .

So by the time Frau Gesstler walked into the library, both of them were sitting there drinking Scotch, Karin dressed in the same blue jeans and the same cashmere sweater she had worn under her raincoat when she arrived, looking down into her glass and saying nothing at all, while Gottfried was obviously well launched into the kind of monologue or tirade we get when he is very angry and then starts drinking to overcome the anger!

Hammerbrook! Of all people, Alexander Hammerbrook is now involved in this story. Herr Doctor Hammerbrook, nephew of the Oberbürgermeister, doctor of jurisprudence, banker, ocean racer, everybody's great friend, the sailor who always knows which way the wind is blowing. First a partner of the Waldsteins. Then no longer a partner of the Waldsteins. Then a good little Wehrmacht officer, nothing but the best assignments, intelligence staff of Rommel's Afrikakorps, hell-for-leather all the way into Egypt with lots of photographs in the newspapers, then the tide turns, the British drive the Afrikakorps all the way back to Tunisia, the Americans arrive from the other direction, in the spring of 1943 the German operation in Africa is finished, Herr Doctor Hammerbrook gets captured just at the right time to spend the rest of the war in Texas drinking real coffee and eating scrambled eggs and corned beef hash and reading good books about the advantages of democracy, and what are the rest of us doing while Herr Doctor Hammerbrook is reading and teaching and enjoying the Texas sunshine?

Frau Gesstler realized that he must have had a drink at the office because he unlocked the big armoire now and took out the photograph boxes. He did that very rarely, and then only late at night when they were alone, or once or twice with other people from the Leibstandarte.

He rarely saw any of them now. Few of them had managed to change in the way Gottfried had changed. Those hard young men who believed so passionately in the Führer, who were perfectly willing to give their lives for their country and their Führer, who really believed almost to the end that they could still win — despite what these particular men had seen in Russia, in Italy, in Normandy, in the Ardennes, and finally in Hungary — very few of these young men adjusted to a world turned upside-down for them, a world in which everything they had been taught was right was now wrong, everything they had been taught was wrong was now right, instead of heroes decorated with Iron Crosses and Knight's Crosses of Iron Crosses, and Swords and Oak Leaves and Diamonds *upon* Knight's Crosses of Iron Crosses — instead of heroes they were suddenly murderers, criminals to be put in prison, put on trial, publicly humiliated, in some cases handed over to the Poles and Russians to be hanged, in other cases just sent "home" to homes and families that no longer existed . . . most of them had just drifted away, to South America, to the French Legion in Indo-China, to the endless wars in Africa. Of course, some of them returned to the farms and factories they had come from, and the lucky few who were princes and barons and other sons of rich men in the West took up their lives, tried to forget, tried to focus their attention upon careers and money and had as little as possible to do with their old comrades.

He had shown her the photographs one evening just after she had come back, when he was still living in the attic of his aunt's farm out in Holstein. The aunt would not let her go up to Gottfried's room! Frau Gesstler had found the pictures uninteresting: grinning young men in uniforms, tanks pushing through Norman hedgerows, tanks in the snow. . . .

Thank goodness Irmtraud appeared at the door to announce dinner. But it was the same at the table.

Herr Doctor Hammerbrook arrived this afternoon, as per his urgent request last night. Why Hammerbrook? It seems that Waldstein Hammerbrook & Co. has now some interest in our Seagull Project. Why? one might ask. Of course, Herr Doctor Hammerbrook has been very close to the Americans since he was their prisoner and behaved so excellently as a prisoner that he was among the first to be shipped home when the war was over, was then ready to reenter the family bank and participate in the organization of the Fourth Reich, Adenauer's democratic Reich, and when the children of Israel returned with their money from London and Zurich and New York, Herr Doctor Hammerbrook and his father just changed the name of the bank right back to Waldstein, Hammerbrook & Co. and happily received their deposits. And now this piece of business, it seems, comes through the connections of can you guess who? Of course Mr. Otto

Waldstein, Herr Doctor Hammerbrook's partner, who spent the war in Eisenhower's intelligence and also has many friends in the United States and one of these friends is Mr. Boris Fleischer, of Rumania and Israel and New York, where he is presently the Chairman and a large stockholder of the Boatwright Corporation, and it seems that despite the opinions we received from Francis Hyde's American lawyers to the effect that German military service of the directors of Hansa Nordamerika Bank over thirty years ago need *not* be disclosed in the filing under the American laws, despite those opinions, it appears that Mr. Boris Fleischer, or at any rate his bankers, already know that when Gottfried Gesstler was seventeen years old, in March of the year nineteen hundred and forty-four, Gottfried Gesstler was assigned to the First Panzer Regiment of the First SS Panzer Division, then being refitted in Belgium. Herr Doctor Hammerbrook did not explain *how* Mr. Fleischer came to this knowledge, but Herr Doctor Hammerbrook wondered if the directors of the Hansa Nordamerika Bank and its American partners had fully considered the implications.

Oh my God, thought Frau Gesstler, not *this* again! When will they ever stop? A generation ago, half a lifetime ago, and every time something happens, they bring *this* up again! But how do they know it in America? Because it was the Americans. It was the Americans who were killed, it was the American army that threw them in jail like criminals and beat them and put them on trial for their lives. . . .

Frau Gesstler tried to change the subject: when do the girls have their spring vacation this year? but Gottfried did not want the subject changed.

The moment Hammerbrook left I put in a call for Francis Hyde. But then of course I had to cancel it.

Why? asked Frau Gesstler.

Why? Because the first thing he would want to know is if we have heard from Mrs. Bromberg here, our missing daughter!

I should have called to tell you when she arrived this morning —

Karin was carefully dissecting the roast squab on her plate.

Frau Gesstler said that really, they were entitled to some explanation. Karin knew that she was always welcome here, this was her home no matter what was happening in America, but it would make it so much easier in this particular situation —

Karin said she had come home to think.

Gottfried Gesstler silently finished his plate, silently finished half the bottle of Clos de Vougeot, and stared at the huge oil painting above the sideboard, blue sky and clouds and whitecaps on the green waves, the *Möwe* heeled over, sailing across the wind, sailing down the Kieler Förde —

After all these years Frau Gesstler was still uncomfortable at the tension between her husband and her daughter. It had nothing to do with this thing today, just a business matter, after all, she did not understand exactly what this was all about, with Francis Hyde and these American companies and now Alexander Hammerbrook; no, Karin had been unpleasant to Gottfried from the very beginning. The girl had only been — what, nine years old? but she had been hurt by the divorce and by their rootless life in those years, first their return to Holland but they would not let her stay in Holland, even her own family hated the Germans so much and she said, "But I have left him," and it made no difference, nobody would speak to her, so she decided to move back to Hamburg and found work as a secretary for that English bank and one day like a miracle Gottfried Gesstler walked into the office — eight years! Gottfried Gesstler in a business suit! He was working twenty hours a day to rebuild his father's works. . . .The German schools were too hard at first although she did well with the music and piano lessons but she had to be put back a year and then when Gottfried wanted to spend all night in the apartment they decided to send her to the boarding school in Vevey and then the singing places in Munich, in Milan, and of course she came back a stranger, a beautiful lady from a fashion magazine, cold and polite to her mother and Gottfried, warm and sure of herself with men, the singing was good for a while, but the crazy riding, the crazy driving, *why?* And then to California to visit her father and married the Jewish boy, Frau Gesstler thought partly to anger Gottfried but the Brombergs are rich, important people who own their own firm and then something went wrong out there, Frau Gesstler could never get her to explain exactly what happened and suddenly they were in Philadelphia — Why Philadelphia? Frau Gesstler had never understood that either, but then there was the business with the lawyer, and now Frau Gesstler began to remember that she had been trying to remember something . . . but then they finished the soufflé and the coffee and Gottfried looked at his wristwatch.

It was midday in New York and Philadelphia. He would have to call Hyde now. Did Karin want to speak to him too?

Karin shrugged. What's the hurry?

For one thing, your fiancé wants to know where you are.

He doesn't need to know where I am every minute.

True love, obviously. And for another thing, I must tell him about this interview with Hammerbrook —

What is the hurry about that? He already knows you were in the SS, because I told him. It didn't seem to interest him very much.

Gottfried Gesstler examined his coffee cup for a moment. Then he looked at Karin: you did not tell him the whole story because you don't know the whole story. Come back to the library and drink something with me.

Why is he doing that? Frau Gesstler asked herself, and remembered what it was she had been trying to remember, but by then it was too late.

EIGHTEEN

A Company Is People

"Do nothing until you hear from me," Hammerbrook said, but Graham Anders wondered if Hammerbrook understood how difficult it would be for Anders to do nothing.

According to the *Financial Times* of London and the *Frankfurter Allgemeine Zeitung*, speculators were buying Boatwright stock in the hope that a tender offer was coming, in the hope that a tender offer would trigger defensive tactics on Boatwright's part, in the hope that the bankers would produce a "white knight," a buyer more acceptable to Boatwright's management. . . . In any case the stock was hot, the computers were focused on Boatwright, the feeling was that the price would go up, and that feeling would of course drive the price up. Anders knew from experience that when a company is "put in play," that company's lawyers cannot just sit around doing nothing — but here he was, eating a half-dozen greenish Brittany oysters in the restaurant of the Hotel Vier Jahreszeiten and looking out of the window at the traffic on the Neue Jungfernstieg, the windblown trees, the gray, wind-whipped waves of the Binnenalster and, beyond the water, the office buildings along the Ballindamm —

At home, people would be getting up now, opening their newspapers, drinking coffee, reaching for telephones. If Boatwright was hot yesterday, Boatwright would be hotter today. The pressure on

Boris Fleischer would be terrific. Of course, Boris could insulate himself by staying in his apartment and refusing telephone calls, but Boris would know that his subordinates at 250 Park could not avoid the calls. Boris would also know that many of his officers — especially the best ones — did not want to avoid the calls because at times like this, some of the calls would be job offers.

When a company is put in play, the most secure and highly paid vice presidents are suddenly not sure to whom they may be reporting in a couple of months — or if they will be working for the company at all — and their peers across the street and across the country are well aware of it. This is the time to repeat offers that were turned down before. The effects can be catastrophic. As the price of the company's stock goes up, its efficiency as a business goes down. From top to bottom, minds are distracted, people turn inward, people focus on their own problems, the gears slip — although this kind of deep internal damage may not be visible for months.

So what do we *do?*

The waiter removed the oyster shells and served poached eel with dill sauce, asparagus vinaigrette, new potatoes, another glass of Pilsen. Anders rehearsed the classic defenses which had been discussed in New York: more cumbersome, embarrassing "shark repellents," such as charter amendments providing for a staggered board of directors? Some of this had been done last year, thank God. It was probably too late for more of such gimmicks.

Put a block of new stock into friendly hands? Maybe, but whose hands? Essentially a "white knight" defense; you wind up being owned by the white knight, who might turn out to be a black knight when he has you locked up. Sell a "crown jewel," an asset like Siegler, thus perhaps removing the point of the takeover? If Boatwright sold Siegler directly to Philadelphia Pharma, would Hyde still need the Germans? Having worked night and day to get Siegler for Boatwright, Anders would be everlastingly goddamned if he would suggest a course like that, and in any case he did not believe either Siegler or Fleischer would go for it. Think of something better!

Anders drank his beer and brooded out the window. The whole idea of a takeover battle made him feel a little sick. Theoretically it shouldn't. Theoretically a corporation lawyer in his prime should welcome the coming clash of arms, the all-night meetings, the frantic telephone calls, the flying around in airplanes to argue in courtrooms all over the country: the excitement, the intellectual stimulation, the flow of adrenaline into his blood — and the flow of legal fees into Conyers & Dean. But Anders knew too much. He knew that once a battle like this begins, the target company is almost always sold to *somebody*.

Did he really care if Boatwright were sold? No more fees to Conyers & Dean after how many years? Eighteen sixty-one to 1978 makes a hundred and seventeen years? So what? At say thirty dollars a share, Caroline would suddenly be rich beyond the dreams of avarice. Instead of being limited to Boatwright's modest dividend, her inheritance would turn into cash. Put the whole thing into tax-free bonds? Her income would make his look ridiculous. Quit the firm? To do what all day? Wouldn't be the first person to retire at fifty. *And do what all day?* Read *The Wall Street Journal* AND *The New York Times* AND *The Philadelphia Inquirer?* Discuss Caroline's investments with the brokers? Have lunch at the clubs? Attend the Orchestra on Friday afternoons?

Anders thought about all the golfers, the tennis players, the squash players, the skiers. . . . How about bird watching? Jogging? Laura Carpenter, paging through *The Sunday Times Magazine:* "John Lindsay jogs, Graham Anders fucks. . . ."

Yeah, and suppose Caroline throws you out? She won't. The hell she won't, she did before. That was different, she won't do it again. Why won't she? Because she knows I love her, she knows how much I need her. You've got a funny way of showing it! *Thin ice!* Thin ice out here and cold black water up your nose and over your head and then you'll be sorry but then it will be too late. . . .Why not turn around, go back to the nice warm cabin on the shore?

The coffee came. What am I going to do? Anders asked himself. I can't just sit here and look out the window, now thinking again about the vice presidents taking telephone calls. A company is people.

A company is people?

Is that maybe it? Take Boatwright private? Get rid of the public shareholders entirely? Borrow the money and buy them out, have the employees own the company. If Fleischer wants to do it, if Caroline wants to do it, and if the employees want to do it, there should be a way to do it in this case. Been done before. Leveraged buy-out. Interest rates horrendous, though. Get somebody to run the numbers. What is Boatwright's cash flow? Aren't the interest rates much lower in Germany? Could Hammerbrook's people figure out how to do this? Make a deal with Germans after all, but different Germans?

The waiter brought a silver tray with the check, and a pen. Anders turned over the check and began to do some numbers from memory. Taking the highest possible price of thirty dollars a share, how much was Boatwright worth? We set up an employee stock ownership plan, there are special tax advantages to make that easier. Have to call our tax guys to check that out. . . . Anders was excited now, so absorbed in his work that the waiter retreated. Anders had never done a leveraged buy-out himself, but he had studied them. There must be an infinite number of ways to do this, ways to capitalize a new company that would belong to the employees and a few big private investors who would borrow the money from the banks, buy out the stockholders of the old company and then merge the old company into a new company. The cash generated by the business would gradually pay off the debt. . . . Would Fleischer agree to this? Caroline asked: What happens when Boris dies? The Jewish charities don't want stock in a private company. They have to have stock they can sell — or cash. This way Fleischer's estate would be completely liquid because under this plan we cash out Fleischer now.

But he won't do that.

Why won't he do that?

Because he wants to keep running the show. Boris Fleischer wouldn't know what to do all day either.

Well, we'll write him a contract. Chairman for life. Would that fly? Something like that. And the charities? We'll have to figure something out. Some kind of deal with Boris's estate where we buy back his stock over a period of time or arrange for a private placement . . . something like that. . . .

The waiter was back. Yes, thank you, the eel had been excellent. First eel he had ever eaten. They don't serve us eel in America. Anders signed the check and walked out of the restaurant. He hadn't really done anything, but he felt better.

What do we do now? Even if everybody agrees in principle, a leveraged buy-out takes time. A lot of players and a lot of complicated interconnected deals. Have we got the time? Hyde and Gesstler's brokers may be buying right this minute. We've got to do something to gain time. What can we do to gain time?

Anders stood in the hotel lobby and looked at his watch. Go upstairs and plug back into the world. Call Hammerbrook, call Conyers & Dean tax partners, call Fleischer — *No!* Call Fleischer first. Tell Boris that Caroline would like to do this. Have him try it out on Siegler. Then we go to Hammerbrook, have Hammerbrook figure out how to do it, but the idea should come from Boris Fleischer, not from Graham Anders.

Riding up in the little elevator, Anders thought that the rest of the day would be spent on the telephone. He was right.

NINETEEN

The View from Bryn Mawr Hospital

— Hello?

— May I speak with Mrs. Graham Anders, please?

— This is she.

— Mrs. Anders, my name is Francis Hyde. . . . I had the honor of serving as a trustee of Dr. Boatwright's Institute at Penn for a number of years —

— Oh, yes, Mr. Hyde, my father often spoke of you. I know who you are. How are you?

— Well, now, that's why I'm calling —

— If you want to speak to Graham I'm sorry he's not —

— No, actually I don't want to speak to him, I want to speak to *you*, and as it happens I'm flat on my back in the hospital, in Bryn Mawr Hospital.

— Oh, I'm sorry!

— Well, they say it's a routine procedure, but here I am flat on my back, only a mile or two from your place . . . and I'm calling to ask if perhaps you'd have the time to come over to discuss something of considerable importance to both of us. Think you could manage that?

— Just the two of us?

— Exactly! Just the two of us.

. . . .

— Are you thinking about it? May I call you Caroline?

— Yes, sure, Mr. Hyde. . . . I guess it would be better if I brought somebody from Conyers & Dean along, Mr. Hyde.

— Yeah. Well. Of course that's the right thing to say, first off, but let me suggest a thought to you: I've been working with lawyers all my life — well, anyway, since I was twenty-five or so, and with all due respect to your brilliant husband, one thing I've learned is that we Americans let the lawyers tell us what to do — or even more what *not* to do — too much! One thing I've learned is that frequently you can make a business deal with another person much more easily if the lawyers aren't there to complicate everything, if the lawyers aren't there to tell you how you can't do whatever it is you want to do, but if you make the deal first and then call in the lawyers and instruct them to figure *how* to do the thing you've agreed you want to do, just call them in and tell them to get it done — it works much better that way.

— I see.

— Been my experience over forty years in business and I haven't gone to jail yet!

— I know you've been enormously successful Mr. Hyde . . . but I still don't think I ought to see you alone at this time.

— Okay, Caroline, I can see you're a Boatwright clear through, but will you let a sick old man just talk to you on the telephone for a few minutes more? You might find it interesting.

— Go ahead, Mr. Hyde.

— Okay, well, this kind of thing is best done face-to-face, but I'll give it the old college try: Caroline, as I'm sure you know, I've made a considerable investment in Boatwright stock this year, together with some German partners who want to put their money to work in the United States. You know that, don't you?

— Yes, I do, Mr. Hyde.

— Yes, of course you do. Well, in that connection, having put this much money up, I am of course interested in what's going to happen to Boatwright in the future, and that's what I'd like to discuss with you. . . . From your point of view, of course, I'm an old, old man, my dear, and right now I *feel* like an old, old man, but Boris Fleischer is considerably older, isn't he? What's going to happen to Fleischer's stock when he . . . ah —

— When Boris Fleischer dies, at least some of his stock will certainly be sold.

— But the lawyers tell me that you have the right to buy it, Caroline.

— Well, I guess that's a matter of public record, Mr. Hyde.

— Are you going to want to do that? Are you going to want all that much Boatwright stock? All your eggs in one basket?

— All my eggs have always been in that basket, Mr. Hyde. My great-grandfather —

— Yes, I know about your great-grandfather, my dear, but the other Boatwrights don't seem to feel that way, do they? The Fords don't have all their eggs in Ford and the Rockefellers don't have all their eggs in Standard Oil and the DuPonts don't have all their eggs in DuPont, and I for one don't understand why Caroline Anders has to have all her eggs in Boatwright.

— What are you really asking me, Mr. Hyde?

— I'm really asking you to name a price for your Boatwright stock.

— It's not for sale, Mr. Hyde.

— Yes, that's what I have understood to be your position, but now some things have happened that might induce you to rethink your position.

— What things?

— I just told you I feel like a very old man right now, a very sad and bitter old man, and I'm going to tell you the reason I feel that way, because I'm angry and I think you and I are being played for a couple of fools and I think we're in a position to help each other. Now this is a very unpleasant story and of course you're free to hang up any time, but don't do it, Caroline. Hear me out.

TWENTY

Defendant No. 18

Alexander Hammerbrook was genuinely thrilled, actually rubbing his hands. "Oh, excellent! Oh, terrific! Yes, we would be very much interested in designing something like this for Boris Fleischer. I must tell you, we have not yet done one of these deals, I think no bank in Germany has done one, but we absolutely have the capability, we are honored, please tell Mr. Fleischer this house is honored to be asked."

"What are we being honored about?" asked Otto Waldstein, as he held open the door for the waitress who stood behind him carrying a tray of coffee, fresh rolls, and fresh flowers. As Anders watched, breakfast was served at the mahogany conference table and Hammerbrook, drumming the table for emphasis, explained the reason for such an early meeting.

Anders had spent much of his life working at night. Night negotiations, nights at the printer — "all-nighters" the young lawyers called them now — are part of every corporation lawyer's life, but Anders didn't like them anymore and this last one had been the worst he could remember, he felt his age this morning, felt actually older than fifty, felt himself sometimes floating like a toy balloon against the ceiling of Hammerbrook's sunlit office, floating then into the Baltic clouds in the photograph of Hammerbrook's racing sloop —

He had started telephoning right after lunch the day before, when it was morning in Philadelphia, in New York, in Boston. He had not finished until past midnight in Philadelphia, New York, and Boston — when it was past six o'clock in the morning in Hamburg — but he thought he had accomplished something. To his own amazement, he had argued Boris Fleischer out of depression; he had persuaded Boris Fleischer to summon six of his best executives from 250 Park to the Waldorf Towers; he had dispatched Tommy Sharp and one of the most brilliant young tax partners from Conyers & Dean also to the Waldorf Towers; he had explained the situation to Walther Siegler in Concord, to one of Walther Siegler's sons and to a skeptical partner in a Boston law firm representing Walther Siegler's sons; he had copied down three pages of numbers, the essential financial picture of the Boatwright Corporation for the year ended December 31, 1977 — and finally, as the sun peeked over the spires and the rooftops on the other side of the Alster, he had convinced Fleischer to let him hire Waldstein, Hammerbrook & Co. to develop a plan for taking Boatwright private, as quickly as possible.

He was hoarse and his right ear ached when he picked up the telephone again, to call Alexander Hammerbrook at home. Yes, Hammerbrook would be glad to see him in about an hour, and Otto always came to the bank very early anyway. They would give Anders breakfast.

Was there time for a nap? No, but there was time to shave and shower and change his clothes, and just as Anders stood naked in the bathroom drying himself with the large bath towel, there was a knock at the door. A loud knock.

Alexander Hammerbrook had lighted his postbreakfast cigar now and was frowning at the sheets of yellow legal paper upon which Anders had carefully copied a summary of Boatwright's financial statements.

"Leveraged buyout," said Otto Waldstein. "Very, very interesting for us, a real challenge for us to think up something elegant. A thing like this can be like a work of art, you know, or like the machinery of a Swiss watch, a thing of beauty in which every part is carefully designed for its exact function. . . . Oh, they will be angry in Wall Street to hear that a bunch of Hamburgers got this job! My own cousins will be *very* angry!" His blue eyes sparkled.

Hammerbrook looked up from the numbers. "Yes, this is an interesting problem, a problem we will solve for you, *but, but, BUT!*" He blew out clouds of blue smoke. "I think there is a considerable bunch of legal paperwork to be done, is there not? You have to have a meeting of Boatwright stockholders? Proxy statements explaining everything? Once we have the principles worked out, how long will the other things take?"

"Ninety days?" Anders knew that it would probably take longer, but he had learned to say that everything takes ninety days and sometimes he was lucky; sometimes it could really be done in that time.

Hammerbrook looked dubious. "April–May–June? What are Mr. Hyde and Mr. Gesstler doing all this time?"

"We haven't even asked you how your interview with Gesstler went," said Anders.

"Not good. Mr. Gesstler has been advised by Mr. Hyde's American lawyers that his military service to his country thirty-four years ago is of no concern to United States regulatory agencies or to United States stockholders. Mr. Gesstler also had quite a lot to say about United States army operations in Vietnam as reported in the press and on television, American soldiers setting fire to grass huts with cigarette lighters, the incident of Lieutenant Calley of your Americal Division who simply shoots a whole village of women and children just a few years ago, and we Germans are still supposed to hear lectures from the Americans about our service as soldiers in very hard battle against other soldiers thirty-four years ago because we wore a black uniform instead of a gray uniform?" Hammerbrook poured himself another cup of coffee. "Mr. Gesstler also permitted himself some comments on the fact that Doctor Hammerbrook spent the last years of the war as a prisoner in America while Mr. Gesstler was in a tank in which the rest of the crew burned up, in Normandy; while Mr. Gesstler's best friend was killed at Mr. Gesstler's side by an American airplane in the Ardennes; while Mr. Gesstler watched eighty-five percent of his battalion killed in hopeless counterattacks against the Russians in Hungary —"

"Hopeless counterattacks personally ordered, *demanded*, by the man for whom the Leibstandarte Adolf Hitler was named," Otto Waldstein interrupted. "A man who became so infuriated by the failure of those counterattacks that he ordered what was left of that division to remove their Leibstandarte sleeve insignia!"

"Yes, in any event not a successful interview," said Hammerbrook. "I asked whether he had considered the fact that important persons in the Boatwright management are Jewish — not only Jewish, but people from Europe with personal experience with the SS, and Mr. Gesstler explained to me that his entire service had been with tank battalions of the First Panzer Regiment, that he had never even seen a concentration camp —"

"Never saw cattle cars full of people?" asked Otto Waldstein. "Cattle cars packed full of people standing up because there was no room to sit down? Cattle cars waiting on sidings while the Leibstandarte's troop trains rushed them back and forth across Europe?"

"I think we can assume that even combat troops of the SS knew perfectly well what happened in the camps," said Hammerbrook. "A product of the Junkerschule Braunschweig most certainly did. But Mr. Gesstler wanted to tell me about the efforts of his father and mother to protect their Jewish dentist here in Hamburg —"

"Oh, for God's sake!" said Otto Waldstein.

"— and about his contributions to your project to help the people who worked in the Gesstler plant during the war —"

"All right, all right." Otto Waldstein held up his hand. "All the usual responses when the subject of the past comes up around here. But have we any indication of Gottfried Gesstler's plans? Does he really contemplate taking over Boatwright?"

"He says no. He says he is only making an investment, on the basis of the advice of his American partner."

"Which is what he has to say, at the moment." Otto Waldstein turned to Graham Anders. "If they put out their tender offer tomorrow, it will be much more difficult to make Boatwright into a private company. . . . We will be in court, will we not? It could take several years, even if we win. Is that right?"

"That's right," said Anders. "But I have something here to show you. Something that might buy us time." He reached into his jacket and withdrew a white envelope. It was already open. He shook it carefully. Two pictures spilled onto the table in front of Waldstein and Hammerbrook.

They leaned forward to examine the pictures. The room was silent.

He was irritated that the maid would knock so early, and so loud, but it wasn't the maid.

"Guten Morgen," said Karin, not smiling at his bath towel costume as he closed the door behind her. She wore high heels, blue jeans, and an English raincoat. Her hair was tied back in her usual black silk scarf, and her stare was so fierce that Anders asked: "Are you okay?"

"No, dear, I'm not okay, will you just hold me for one minute, please?" and she was in his arms, shaking, her head on his naked shoulder, and in the tall mirror on the closet door he saw that she had closed her eyes.

"Hey, what's wrong?"

As she clung to him, she gradually stopped trembling. He felt her lips, cool against the side of his throat.

"Tell me!"

"Oh dear, I think perhaps I'm going crazy!"

He held her at arms length, put his hand under her chin, and looked into her eyes. "Tell me!"

She looked back. She took a deep breath. "Okay." She stepped away from him, unbuttoned the raincoat, and drew a white envelope from an inside pocket. "Here is a little present for you. Not so little, really."

Anders stood there, holding the envelope with one hand and the towel with the other.

"Well, open it!"

He walked over to the desk by the window, tore open the envelope, and spilled a little glossy snapshot and a yellow newspaper clipping upon the desk. Frowning, he picked up the snapshot first. It was bent convex. Dried paste and bits of grainy black paper stuck to its corners. A blond young man is smiling down from behind a machine gun atop an armored personnel carrier. He is wearing a loose, unbuttoned camouflage parka over a black wool tank jacket. Driving goggles dangle around his neck. His collar is open, and on his right collar tab are the stylized twin lightning bolts. A black overseas cap is cocked over one eye. On the front of the cap is the silver death's head, tilted sideways. In the background: a snow-covered field, a dark pine forest, a line of helmeted Panzergrenadiers, also wearing camouflage jackets, passing gasoline canisters up to the crew of a Mark V Panther tank. . . .

He put it down and unfolded the fragile piece of newspaper, but he had to pad barefoot across the room to get his glasses before he could read the caption under the picture. Karin had slumped into an easy chair, from which she silently watched him as he sat down again.

The picture and the caption below it had been carefully clipped from a German newspaper dated May 17, 1946, now dried almost orange. Six rows of bareheaded men sit on folding chairs and stare into the camera with various expressions: disdain, amusement, boredom. Their chairs are set upon some kind of bleachers rising back against the wall. The men, mostly very young, are wearing miscellaneous bits of German and American uniforms, but no insignia of any kind. Suspended around each man's neck, by a white string, is a large white tag with a large black number on it.

Anders read the caption: Defendants at the war crimes trial conducted by the U.S. Army in the former Dachau concentration camp . . . former SS-Obersturmbannführer Joachim Peiper (No. 42) and members of his battle group accused of shooting American prisoners near Malmédy, Belgium, in December 1944. . . .

"Where did you get these?"

"Where do you think?"

"He gave them to you?"

"No, dear. I took them while he was asleep. I stole them for you."

Anders felt cold. He got up, he walked across the room again, he threw the towel into the bathroom and began to get dressed. "I've got to have breakfast with Waldstein and Hammerbrook in a few minutes. Do you want to tell me what's going on?"

"What's going on is you asked me to help you with what you called this attack on Boatwright, and now I have brought you pictures that should be quite some help to you, I think!"

Underwear. Shirt. Trousers. Anders sat down on the sofa to put on his socks and shoes.

"Last night, Gottfried Gesstler told me the story of this Malmédy trial, what you see there in that newspaper story," said Karin. "I never heard of it before. After the war was over, the Americans put those men on trial for shooting American prisoners. Gottfried and the other men in that picture were convicted of murder, by American judges, but Gottfried was miles away from the place where the prisoners were shot. . . ."

Karin lay back in the chair and closed her eyes and told Gottfried Gesstler's story, and she told it so vividly that Anders stopped dressing and sat silently listening.

"This was just before Christmas, the last Christmas of the war. Hitler decided to gamble everything on a huge attack in the west, a surprise attack through lonely mountain forests in the snow . . . hundreds of thousands of the best troops, the best equipment, and they were supposed to drive all the way to sea, to capture the port of Antwerp, to split the Allies in half. And in the point of the attack — one of the points — was this lieutenant colonel name of Peiper, twenty-nine years old, six years at war, a very tough and smart experienced guy with his battle group, Panzers and grenadiers from the Leibstandarte, and Gottfried Gesstler was a gunner and radio operator, eighteen years old, and their orders were to break through a hundred kilometers to the river Meuse — no matter what!"

Her eyes were still closed. Karin described the desperate drive of Kampfgruppe Peiper through the wooded mountains, the capture of too many surprised, outnumbered American soldiers, the frustrations of maneuvering heavy tanks along the narrow river valleys, finding the bridges blown by the Americans, running out of fuel and ammunition, being bombed and machine-gunned by American airplanes ". . . and then in the middle of all this, the word came that at some crossroads back behind them, there had been a 'mix-up' — that is what they were told, a mix-up — and a bunch of American prisoners had been shot. Well, most of these men had been in Russia three years, they had seen prisoners shot before, even Gottfried Gesstler — who had not been in Russia — admits in their situation, nobody had time to worry about what happened to some prisoners. . . . "

She told how the whole massive Ardennes Offensive collapsed.

She told how the Americans finally fought Peiper to a standstill, how he had to abandon his vehicles, how he withdrew his column on Christmas Eve, walking silently back through the snowy forest nights.

She told how the Leibstandarte was pulled out of the west and transferred to Hungary, to hold off the Russians.

She told how the Leibstandarte lost most of its men in Hungary, fell back from Budapest, fell back from Vienna, and finally surrendered to the Americans.

She told how the Americans combed through the armies of prisoners for people from Kampfgruppe Peiper, how they found them, locked them up, interrogated them. . . . "Well, they had been defeated in war, but they were still SS, still Leibstandarte Adolf Hitler, still arrogant, and at first they wouldn't tell the Americans anything at all. So then the Americans got tough, they locked these men into solitary cells, they threatened them with all sorts of things, some of them they beat up, some of them they promised to release if they testified against others. . . . They used third-degree tactics, and then they got confessions. And some of the American officers who did this work were Jews from Germany and Austria, whose own families had been killed by the SS, so you can imagine the atmosphere in that prison, and at that trial."

"What happened then?" asked Anders. "Were they convicted?"

Karin nodded. "The judges were American officers, and they convicted them. Peiper and some of the others were sentenced to be hanged. The younger ones, like Gottfried, got prison sentences. But nobody was hanged. The American officer who was appointed to defend them went home and made a terrible fuss — he was an American lawyer and he said the trial wasn't fair — and then Congress investigated, I don't understand what happened exactly but the thing dragged on and on, and the Americans just gradually let them loose. . . . The youngest first, so Gottfried got out already in 1948. Peiper they kept a long time, the longest of all. But nobody was hanged."

Anders finished dressing. Then he sat down at the desk and looked again at the prisoners with numbers around their necks. He had been in high school when the Battle of the Bulge took place. He had been in basic training in Kentucky when these trials were held in Germany. He vaguely remembered — was it in college? — newspaper stories about SS men having been beaten up — accusing people of beating them up — in connection with what came to be called the Malmédy Massacre. . . . Is anybody going to give a damn about this? Today?

Anders picked up the clipping. Faces and numbers. Without the death's head cap, without the SS runes, without driving goggles, without the leopard-spotted camouflage jacket, without the machine gun, without the smile, Defendant No. 18 looked even younger. He wore some kind of American fatigue jacket with an open collar revealing a white T-shirt. His blond hair was wetly slicked down and combed, and he was thinner. He sat up straight in his chair with his hands folded on his lap, a disciplined, attentive German schoolboy. With those memories, what in God's earth possessed this man to make a business arrangement involving Boris Fleischer? Involving Walther Siegler? Did he even think about them? Did he think they would be gotten rid of? Bought out? Fired? Did he think this story would never come up? Indeed, *would* it have come up if Graham Anders didn't happen to remember something?

"Why did Gesstler suddenly tell you all this last night?" he asked.

"He wants me to go home and explain this whole thing to Francis."

"Francis Hyde doesn't know that Gesstler was put on trial, doesn't know that Gesstler was actually convicted of shooting American prisoners?"

Karin shook her head. "It's really a very complicated story. Books have been written about it —"

"It's not going to look very complicated to people who see these pictures you've brought me, who see this smiling face under the death's head blown up to the size of a newspaper page, combined with an insert of these guys with their numbers, combined maybe with another insert — all those bodies lying in a field, and what would the caption be? '*A new partner for Philadelphia Pharma?*' "

She dropped her eyes. "I know what I have done."

"Why doesn't Gesstler explain his own story to Francis Hyde?"

"Because he thinks it would look bad, it would make too much of it, if he suddenly flies over there and makes this great confession. He thinks another person can explain it better."

"So he picks *you* for the job?"

Karin smiled, but it was a sick, bitter smile. Karin shrugged. Karin chewed her lips.

"I thought you didn't like him," said Anders.

Karin produced a handkerchief and blew her nose. "I guess I have just proved I don't like him."

"But he trusted you enough to tell you this whole story, to show you his pictures from the war, his newspaper clippings from his trial?"

"He did, yes. He was upset about Hammerbrook, you see. These things, they are not secrets in Germany, after all, and Dr. Hammerbrook's people will find them out quickly anyway, so he wants Francis to hear it first from him, so should he go himself? No. Should he telephone? No, not something like this. Should he write a letter? Not time enough, the story is too complicated. Should he send a German lawyer? Or should he send the girl that Francis asked to marry him, to explain this story? And what does the girl do? She gets up in the middle of the night and goes down into his library and finds the photographs that he has shown to her, and she takes just one photograph and one newspaper clipping, but she knows the right ones to take, doesn't she? She knows the ones that will be the most effective in the hands of Mr. Boris Fleischer's lawyer!"

The morning sun was streaming into the room, but she sat in the shadowed corner. Her face was dark and her eyes seemed too bright until he saw that she was crying. "You think I'm really crazy?" she whispered.

Anders looked at his watch. "I've got to get over to the Ballindamm. They're expecting me. You really want me to have these pictures?"

She nodded.

"When are you going home?" he asked.

"Right now this minute! I have to fly out of there in half an hour to make the connection in Frankfurt, to be in Kennedy this afternoon. They will have a limousine at Kennedy. Gottfried wanted to drive me to the airport, but I talked him out of it, I took a taxi so I could give you these." She stood up and looked at her watch, then looked directly into his face and smiled the saddest smile.

Jesus Christ she's brave, she really loves you! "You're going to tell Francis Hyde about the Malmédy Trial? Gesstler's version of the Malmédy Massacre? What about these pictures? Francis Hyde is the one who ought to see these pictures!"

"Don't ask me to do that too, Graham! How can I tell him what Gottfried wants me to tell him, and at the same time show him these pictures? They are for you. *You* do what you want with them."

"I want to show them to Francis Hyde."

"Then do it, show them to Francis, just don't ask me to do it."

Anders could not stop staring into her eyes, which seemed to be gray now, not cornflower blue. "Whose side are you on?"

"I have to be on both sides! This whole thing is my fault in the first place."

"Why is it your fault?"

"Because I suggested Boatwright, I mean I didn't mean to do it, but they were looking for an American investment, Gottfried wanted Francis to suggest something and Francis wasn't really interested but I was thinking about you — Yes, I was, I was thinking about you being back with Caroline, and I said the name 'Boatwright' to him, to Francis, and *bang!* suddenly Francis was very interested —"

"Are they still out there buying Boatwright stock?"

"Yes, *No!* I mean, they bought some more on Monday, but when Dr. Hammerbrook came over yesterday, Gottfried suspected there might be trouble about this Malmédy thing but he didn't call Francis right away, because of me."

"Because of you?"

"Well, Francis had been calling there to see if I arrived but they didn't know where I was, so Gottfried waited until I showed up, you see, and then he spent the whole evening telling me this Malmédy business, how should I explain it to Francis, so we called after that, and something now has changed over there —"

"What do you mean? What's changed over there?"

"I don't know. For some reason we couldn't get through to Francis at the hospital, so we called the investment bankers in New York. They said the New York Stock Exchange was closed but they could still buy in San Francisco and then suddenly they couldn't, somebody told them they had instructions not to buy anymore, maybe from Francis, so now we don't know what is going on, and that is why I must not miss this plane, Graham!"

TWENTY-ONE

John the Baptist

Anders walked in the streets of the city. At the moment there was nothing more for him to do at Waldstein's. There was no point in calling Philadelphia or New York, where it was four o'clock in the morning, and the hotel would be buzzing with maids and vacuum cleaners. Confused and depressed, Anders walked along the Binnenalster. A wet wind blew from the North Sea. The city teemed around him. Trailer trucks roared across the bridge. Buses. Diesel exhaust. Cars. HH license plates: Hansastadt Hamburg had been burned to ashes in 1943. He remembered the photographs on the walls of Otto Waldstein's office. New buildings, and new trees along the water. Not so new now; new in the life of a tree, not so new in the life of a man . . .

Another cup of coffee? A drink? When you start wanting a drink at ten o'clock in the morning, it may be time to stop drinking! Just keep walking for a while.

Blue Lufthansa signs. Time to go home. They were getting him a ticket for next morning. Nothing more to do here, unless Boris Fleischer wants interviews with Hammerbrook's investors? No. Wrong thing, we have to rely on Waldstein and on Hammerbrook now. But they will have to send somebody to New York, to meet with Fleischer's operating people. . . .

Walking along the Alster — not a lake, a dammed-up river — this leveraged buyout thing will *not* be easy, it will have to be sold. First of all to Fleischer's vice presidents. This is not being done by Morgan Stanley, this is not being done by First Boston, this is being done by Waldstein, Hammerbrook. *Who?* From *where?* Fleischer's vice presidents are mostly new young men, not old friends of Graham Anders, not old clients of Conyers & Dean. They are not going to do this on trust. They are only going to do this (a) to save their jobs and (b) to get rich. Somebody has to convince them that they will indeed secure their jobs, this way, and that they have a good chance of getting rich. Not Boris Fleischer. Not Alexander Hammerbrook. Graham Anders has to go home and do that job.

Can you do it?

Anders stopped on the bridge and looked across the Aussenalster, the outer and much larger expanse of water. A silver 727 was climbing into the distance, climbing west. Amsterdam? London? Where would she be now? In Frankfurt, waiting to board a 747. What did she mean, something is changed over there? Well, she didn't know herself. Or did she? *How can you believe a word she says?*

On the other side of the bridge he found a newspaper stand. He bought a *Paris Herald*, a *New York Times*, a *Financial Times* of London and a *Frankfurter Allgemeine*. Then he continued down a side street until he came to a modern steel-and-glass shopping arcade, and inside he saw a terrace where people were already eating cakes and drinking coffee, so he sat down, ordered coffee, and began to flip through the papers, looking for the financial pages.

Boatwright's price was down a dollar at yesterday's close, but he already knew that, and there was nothing else. Nothing. Is that good news or bad? Presumably nothing happened. They haven't had to file their 13D for Monday's purchases yet. Whatever Karin thinks happened over there has not been reported yet. Had not been reported when these papers closed. Why is the price down? Ask the Arbitragers. Arbitrageurs? Arbs? Your mind is out of gear.

On the other side of the arcade, he noticed the familiar orange AGFA sign, a window full of Leicas and Japanese competitors. He paid for his coffee, crossed the hallway and entered the photo store.

The clerk was a dark young woman in jeans and a gray sweater, who insisted on English. Anders took the envelope from his breast pocket and dropped the pictures on the black velvet.

"I'd like to have these rephotographed and then blown up." He looked around. On the wall behind her was a color print, about twelve by eighteen inches, a white Bavarian church in front of blue snow-capped mountains. "Blown up to that size."

She glanced at the faces of Kampfgruppe Peiper. "Yes, sir, that can be done." No reaction at all.

"But I've got to have it done today. I'm leaving first thing in the morning."

Now there was a reaction. The pictures would have to go to a laboratory, sir, and it would take a week. They would be glad to send them anywhere —

Anders smiled his best smile and said he would be glad to pay a surcharge for special service.

"Just a moment, sir." The girl picked up the snapshot and the limp yellow piece of newspaper, turned, and disappeared through the door. Anders felt his heart stop. A blast of white-hot panic. A dozen old spy movies. Voices behind the door. The girl came out first, and behind her came a man. . . . Anders had only the dimmest impression that the man was also dark and quite fat, dark eyes behind heavy spectacles, perhaps, but Anders had already grabbed his envelope and now he reached across the counter and snatched the picture and the newspaper clipping from the girl's hand and put them back into the envelope and was out of the shop before anyone could say a word, walking as fast as he could toward the entrance of the arcade and the open street where the cold wet wind blew off the Alster.

It was crowded in the field, and very cold. A hundred men were milling around in the snow, all looking at the Germans on the road. There were only two vehicles up there at the crossroads: a Panther and a half-track armored personnel carrier. Each of them had apparently thrown a track, and their crews were in the road yelling instructions and working with hammers and wrenches to get the tracks back on.

"We could jump the fuckers," somebody muttered, and he was right. The main German column was long gone down the road to Stavelot, leaving only these ten men with their immobilized equipment to guard a field full of disarmed soldiers. The cannon of the tank was pointed into the field, but there was probably nobody inside the tank. The crew was out in the road, struggling to force the heavy steel-link track back over the wheels on the far side. Only two Germans were paying any attention to the prisoners in the field: one was an officer who stood in the road, scowling and trying to light a cigarette in the wind, turning from the prisoners to the work his men were doing and then back to the prisoners again; the other was a boy behind the machine gun atop the half-track. The boy wore earphones and a black overseas cap with a silver skull in front; he kept looking over his shoulder, watching for airplanes. . . .

A telephone rang. The sky turned yellow. The officer whirled, drew his pistol, and began to fire. The people in front were running. Somebody was yelling "*Stand fast! Stand fast!*" but everybody was running now, trying to reach the woods, and then they heard the earsplitting *baaa-rip! baaa-rip!* of the machine gun and saw what must have been their own black blood splattering into the snow —

— and he was awake, his shirt and his pillow soaked with sweat, reaching for the telephone.

"Mr. Anders, you wanted to be called at noon? It is noon now. Shall we place the call for you?"

— Good morning! I'm sorry to wake you up so early, but it's noon over here and I wanted to tell you what's happening.

— Well, I've been sort of wondering when I would hear from you. I gather you've talked to your office.

— I tried you a couple of times last night, but the line was busy twice and I had to call a lot of other people. . . . Caroline, I think we've come up with an answer to this thing. It's too complicated to explain over the telephone, but essentially we ought to take Boatwright private, do what they call a leveraged buyout. Otto Waldstein and his partner Hammerbrook over here are going to work out the mechanics, but essentially we're going to borrow the money to buy out the public stockholders for a good price, and when the thing is done, Boatwright will be owned by you and Boris and the employees and some German investors that Waldstein and Hammerbrook are getting together —

— Graham, when are you coming home?

— Tomorrow, but they can't get me a direct flight into Philadelphia tomorrow. So I'm coming into Kennedy and I'll get another flight there or I'll take the train, but I'll call you from Kennedy —

— Graham, don't make any commitments for what happens about my Boatwright stock.

— What? What do you mean? How could I make a commitment —

— Well, don't start on a project that depends on my stock, because I've decided to sell it to Mr. Hyde, at thirty-five dollars a share.

— You have *what?*

— Graham, I think we'd better discuss this face-to-face.

— Now wait a minute, Caroline, of course it's your stock and you can do whatever you want with it, but Christ Almighty, this is one hundred and eighty degrees the opposite of what you've been saying all your life —

— Maybe it's time for a change of course for me. For all of us.

— Caroline, are you all right?

— No, I'm not all right. I'm very, very miserable!

— Would you mind telling me why?

. . . .

— Caroline?

— Graham . . . I think you know that Fanny Hyde, the Lady St. Eustace, and her sister — whatever her name is — you know that they don't like your blonde geisha very much.

— My what?

— They had her followed, Graham.

— Had her followed? Where to?

— Everyplace she went on her little trip, including your room at the best hotel in Hamburg, where she may be sitting on your lap right now, for all I know.

— She's not sitting on my lap; she's on her way back to Francis Hyde.

— Well, she's going to get a cool reception, because Mr. Hyde is heartbroken and very bitter. Did she tell you that she asked him for your head on a silver platter? I must say I never thought of you in the role of John the Baptist before!

— I don't believe a word of this! Those Hyde girls would stop at nothing —

— I didn't talk to the Hyde girls, I talked to their father, they gave him a written report from their detectives. . . . Four Seasons Hotel, Room 322, is that correct? Graham, I'm really sick of this whole thing and I think I'd better just take my money and run, as the saying goes.

— Run where?

— I don't know. What difference does it make? Isn't that what you always say?

— Caroline, can you calm down and just please listen to me for just a minute?

— I'm perfectly calm. I've been waiting five days to hear from you, calmly wondering what you would be telling me about our future when you finally called, and now you do call and all you want to talk about is going private, or leveraged buy-outs, or whatever!

— Caroline . . . All right you're mad at me, but don't make the decision of your life, don't make a decision like that because you're mad at me! You're going to take your money and run? Where will you run to? And what are you going to do with that much money? You'll be just another rich woman on the Main Line, with everybody and his brother sucking up to you for money for this and that wonderful cause. This is the same old Philadelphia story, you know. What happened to the Curtis Publishing Company? What happened to the Pennsylvania Railroad? What happened to Philco? What happened to Saunders? What happened to Lippincott's? What happened to Wanamaker's?

— Graham, I don't *care* what happened to Wanamaker's! I don't *care* what happened to the Pennsylvania Railroad! What I care about is what's happened to you and me, that you cannot get that woman out of your system. . . . After all this time? Have you really been seeing her all these years?

— Of course not, Caroline.

— You expect me to believe that? You're supposed to be on a vital mission to Germany for Boris Fleischer, for Boatwright, and she gets to go along for the ride?

— She did *not* go along; if somebody followed her they surely know —

— Followed you the next day, I'd call that pretty close communication.

— There was *no* communication!

— Oh stop it, Graham, don't take me for such a total *sap!*

— Oh sugar, I wouldn't ever, *ever* —

— You have made an *ass* out of me in front of the entire *world!*

— Entire world knows I love you very, very much!

— In front of the children!

— The children are fine. . . .

— And all you want to talk about is my Boatwright stock! I'm not a human being that you stood up and married in Germantown Meeting and said you would forsake all others until death shall separate us? And that you still screw once in a while and that had your children? No! All I am . . . all I am is the owner of the biggest block of your biggest client!

— Caroline! You *know* that's not true! I met you before I even went to law school —

— That's the very first thing you ever said to me, the first words out of your mouth, you said I was the Locomotive Works!

— That was after you said whose son I was, whose grandson I was.

— No, you said it first!

— Oh Caroline, *please* —

— What *is* it about her, Graham? What does she know how to do? Is it really the German songs?

— What was all that about John the Baptist? I never claimed to be John the Baptist, but I think you know how badly I need you, I can't function without you. . . .

— Well you're going to have to learn and there will be plenty of people eager to help you because I've really had it, Graham. Up to here! And I don't want to talk anymore now, we will have to work out the mechanics when you get home. . . .

— Caroline, will you just please listen to me for one more minute? Have you actually signed an agreement with Francis Hyde?

— His lawyers are working on it. Bill Pennington's firm.

— Caroline, when I get home I'm going to put some things on Bill Pennington's desk that will stop their whole deal dead in its tracks, so will you please please please not sign anything at least until I get there?

— Is this something about the SS business you were talking about?

— Yes.

— Something Karin got for you?

— That's right.

— Something we are supposed to be grateful to Karin for, is that right?

— No, that is *not* right, there's not one word been said about anybody being grateful to her —

— Then why did she do it? Whatever she did?

— Look . . . I can't explain why she does or doesn't do something, because most of the time she doesn't know herself!

— She is self-destructive, and so are you, and that's what the two of you have in common! You are very much alike, you are a perfect matched pair, you were made for each other, you can't stay away from each other, and now you are both going to be free to ride off into the sunset together! And the Boatwright Corporation is going to get along without the last Boatwright.

— You aren't the last Boatwright! You've got a son called Boatwright. And now you want to throw it all up. You're going to sell Boatwright to Francis Hyde and to the Leibstandarte Adolf Hitler because you're pissed off at me for seeing another woman? Caroline, *I'm begging you!* Don't sell your birthright because you're mad at me. I'm the way I am. I can't help the way I am, you've got every conceivable ground for divorce if that's what you want, but you've put up with me all these years, I can't make myself into a better person!

. . . .

— Caroline?

— I told them to get the papers ready, Graham, and that's what they're doing —

— Caroline, just think a minute: with all the stock dividends, with all the splits, at thirty-five dollars a share, you are worth more than all the Boatwrights who have ever owned Boatwright stock, including your Aunt Susan, including your great-grandfather, including your grandfather, including your father, including your sister and your cousins and your aunts and their children . . . your whole God-damned clan, and the reason you are is that you held on, you did not sell, you kept a very substantial piece of the American economy in your hands, and it grew with the American economy, and while the dollar is worth less and less every year, an efficient money-making machine is worth more and more every year, and when you exercise some control, when you sit on the Board of your own machine, a machine that bears your name —

— Graham, I've never heard you go on this way! You are more sentimental about the Boatwrights than any Boatwright ever was.

— I'm not sentimental about the Boatwrights, I'm sentimental about *Boatwright*, for which my grandfather was the lawyer from I think about 1917 until his death, and for which I have been the lawyer — one of many, these days — since even before I was made a partner in the firm, when I worked under Ellsworth Boyle —

— Oh, I know that, Graham!

— And I am particularly proud of the fact that I continued to be the lawyer for Boatwright when the whole management changed, when Fleischer took over, when they got out of the locomotive business, when they moved to New York, and now I am right in the middle of a most desperate maneuver to save the company *again*, for you, for the firm, for our children . . . and you want to . . . and you tell me . . .

— Calm down, Graham!

— You have to realize I was up all night trying to arrange this deal and I only slept a few minutes just now and I had a crazy dream and I apologize for yelling at you but I feel like I'm at the end of my string!

— It's too late, Graham.

— I never held myself out as John the Baptist!

— I never thought of you in that role, frankly.

— If you don't want me to come back to the house, will you explain the thing to Boatie?

— I am to explain your behavior to your son?

— Caroline, how in God's name —

— Graham, maybe you had better get some sleep now.

— Well, it's just lunchtime here. I could leave now, but the flights are all in the morning. I'm leaving tomorrow morning.

— Yes, you said that. I'll see you tomorrow night then?

— You want me to come home?

— Well, we have to talk about this thing face-to-face and get ourselves . . . We can't do this by telephone. . . .

— Okay . . . Caroline?

— Yes, Graham?

— I would trust you with my life. Do you know that?

. . . .

— Do you know that?

— Is that the most important thing?

— Yes, that's the most important thing. There's nothing more important than that.

— I wonder. You should see how you light up when she walks into a room!

— I don't know how . . . I don't know what you want me to say to that.

— There's nothing you can say to that, Graham. Have a good flight. I'll see you tomorrow. Get some sleep.

TWENTY-TWO

False Alarm

Francis Hyde was almost sixty-nine years old. He had thought of life as having the shape of a rainbow, and he knew that he was sliding down the right end, which was the wrong end of the rainbow. He had seen bad times before, but this last week was the worst week he could remember. Maybe it only seemed so bad, because it ended the best winter of his life. Pretty sad when you have to wait that long for the best winter, but better late than never . . . Perhaps it was his own fault. Too much time devoted to work. He realized now that building the Company had been the only thing he enjoyed. More than enjoyed: loved. The harder he worked the better it went, and the better it went the harder he worked. He was a maker of drugs, and he gradually understood that the inventing of drugs, the manufacturing of drugs, the selling of drugs — and the making of a great deal of money from it all — had become to him the most potent and addictive drug of all. For a man who lived from medicine, he hadn't been sick much, which was why this thing now had been such a shock.

The winter with Karin had restored his life. She showed him what he had been missing. His life with Marjorie had been no life at all. Marjorie liked bridge and golf and Chesterfield cigarettes and Beefeater gin. Marjorie cringed away when he touched her. Marjorie spent so many hours a day on the golf course that the skin of her face and her neck and her arms and her lower legs turned gradually to brown wrinkled leather, and Francis Hyde could not remember why he had asked her to marry him. After their second daughter was born, Marjorie began to slip more and more into another world, sitting silently through dinner, staring down at her plate. . . . After Marjorie's death, he sold the house and bought a comfortable condominium near his office. His friends invited him to go after trout in Colorado, salmon in Scotland, chamois in the Tyrol, tigers in Bengal — but now the men of his age were dropping off. People tried to fix him up with the widows and divorcées of his generation. Some of them were still handsome, all of them were enthusiastic, a few were surprisingly aggressive physically, but Francis Hyde was too suspicious, too set in his ways, too accustomed to being alone, and nothing happened until Karin Bromberg simply overwhelmed him. It wasn't only the skiing in Switzerland and the tennis and the sailing and naked night swimming in Barbados and the theater trips and the suddenly cheerful restaurants in New York and the things in bed he had read about but never experienced; it was the sound of her laughter, the sound of her singing, the sound of her playing the piano — the sounds of life after the stillness of death. He had never before met a woman whose only interest seemed to be pleasing him. She wouldn't move into his apartment because of her girls, but she let him visit whenever he wanted to, and she traveled wherever and whenever he wanted her. He had never traveled with a woman other than his wife and was at first embarrassed in front of blasé hotel clerks. Karin laughed at him. He became accustomed to her hand in his elbow, to the pressure of her shoulder in the next airplane seat. . . . Shyly, he began to introduce her to his friends. A trophy. One bank chairman almost dropped his eyeballs; the chairman's wife squinted, then inquired about Francis Hyde's daughters.

The plan to take over Boatwright with German money was something extra that winter, something to keep his hand in. Younger men were running Philadelphia Pharma, theoretically he was retired, but he couldn't play tennis and read the papers all day, and he ached to get into medical high technology; it was the perfect match for a pharmaceutical company and Siegler would be a fine beginning. Boatwright seemed to suit Gesstler's requirements too, and of course a combination with Boatwright would more than double the size of Philadelphia Pharma — not the worst way to sign off. A good winter.

And then?

And then Freddie Hill stuck a finger up his asshole. Freddie Hill grunted. Freddie Hill had been taking care of Francis Hyde since both of them were in their thirties, giving him occasional physicals, prescribing more exercise and less alcohol, helping to find all the different headshrinkers and drying-out academies for Marjorie, providing unsolicited comments on Philadelphia Pharma's new products. . . . Well, this didn't mean a thing, but at our age most men begin to have some trouble with the prostate and there's nothing to do but check it out, perfectly simple procedure, a few days in the hospital so they can take a biopsy —

Francis Hyde knew better. His own father had gone in for a prostate operation and had come out a senile old man. Two of his friends couldn't hold their water after this thing. Had to wear a rubber tube inside their pants. How long would this girl stay with a man who had to wear a rubber tube?

And that wasn't the worst of it: Francis Hyde knew a man whose carcinoma had to be treated by castration!

Before this happened, he had not worried about the prenuptial agreement. Bill Pennington, pushed by the girls, had delivered an earnest lecture: absolutely standard in this kind of a marriage, you've got to provide some security for the girls, Karin has her own income and these arrangements are more than generous — the Hyde Place alone, just think of it, "Hyde-a-Way" back in the family! and when she flat out refused to sign the thing, Francis Hyde had been at heart a little impressed, although of course he could not admit that to Bill Pennington or to the girls.

But then Freddie Hill put him into the hospital, the urologist came, the pathologist came, his daughters came — and Karin disappeared. She said she wanted to see her mother but when he called Hamburg, Gottfried didn't seem to know anything about it, and then his daughter Fanny came into his room in her mink coat and her black gloves and shut the door to the hall and sat down beside the bed and pulled off her gloves and lighted a cigarette just like her mother and said: "Daddy, I'm afraid I've got some bad news for you!"

Francis Hyde lay in the hospital bed all afternoon and evening, staring at the television, seeing nothing, feeling fury burn his insides. He didn't think he had ever met Graham Anders. Until recently he had been dimly aware of the man, a successful younger man but not in Francis Hyde's field of vision: Conyers & Dean . . . grandson of the redoubtable George Graham . . . married to a Boatwright . . . but then Graham Anders had flown up to Boston and sweet-talked old Walther Siegler into Boris Fleischer's tent while Francis Hyde's own people were standing around sucking their thumbs, and now this winter Karin had cried all over him about what a complete bastard and shit Graham Anders was . . . and now this?

Alone in the night, Francis Hyde called Caroline Anders.

When he hung up, he felt a little better. He still knew how to persuade, apparently. Especially when he knew he was right. He picked up the telephone again. When Bill Pennington was really awake, when Bill Pennington recovered from his surprise, he promised to deliver the agreement to Caroline in person, at her office, before lunch tomorrow; he promised to watch Caroline sign it; he promised to stop the investment bankers from buying any more Boatwright stock until Caroline's agreement had been filed with the SEC, maybe the same day. "Jesus Christ, Francis, *what a triumph!*" he shouted, climbing out of bed. "I'm going to draft it right now, I can't go to sleep after this. My God, how did you ever do it?"

A mild sense of satisfaction permitted Francis Hyde to nap in the gray dawn until they woke him for breakfast. He was alone. Shamed, enraged, he had finally exploded at the girls and told them to go home, so they did, and now he was alone again, waiting for the doctors. Something had to be done about Graham Anders. Impotent? Was that all a lie, to make Francis Hyde feel confident with a woman who was thirty years younger? To make Francis Hyde think she's after more than his money? And now it might be Francis Hyde! Don't think about it. . . . Is thirty-five dollars a share too much? Worth it if it works. What do they do now? Better stay one move ahead. Pennington kept complaining that Conyers & Dean had a conflict of interest representing Boatwright Corporation and Caroline Anders, one of its biggest stockholders, in a situation like this, but so far Pennington hadn't done anything about it.

Conyers & Dean?

Maybe the time had come to try another tack. He picked up the telephone, called Information, and was pleased to discover that Ordway Smith's home number was listed. It was still only 7:30 in the morning, and if he could catch Ordway before he drove to the station, Ordway might be persuaded to visit a sick old man. . . . No, that wouldn't be the right approach. This is old Walter Smith's son, always polite and friendly without sucking up to Francis Hyde the way so many people do. Best thing would be just to say come see me this morning before you go to the office because I want to talk to you. See what happens.

He woke up when somebody came into the room.

"False alarm," said Freddie Hill, grinning. Freddie Hill wore a long white coat. Freddie Hill looked pleased with himself.

"You're kidding." Francis Hyde heard the tremor in his voice.

"No, hell, I *told* you this was just a routine test because we can't take chances, but the thing's benign, Johnson says we don't even have to operate, so you got yourself into this sweat for nothing, skipper. Put on your clothes and go home."

"Jesus, I can't believe it," said Francis Hyde wishing that he believed in God so that he could thank somebody for the way he was suddenly feeling.

BOOK IV

TWENTY-THREE

Can the Leopard Change His Spots?

The flight attendants were still clearing the lunch trays when the English girl's voice came out of the speakers; they were over Boston ten minutes ahead of schedule, the captain was starting his descent into the New York area, the seatbelt sign was on, British Airways and the entire crew very much hoped they had enjoyed their flight in the Concorde. . . .

The plane was smaller than Anders had expected. At the gate in London, the drooping needle nose made him think of an aluminum anteater. Inside, he was reminded of the tubular cabin of the British Comet, the very first commercial jet. How long ago had that been? He couldn't remember. The passengers around him looked prosperous and busy; he guessed that none of them had paid with their own money. Neither had he.

"Isn't this quite unbelievable?" asked Otto Waldstein, returning from the toilet. "When I began to shuttle back and forth across this pond it was almost a week at sea, and now it's champagne and a leisurely lunch." He settled into his seat, snapped the belt lock, and began to set his wristwatch back. "I'm not at all sure I prefer this. We arrive before we left, so to speak. Perhaps it makes us younger, but by the time we are in Manhattan we will have to have lunch again!"

The Concorde had been Otto's idea. The night before, at his candle-lit dinner table, he announced that he hadn't seen Boris Fleischer for a couple of years, he didn't like the way Boris sounded on the telephone, perhaps it would be a good idea if they had a long talk, this Boatwright project was a fine excuse to try the new Concorde, they would hop over to London first thing in the morning, the office had already arranged the tickets, if Graham would not mind his company . . . so at dawn Anders was picked up at the hotel by Otto Waldstein and his driver. Now it was only nine o'clock in the morning Eastern Standard Time, and they were sinking toward Kennedy.

Anders was glad to have Otto Waldstein's company; it kept him from thinking about the stiffness in his knees and the pain in his feet; once in a while it even distracted him from despair. Otto Waldstein was three years older than Boris Fleischer, but he seemed younger. He didn't actually drink any champagne, but he chatted happily all the way through lunch, all the way across the Atlantic. He talked about the glories of the *Berengaria* (which had been the Hamburg-Amerika Line's *Imperator* before the British confiscated her in 1919) and the *Île de France* and the *Queen Mary* and the *Liberté* (built in Hamburg as the *Europa* for the North German Lloyd, confiscated by the French in 1945). He talked about his adventures with the Tenth Mountain Division in Italy, his work on General Eisenhower's staff in France, his reasons for returning to Hamburg after the war, the rebuilding of Waldstein, Hammerbrook & Co. . . . and he talked with special enthusiasm about taking the Boatwright Corporation private.

But he also asked questions: What *is* the matter with Boris? Depressions? Hmm. If we are going to put our clients into this company of yours, if we are going to the Deutsche Bank for a loan this big, we have to be satisfied about the management, you know. . . . Hmm. How much authority has he actually delegated to these younger men? What happens when Boris is out of the picture? You think they can? Any one man in particular? We are not so crazy about "teams," you know.

And what about your wife? (Anders almost closed his eyes.) Well, my dear fellow, if Mr. Gesstler and Mr. Hyde do make a tender offer for all of the Boatwright stock at say thirty dollars a share, your wife would collect a fortune, would she not?

Tell him! You owe him the full story, and you'll feel better if you tell somebody. No, if I tell anybody, I have to tell Boris first. Nothing has happened anyway, there's nothing to tell! *Nothing to tell?* Suppose she has signed with Hyde by now, and Pennington's messenger is on the train to Washington? First Amendment to Schedule 13D. Press release the minute they file it with the SEC . . . Could be on the Dow tape by the time we meet Boris. . . . They see on the tape that Caroline has sold her stock *and they ask you why?*

He remembered Otto Waldstein's reaction to the Gesstler photographs yesterday. Hammerbrook's reaction. Silently looking down at the pictures, looking up at him.

Frowning, puzzled, still frowning at his halting explanation of how he got these pictures, then embarrassed, let's get on with the deal, do what you want with these things. . . . And now Hyde has Caroline's stock? Anders could just imagine Boris Fleischer and Otto Waldstein staring at him, and he had to force his mind away from their eyes. . . .

Where the hell is Karin? What will Hyde do to her? Don't think about it; she was supposed to get home last night and whatever he did is done. Where is she?

Anders had been trying to reach her since he finished his conversation with Caroline yesterday. He had to tell her that Francis Hyde knew. He called Lufthansa in Frankfurt and told them he had an emergency message for Mrs. Bromberg on their ten o'clock plane to New York and they were polite and helpful until it turned out there was no Mrs. Bromberg on their flight manifest. Try TWA. TWA Frankfurt first put him on hold with Viennese waltzes for a while and then had a policy against giving out passenger flight information, except in emergencies. Well, what was the nature of the emergency? Anders told her Mrs. Bromberg's father had just died and she then confirmed that Mrs. Bromberg would arrive in New York at 1:30 Eastern Standard Time, they would radio the plane to have her call Mr. Anders, Hotel Vier Jahreszeiten Hamburg. By that time, it was 7:30 P.M. in Hamburg and Anders was late for dinner at Otto Waldstein's house. Karin had not called. He left a message for her with the hotel operator ("Mr. Hyde has been fully informed"), but she still had not called when he returned to the hotel at eleven. It would be five o'clock in the afternoon in Philadelphia now, and Karin should be in her house. . . . Anders called and called. Nobody answered. Could it be spring vacation? Children with Bob in California? He woke up at five o'clock this morning and called again. No answer. As he stepped out of the bed, his left knee did not bend properly, and when he put his weight on his feet he felt the sharp, familiar stabbing pain, as if a needle had been inserted an inch below his left ankle. He swallowed four aspirins, shaved, showered, dressed, packed his bag, rode downstairs on the elevator, and checked out just as the chauffeur came up the steps into the lobby.

Now he parried Otto Waldstein's question about Caroline, and talked instead about Boris Fleischer's fears for the future of the United States. Otto Waldstein stopped talking and listened intently as Anders projected Fleischer's nightmares: wholesale unemployment, fire in the streets, America is an island but the water is rising. . . .

Otto Waldstein was gazing past Anders at the rising ocean of eggshell-colored clouds. There was a moment of silence. Then he said: "Boris is not the only one who has such nightmares. But —" A pause for thought. "But, unless we take arms against the sea of troubles — is that from *Hamlet*? Unless we can actually do something about these issues, it is better to put them out of your mind and do your work, don't you think?"

"I told him he should go into politics," said Anders.

Otto Waldstein smiled. "Nobody trained Boris Fleischer to be elected to public office. And not me either. At our age it's too late to learn, I think. Old shoemakers had better stick to their last." He paused. "But old shoemakers don't need to worry about things they can't help."

The plane dipped into the clouds. The pitch of the engines changed, there was a bump and rumble of adjusting machinery, they emerged into blazing sunshine again, tipping left, and for the moment Anders thought he recognized Montauk Point.

"Boris is sending out a car for us," said Otto Waldstein.

Okay, thought Anders, I'll tell Boris and Otto when we're all together, at the second lunch, but that is not the way it happened, because when he and Otto Waldstein came through the United States Customs booth and faced the line of chauffeurs and limousine drivers holding up handwritten signs — *Mr. Walt Stein & Mr. Andrews* among them — he felt an electric shock of delight as he recognized a small beaming seventeen-year-old boy wearing a blue school blazer and very large eyeglasses.

"Whose car is this?" asked Anders, gritting his teeth, trying not to limp as he marched through the parking lot beside Boatie, who now stopped to unlock a little red Toyota.

"This belongs to a guy in my class, Dad. He let me borrow it." The boy threw the overnight bag into the back seat and held the door as Anders climbed in.

"Your mother doesn't know you came to get me?"

Boatie settled back into the driver's seat, started the engine, glanced into the mirror and eased the car out of the column. Then he smiled at his father. "I thought we would surprise her."

Otto Waldstein had been delighted to meet the boy. "Your father didn't tell you what plane he was coming on?"

"No sir, I called your office in Hamburg and they told me."

Otto Waldstein turned to Anders. "Go home to your wife, my friend. I will have my talk with Boris now and we will telephone this afternoon. Good-bye, young man, I hope to see more of you." They rode in silence for a while. Verrazano Bridge. New Jersey Turnpike.

"Dad? There's trouble again, isn't there?"

"Is your mother . . . what did your mother say?"

"You *are* coming home with me, aren't you, Dad? She says you're moving out again."

"Boatie, it isn't up to me, it's up to your mother! Your mother is angry with me, she's got good reason to be angry with me —"

"Do you want to live with Karin again?"

"No, I don't, and anyway she's getting married to somebody else."

"Mother says she's not."

"Well, we don't know exactly what she's doing, to tell you the truth, but no, I want to stay at Juniper Lane, I want to stay with your mother, with you. . . . I hope you believe that, buddy."

Anders was staring past the boy's desolated face, at the oil refineries, at a United plane tilting toward Newark. "I'm afraid it's become rather common, people think they can't live together anymore, they get sick and tired of each other, they just can't live together, anymore, all sorts of reasons. . . . But that doesn't apply to *us*, honest to God, boy, I love your mother very much, I need your mother to take care of me —"

"Well, why do you have to see other people?"

Anders looked down the Jersey Turnpike. He's asked you a question and he deserves a straight answer. What *is* the answer?

Anders used to think his problem was unique. He had even made up a name for it: He called it the Good Girl–Bad Girl Problem, but then, in black depression, he had consulted a psychiatrist and learned that his ailment was so common that they had a medical term for it: the Whore–Madonna Complex. He remembered wondering why they put the Bad Girl first. They had a fancy name, but they didn't have a cure. In effect, he was told to relax and enjoy it, and given pills for his depression. The pills eventually worked, but how do you explain all this to your son?

He tried. "I don't know exactly how to answer your question. Maybe some people need one person to love and live with and have children with and respect —" Anders sighed from the effort of actually putting this into words "— and somebody else to play with. Maybe somebody they don't look up to so much. You love them *all*, but you love them in different ways. You understand that?"

"No!" the boy said, fiercely.

"No, of course not, why should you? What more can I tell you? I wish I wasn't the way I am, but I've never been able to do much about it."

"You hurt a lot of people, Dad."

"I know it."

"You told me a gentleman never hurts another person's feelings unintentionally."

"No!" Anders replied without thinking. "Somebody else told you that. The man who is always explaining what a gentleman doesn't do just proves he isn't one, you know!" but he instantly regretted having said it. "Boatie, I don't know if I'm a gentleman, but I know I'm your father, I know I love you very much, and I know I'm very proud of you — This is a hard thing to talk about. Maybe I should say that you've got to take your old man as you find him. The leopard can't change his spots. That's from Kipling, isn't it? *Just-So Stories?*"

"I think it's from the Bible, Dad. The prophet Jeremiah asks if the Ethiopian can change his skin, or the leopard his spots."

It was just after noon when they crossed the Delaware, so they drove directly into the center of town and stopped the car in front of the Franklin Tower.

"I have to leave you here, kiddo. I really appreciate your coming to meet me."

"It's evening for you, Dad. Why don't you come straight home with me?"

"No, I'd better find out what's happening upstairs, and your mother is at her office anyway. I'll give her a call, and we'll see how things are. You can go back to school." He opened the door and started to get out. His right knee felt as if it were stuffed with cotton wool. "No, wait a minute! There's an important job you can do for me this afternoon." He sat down again, reached into the pocket of his jacket, and withdrew the white envelope. It was soft and wrinkled by now.

"Welcome back, Mr. Anders," said the handsome, matronly receptionist on the thirty-first floor. "You've been missed." Looking into the eyes of George Graham as he walked slowly past the portrait, he felt as if he had been gone for a month instead of a week. . . .

"Welcome back, Mr. Anders," said his secretary, and stood beside him looking down at the orderly stacks of mail and *Wall Street Journal*s and pink telephone slips.

He dreaded the telephone slips, and something was bothering her.

"Tom Sharp and his whole group are in New York, Mr. Anders. They've been there for several days and they thought you would go directly to Mr. Fleischer's office — Oh Mr. Anders, there's been a terrible fuss about your time records and the checks were returned —"

"What? What time records? What do you mean my checks were returned?"

"Remember before you left I told you they were after me because we hadn't turned in the time for January yet? Remember I did speak to you about it a couple of times, because they called me from the administrator's office, Sherman Shapp's secretary called me, but then you had to rush off to Germany in such a hurry, so what happened is they didn't transfer the money from your draw into the checking account, but that's supposed to be automatic transfer on the first of every month, that was the whole idea when they put in that system so every partner wouldn't have to draw his own checks, but now they say if your time is more than thirty days overdue the computer is programmed to stop the transfer. I mean it automatically doesn't transfer the money because they say that's the rule the firm adopted to make people turn in their time, but they didn't *tell* me they didn't make the transfer, Mr. Anders, so I sent out all your personal checks and the bank returned them for *insufficient funds*. . . ."

"All right, all right, come on now, let's not get all out of control here, it's not your fault, it's the fault of this goddamned squirrel cage system we've constructed for ourselves. . . . Come on now, it's really okay —"

"I went straight in to Mr. Smith and explained what happened and he called Sherman Shapp and made him transfer your money that very same day but now I don't know —"

"Well, okay then, it sounds like you handled it beautifully, we'll write a little note and send out new checks, but would you do me a favor first? Would you go over to the library and see if Judy can find us *Bartlett's Familiar Quotations* . . . and a Bible?"

"A Bible, Mr. Anders?"

Mr. Thomas Sharp — at Boatwright NYC — please call.

Mr. Gordon (*Wall Street Journal*) — please call.

Mr. Fleischer — please call.

Mr. Ordway Smith — lunch today?

Mr. Bennett Williamson Exec VP Boatwright NYC — lunch tomorrow?

Mrs. Bromberg — please do *not* call — will call back later.

Jeremiah 13:23: Can the Ethiopian change his skin, or the leopard his spots? then may ye also do good, that are accustomed to do evil.

Accustomed to do evil? His eye dropped down the half-column of print, to verse 27:

I have seen thine adulteries and thy neighings, the lewdness of thy whoredom, and thine abominations on the hills in the fields. Woe unto thee, O Jerusalem! wilt thou not be made clean? when shall it once be?

He decided it was time to call his wife. He reached for the telephone, but then he looked up. Ordway Smith was standing in the doorway.

TWENTY-FOUR

Billable Time

As managing partner, Ordway Smith had to have lunch on office administration matters once or twice each week. He also had to eat with the Orchestra board, the Museum board, the directors of Mo Patterson's investment company, the directors of the William Penn Trust Company, the United Fund Allocations Committee, the Trustees of the University, the Committee of Seventy. . . . Ordway's lunches were scheduled months in advance, which was why Graham Anders was surprised to find himself invited so soon again.

Same room, same table, same waiter.

"Just iced tea today, Tony," said Ordway Smith. "Six bluepoints and a club sandwich, please."

Anders ordered the same thing, and the waiter withdrew.

Graham Anders had already given a report on his trip to Hamburg. He told about Waldstein and Hammerbrook; he told about Gottfried Gesstler and the Kampfgruppe Peiper; he did not tell about Caroline Anders and Francis Hyde.

"So Boatwright goes private?" asked Ordway Smith.

"Looks like it. Otto Waldstein is with Boris and Boris's officers this afternoon. I plan to go over there tomorrow. They haven't agreed on the price yet, but word seems to be out, the telephones are ringing off the hook, the stock was trading over thirty when we left the office, it's really impossible to keep this kind of thing under wraps even if we don't have all the details nailed down —"

"And the management is still going to work with Conyers & Dean?"

"Sure, it's the same people. Boris is still the chairman, the rest of the team remains in place — but, Ordway, we've got to set up a New York office, the younger executives really don't see why they have to call Philadelphia for legal advice —"

"I don't know, Graham. You're not the only partner agitating for a New York office, but does it make economic sense? The expense would be terrific. If we could hook up with an established firm that can carry itself, but if they can do that, they might not need us; it's a question of finding the right fit — but if you succeed in taking Boatwright private, won't Caroline still be one of the biggest stockholders? When Boris retires . . . I mean, why does Boatwright have to stay in New York?"

Better tell him! If you don't tell him this very moment and Caroline signs with Hyde — has already signed while you're sitting here eating lunch — he is never going to forget it the rest of his life!

But he couldn't do it. "Anything can happen in one of these things," he said. "We've got months of work ahead of us. We'll have to set up a committee of independent directors to evaluate the price being paid — and of course anybody can come out of the woodwork with a lawsuit —"

"Think Francis Hyde might sue?"

"No."

The oysters were served, and they ate them.

Ordway Smith looked over the tops of his glasses. "Graham, Francis Hyde is not one of your greatest fans."

"He's still not going to sue," said Graham Anders, and sipped the liquor from an oyster shell. Ordway Smith gazed out the window. "And how are things with Caroline?"

Oh Jesus! "What's on your mind, Ordway?"

A bleak smile. "Can't we have lunch without —"

"We could — and did — for twenty-five years."

"But not anymore? I'm sorry if you feel that way," said Ordway Smith.

Anders said nothing, watching the oyster debris being taken away and the sandwiches served. Salt? Pepper? More mayonnaise? They ate in silence for a few minutes. Then Ordway Smith wiped his lips with his linen napkin, and sighed. "Okay, you're right, there *is* something. . . . What did I tell you . . . ask you . . . at our last lunch, what did I most respectfully suggest that you *not* do?"

This time, Anders looked out the window. "Well, I didn't."

"Come on, Graham!"

"*I didn't!* I don't want to go into details, Ordway —"

"I'm not asking you for any details, but I had a most extremely unpleasant interview with Francis Hyde —"

Anders frowned. "When was this?"

"This was yesterday. He was in Bryn Mawr Hospital, he called me at breakfast, he more or less commanded me to see him immediately — well, everybody jumps when he calls, he's used to that, and I jumped too, drove over to the hospital, went up to see the great man —"

"Who wanted my head on a silver platter?"

"He didn't mention any silver platter, but your head — yes, he wants your head, Graham."

Anders continued dissecting his sandwich with his knife and fork. "Everybody seems to want my head these days. Did he offer to send us business?"

"He made some hints in that direction. He's not happy with the way their trademark litigation is going, he's heard of Harry's success with the soap company cases —"

"Right on the verge of taking over our client, he wants to hire us — and I'm to be gotten rid of, is that the idea?"

"I told him it was out of the question, Graham, not even to be *discussed* —"

"Not even to be discussed? With your partners?"

Ordway Smith sighed again, shifted in his chair, drank some iced tea, wiped his mouth, and looked uncomfortable. "Well, of course this was only yesterday, I'll have to speak to a couple of people on the management committee —"

"Who?"

"Graham, he might say something to somebody else —"

"Who are you going to talk to?"

"Well, Ames Mahoney, of course, and Harry. And Pat. Separately. Of course it is a perfectly outrageous suggestion —"

Anders thought about Ames Mahoney. Anders thought about Harry Rex. And Pat. And the others . . .

"What do you think Bill Pennington pulls in from Phila Pharma these days?"

"I haven't got the slightest idea, and this subject ought to be beyond discussion, Graham, and it *would* be beyond discussion if you could just . . . nothing will come of it, of course, but I've got to tell them that the old boy put up this balloon . . . as a matter of fact, we just had a meeting about you!"

"Dessert, gentlemen? Some coffee?"

"Thank you, Tony, we're both okay. . . . Graham . . . the feeling seems to be that you're not doing a good job as head of your department. This matter of time records, just one example: you are supposed to know how many hours each lawyer in your department is working and how much money he or she is bringing in, and you don't, Graham! You're not even keeping track of your own time. Last month Tommy Sharp sent a bill to the underwriters for the Amoeba stock issue, they paid the bill and the syndicate closed; *now* it turns out that you had some fourteen thousand dollars' worth of time that you — or your secretary — never bothered to turn in and there is nobody to pay it, so that time is simply lost. We've had to write it off. Now in the first place, you've cost the firm that money, and in the second place, what kind of an example is that for a department head to set?"

Anders rubbed his hand across his eyes. When did they have this meeting? What are they going to be saying at the next meeting?

"And that isn't even the worst of it, Graham. In January, you billed Schuylkill Steel for their acquisition down at Sparrows Point, and it turns out you didn't include nearly ten thousand dollars of time that Tommy Sharp spent on that matter —"

"That's ridiculous, we got an excellent fee for that deal!"

"But Tommy feels that you gave away his time!"

"*I gave away his time?*"

"That's how they think about it now, Graham."

"Gave away his time, and his time is his life, so I gave away part of Tommy's life because I decided to bill Schuylkill Steel forty thousand dollars for a job that was worth forty thousand dollars, instead of extracting fifty? Is that what we've come to?"

Ordway Smith nodded.

"Boy, that is really great! Do you mind if I have a drink?" Graham Anders turned to look across the room at the waiter, who hurried over. "Tony, I think I need a glass of Cognac, please."

Ordway Smith looked at his watch. "Graham, I've got another meeting. . . . Remember they didn't even have departments when we came to the firm. We would work for this partner on one case and that partner on another and it was catch-as-catch-can, we learned to do the work and the work got done, but it was not efficient, and when the departments were organized, that didn't happen overnight, departments sort of gradually formed themselves around the best and most active lawyers, and that's how you got to be the head of your department, the first one."

"Best and most active lawyers, obviously the *last* people we want to run the departments!"

"Graham, there's no point in getting sarcastic about this. Times change. We have five or six times as many lawyers now. Department heads have to be administrators who keep the troops happy, get the work done, get us all paid. You have great talents which we all recognize, but administration isn't one of them. I hear you sometimes don't show up for your own department meetings —"

"Who is going to be the department head?"

"Well, this won't be done tomorrow, but when the fiscal year begins, I would think that Tommy Sharp would be the obvious —"

"So I'm working for Tommy now, is that right?"

"No, you're not working for Tommy, you are being relieved of burdens that you obviously don't want —"

"And how much of my percentage am I being relieved of?"

"Graham, I haven't the slightest idea, I assume there will be some adjustment —"

Some adjustment, thought Anders. There's going to be some adjustment, all right. The thing could be on the tape right now. Back there all the telephones could be ringing. . . .

"You didn't want a drink, did you, Mr. Smith?"

"No thanks, Tony, I'm late now. I take it you're not coming back with me, Graham?"

"Not quite yet. I don't feel so good."

Ordway Smith frowned at his watch again. "It's what — eight-thirty at night for you, isn't it? Why don't you just go on home, Graham?"

"Ordway, let me just say one thing: You're doing your job and you're doing a good job, and I know that. I may not act like I do, but I do."

Ordway Smith was on his feet. Without another word he touched Graham Anders on the shoulder and marched toward the door.

TWENTY-FIVE

Your Looks and My Brains?

At first she was hostile.

"What is this, anyway? I don't hear from you for over a week, not one fucking peep, when *I* call I get told Mr. Anders is on a business trip to Germany — and we can guess who else is in Germany — and now I'm supposed to leave work early because you need a quickie in the middle of the afternoon . . . are you *drunk?*" but then the tone of his voice changed the tone of hers. "Graham, are you *all right?* Is this something about Boatwright? Our traders are going bananas, there's supposed to be an announcement tomorrow. Shouldn't you be in your office? . . . Okay, give me twenty minutes to finish up here. . . . He's in — where the hell *is* he today? He's in Montreal, I think, but he'll be home for dinner, his plane gets in around six so this is no big party, okay?"

The pale spring sun had melted the snow into glistening puddles. A warmish breeze blew across the Square. Anders sat on a park bench and tried to focus on cartoons in *The New Yorker*, feeling lightheaded from the Cognac, feeling alone and desperate, knowing that he should not be sitting here paging through a magazine in the middle of the afternoon with the bums and the baby-sitters and the retired people feeding the pigeons, but his feet hurt too much, pretty soon he might be sitting around like this all day, he should have called Caroline, Caroline might be at Bill Pennington's office right now, maybe he really was going crazy, and then he saw Laura Carpenter striding swiftly toward him, wearing the mink hat she had bought with her own money and a belted English trench coat, carrying a thin leather attaché case.

He stood up, and winced. "I'm glad to see you. Thank you for coming."

"What's wrong, Graham?" She frowned, standing very close. She stared into his eyes. She sniffed. "Cognac? You don't drink Cognac at lunch. . . . Well, come on up and tell me about it. Is something wrong with your legs?"

"Is that all? Is that what you're making this fuss about?"

She was vigorously brushing her hair in front of the mirror while Anders sat on her bed in his shirtsleeves, drinking more Cognac and telling her about his lunch with Ordway Smith.

"They fired me as department head, they're going to cut my percentage —"

"So what? This is bullshit! You hated being a department head, you were a lousy department head even when I was there, they should have done this years ago —" She was incredulous. "My God, you sounded like you got run over by a truck when you called. Is this all that's happened? If you just got off the plane, why aren't you home with Caroline? Take your shoes and socks off."

Then she was on the bed beside him, leaning over to unlace his shoes.

"Ouch! Take it easy —"

"Oh Christ, Graham, it's come back! You'd better go right to the hospital, I'll call a taxi —"

"No, the hell with it, they won't take me unless the doctors see me first, and they don't know what causes it anyway. Can I have some aspirin?"

Laura went into the bathroom and returned with a glass of water in one hand and four pills in the other. Anders swallowed the pills, drank some water, stretched out on the bed and closed his eyes. Laura sat down beside him again and put a cool hand on his cheek. "Where's the German chick?"

Anders took a deep breath, and then told her essentially what happened. He had not been able to reach Karin. Apparently she was back, but he didn't know what happened with Hyde. And Hyde had offered to send a lot of business to Conyers & Dean if the firm —

"Who is Hyde?"

"He's Francis Hyde. He's your husband's boss. He's Chairman of Phila Pharma."

"Oh, *that* Mr. Hyde," said Laura, standing up. "So that's really what you're pissing and moaning about, isn't it? Not all this garbage about Ordway Smith and who is going to run the Corporate Department and what happens to your percentage . . ." She walked over to the window and looked down in the Square. "You hurt because that crazy piece has put you into a *real* mess this time, so I've got to rush home from work to make you well, my function since I was twenty —"

Anders shook his head. "The firm has really been my life, and now they're going to kick me out. Caroline is going to sell her stock and Hyde will wind up in control of Boatwright and the only way the firm will be able to keep Boatwright business — never mind new Phila Pharma business — will be to get rid of Anders!"

"All right, let's not get carried away here," said Laura.

"You know, these old men we have wandering around, am I going to become like that? Taylor Chew began to cut himself shaving all the time. Razor nicks. And their necks shrink so their collars look too big."

She turned and put her hands on her hips. "What the hell are you talking about, Graham? Your shirt collar looks fine to me! You really think those guys you worked with all your life are going to sell your head to Mr. Hyde? Aren't you still in charge of Schuylkill Steel? And the soap company?" She had unbuttoned her dress, and now she walked across the room pulling it over her head, and Anders, looking up to watch, noticed for the first time how thick her waist had become, how her breasts had swollen.

"Ellsworth Boyle would forget to zip up his fly when he came out of the men's room, and we wouldn't know who should tell him —"

From the closet, where she was hanging up her dress, Laura said, "Maybe you'd better zip *down* your fly, because we haven't got all day, as I told you."

Anders stood up very slowly and carried his drink toward the bathroom. "Let me just look at you a minute."

"Well, I can see what you want to look at, you dirty old pre-vert," she said, trying not to smile as she peeled everything off in what seemed like ten seconds, bent over gleaming white to put her shoes into the closet, and then stepped into the bathroom carrying her stockings and her underwear. "Doesn't show much for five months, does it?"

"I think it looks nice."

"Take your clothes off." She moved so that her nipples and her swollen stomach just touched him, and looked up. "Care to dance?"

Anders swallowed. "Can we still do it?"

"*I* can still do it. I don't know about you, if you keep boozing it up like that. . . ." She took the glass out of his hand, threw the drink into the toilet, put the empty glass on the sink, led him back into the bedroom . . . and stopped, frowning. "Maybe this isn't such a brilliant idea, today."

"What?" His thumbs were in her armpits. She stared hard into his eyes. "How many drinks did you have on the plane? You had a Cognac at lunch, you had another up here, you just had four aspirins, your arthritis has come back. . . . *No!*" She pushed away hard. "What time is it in Germany now? What time did you have to get up this morning?"

"Oh come on, we've passed the point of no return —"

"Ain't no such thing, boss." She whirled across the room, grabbed a sky-blue silk kimono out of the closet and wrapped herself. "No deal is done until it's done, isn't that what we say in the takeover business?"

His feet hurt. He knew he couldn't catch her. He stretched out on the bed and put his hands over his eyes. No deal is done until it's done. He felt the bed move as she lay down beside him.

"You won't feel like it twice tonight, hotshot. Quit trying to impress people, it isn't necessary, we're not running a contest."

"I want to do it!"

"Sure you do, but how will you feel fifteen minutes from now? Just cool it. Calm down and relax and we'll figure out how to get your act together. Quit that now! Just hold me and relax. If you straighten yourself out with Caroline the thing is going to be all right, isn't it?"

"I don't know."

"You went to Germany to find the answer, and you found the answer, didn't you?"

"I don't know yet. Everybody else is talking about it, and I'm lying down on your bed."

"You want to tell me at what price you're taking Boatwright — don't clench like that, you asshole, you know I'm only kidding! I haven't told you about my new job yet. We're setting up an anti-inflation fund: oil, gas, real estate, lumber, precious metals — a mutual fund for people who are scared of inflation. The guy who'll run it liked my reports, so I'm going full-time with him as a lumber and mining watcher, I do nothing but study companies in those two industries, and I'm getting sixty thousand plus options to buy the management company's stock. That's not bad for Miss Jersey Cranberries, is it?"

"That's terrific, but what about this?" said Anders, stroking her tight belly.

"No problem. I can do a lot of the work at home, it's reading stuff and talking to people on the telephone, mostly. I plan to be back in the office after Labor Day."

"And what's your husband think?"

"What do you mean what does he think? About this? I told you, he thinks he knocked me up by remote control, artificial insemination, and he's pleased as punch, he's getting so he can do it pretty good now —"

"Well, maybe it really was the artificial —"

"What are you, crazy? You think I'd really let anybody stick a syringe — only insemination I got was from this thing here! I'm thirty-eight years old this summer and this is my last chance to have a kid —"

"I think we may still have some problems," said Anders. "What's the baby going to look like?"

"The baby's going to look terrific! What did you tell me Isadora Duncan said to George Bernard Shaw? My looks and your brains, right? Or was it the other way around?" Laura giggled, and as she wrapped her naked arms around his head, Anders closed his eyes. . . . *Later:* "Hey, don't fall asleep on me!"

"Oh . . . Just let me sleep a few minutes —"

"No sir, not tonight!"

"Just ten minutes —"

"Out, out, *out!*" She began to push him with her feet. "It's time to go home, old boy."

"I can't go home. If I can't stay here, I'll get a hotel room."

"You can't stay here and you can't go to a hotel, either." She was standing up and pulling him. "You're going home to Juniper Lane."

"No, Laura, I can't, she doesn't want me there."

"*Bullshit!* Of course she wants you there, the boy drove all the way to Kennedy to make sure you go home tonight, and that's where you're going!"

"I haven't even talked to her today —"

"There's the telephone."

"From here? I can't —"

"I'm going into the bathroom to take a shower and you're going to pick up that phone and tell the Girl Scout that you're coming home in a taxi, is that clear, Graham? If you don't get this mess straightened out this evening you're going to regret it for the rest of your life, and I don't want you to come crying to me, because I'm telling you what to do now, and by Christ you'd better do it!"

TWENTY-SIX

Good Girls Finish First

The elevator doors opened on the thirty-first floor, and half a dozen women began to crowd aboard before they saw him trying to get off.

"Mr. Anders! Welcome back!"

"Mr. Anders, it's too late to start at five o'clock. . . ."

It was actually quarter after five, and the first-shift secretaries were leaving. Anders had made his way back to the Franklin Tower, moving slowly through the rush-hour streets. He had still not located Caroline, and he wanted to find out what was happening at Boatwright. He waved to the receptionist and started down the hall, but now his left foot hurt so much that he had to sit down on a straight-backed refectory chair just opposite the portrait of his grandfather.

George Graham wore a gray suit and a striped shirt and a navy blue necktie. He held his reading glasses in one hand and looked at something over the painter's shoulder with an expression of restrained amusement. How old was he when Peter Ellis painted that picture? Sixty? Sixty-five? Managing partner. What would George Graham have done in this mess? He wouldn't have gotten into this mess. Are you sure?

Anders stared at his grandfather. Tell me what to do. Caroline hasn't even told her secretary where she is. . . . Wasn't there a slight chill in Rosemary's words of welcome? If you think Caroline is in Bill Pennington's office signing the agreement with Hyde, you'd better call there.

No way.

Beams of evening sunlight streamed through the open doors on the western side of the block-long hallway, casting yellow rectangles across the orange carpets. Well, this is the end of the road, old buddy! If she has really sold her stock. . . . Thinking of the scene: Waldorf? 250 Park? Boris and Otto Waldstein. Somebody comes in and shows them the tape. They look at each other. . . .

"Are you all right, Mr. Anders?"

A kindly looking middle-aged woman: glasses, black hair, overcoat, gloves — a litigation paralegal? Anders could remember when every lawyer at Conyers & Dean knew the name of every secretary. Now he didn't even know all the lawyers.

"Oh, yes, thank you very much, I'm just tying my shoelace."

He stood up and limped the rest of the way to the corner. His secretary had gone home. She had drafted a letter to go with the checks replacing the checks that had bounced. Computer error, regret any inconvenience . . . A few pink telephone slips, but none from Caroline and none from Karin. "T. Sharp, Boatwright NYC."

Anders sank into his leather chair, punched in the client number and the deal number and the telephone number and swiveled around to put up his feet, to look across the city at the blood-red sun now sinking through the refinery smoke, sinking slightly to the west of Wilmington. . . .

"My God, Graham, where have you been, we've been looking all over for you —"

The future head of the Corporate Department ticked off exactly what was being done: committee of independent directors appointed, committee has hired still another firm of investment bankers, this one to advise as to "fairness" of price at which the Boatwright management and Waldstein, Hammerbrook's clients will take out the public shareholders; draft of proxy statement is already at the printer but of course the exhibits — the basic agreements — can't be finished until the deal is actually set. Did Graham want to speak with Boris Fleischer? He's at his apartment. . . . The main problem has been with Walther Siegler's sons: Graham, they are really a couple of perfect pricks and so are their lawyers, they act like maybe they want to back Siegler out of this, take Siegler private themselves — but *wow*, this Mr. Waldstein from Germany is making them toe the line now, he's gone back to the Waldorf to go to sleep but Boris Fleischer was really glad to see him —

The other line rang.

"Wait a minute, Tommy, I've got to put you on hold. . . . Hello?"

"Well! Guten Abend! After two days he answers his telephone —"

"Jesus! Where are you?"

"This little airport, flying club out here, what do they call it? Wings Field? We fly in his Learjet, he has gone to the bathroom before we take off, so I thought I would try just one more time."

"Where have you been? I've been calling and calling, I couldn't . . . Listen, what's going on? You know he knows?"

"He knows? Who knows? What?"

"Wait a minute, I've got to get off the other line. . . . Tommy, I've got to call you back, I've got something else here —"

"Well, I think you get the picture, Graham; we'll see you here tomorrow, right?"

"Yes, I guess so, I'll let you know, Tommy, thank you. . . . Hello?"

"You say he knows?"

"His daughters had you followed!"

"Had me followed?"

"He knows you were in my room that night!"

"He knows I was with you?"

"He told Caroline and she told me and I tried and tried to reach you. . . . Are you all right? Where the hell have you been?"

"He knows? . . . *Shit!* But he didn't say anything. . . . But I told him —"

"Told him what?"

"I told him I saw you in Hamburg. That I gave you those pictures."

"You told him about the pictures after all?"

"Yes . . . On the plane, you know, coming back . . . Well, I missed the Lufthansa connection in Frankfurt, I had to take a later flight, a TWA flight, and then they had trouble with their plane, we had to go to London to get another plane — oh, it was one of these endless stupid things, took twice as long as it should, but I didn't sleep on the planes, and I didn't drink anything except Perrier, and I didn't even take a Valium, I just looked at the sky and the ocean and I thought why have I so fucked up my life? I thought maybe I can be a Good Girl too. You think I can, Graham?"

"A Good Girl too?"

"Why not? Why do I . . . Why must I always be the Bad Girl?

Why must I always be *die Lorelei* who causes shipwrecks? This old man, he needs me, he loves me even now, I think, and he'll take care of me! Why can't I take care of him a little? He hasn't had much fun. *You* don't need me. I'm a toy for you to play with. I cause you trouble. So why don't I just marry him? I brought him his agreement — signed — and I told him Gottfried Gesstler's whole long story about the Leibstandarte in the Ardennes and shooting the prisoners and the trial at Dachau and I told him I gave you those pictures and I explained to him exactly what is on those pictures and he can kick me out into the street if he wants to do that but if he still wants me I will promise not to see you anymore and I really meant it, he *saw* I meant it, so he says he still wants to marry me but he just got out of the hospital, he wants to sleep in the sun right now, so we are flying to some island, it belongs to a friend of his, I don't even know exactly where it is, perhaps in Georgia? He will be back in a minute . . . wait, I have to put another quarter in —"

"Do you want me to call you back?"

"No, no, he's going to be here any second and I don't want him to see me on the telephone. I just wanted to say good-bye, dear. Will you think of me?"

"But what about Gottfried Gesstler? What did Francis Hyde say about —"

"He said, 'What does Anders say?' "

"What? I don't understand?"

"Francis asks: 'What is his opinion of the Waffen-SS? Are Graham Anders and his clients persuaded by all your fine distinctions between different kinds of SS?' and I say, 'They're not *my* fine distinctions, I was two years old, I'm delivering a message from Gottfried Gesstler' —"

"But what's he going to do about it?"

"Do about what?"

"About Gesstler! About this whole thing!"

"How can I ask him that if he thinks I talk to you, and I have not talked to Gottfried, I've been running around all day, I just got back and now I fly away again, I'm afraid to talk to Gottfried, but I will try to be a Good Girl now, the Good Girls always finish first, I think! Why must I always be the Bad Girl who goes to bed with everybody?"

"You're not a Bad Girl —"

"I'm really not, you know! A boy in Hamburg, a boy at the opera in Coburg, then Bob . . . then you, dear, then a couple of men when I was trying to forget you, didn't mean anything, now Francis . . . Does that make me such a whore? All right, I know, I left him out, but he is dead now and maybe God forgives me if I take good care of *this* old man. . . . Do you think it's possible, dear?"

"Yes! Of course it is!"

"You think I can do it?"

"Yes, you can do it."

"But without you, dear. I can't do it if I see you. Will you wish me luck? Oh, God there is one of the pilots looking for me, good-bye, dear!"

The sunset was deflected now. A thin blanket of puffy silver clouds had floated across from the north, that is from behind his head, but some rays from the vanishing sun peeped through the fissures. . . .

Relief? Is that what this is? Had he truly been worried that Hyde would do something to her — or only that he would kick her out into the street, as she so graphically expressed it? And who would have to take care of her then? Or does it just plain hurt?

He heard her playing the piano, he heard the dark voice singing "*Wie man sich bettet, so liegt man,*" yes, and the last line of that translates "If somebody gets kicked, it's going to be *you!*" and what did you expect her to do, that's Bertolt Brecht talking directly to the son of Gustaf Anders, she said it was your theme song and she isn't one to get kicked so she signed on for the Hyde Place and for the five million dollars if she can keep him happy for the rest of the trip.

But what happens now? The light was gone from the horizon and gusts of wind slammed against the glass. What does it feel like when you die?

Caroline sells him ten percent of Boatwright, he's already got over five percent, he may well have picked up another five in the market by now, he says forget those photographs, who cares who got shot after a battle thirty-four years ago, who cares who wore that kind of cap insignia thirty-four years ago, he hires the right public relations firm, he goes into the tender offer holding say twenty percent of the stock, the rest will come in, all right, and then he sends for Ordway Smith again and tells him his new people at Boatwright in New York don't see why they have to use a Philadelphia law firm. . . .

What did she say? Those guys you've worked with all your life? Seeing their faces: Graham, we've got to pay the rent. . . . Fifty is a little old to be looking for a job! You've overdrawn your accounts —

His telephone rang, and he jumped. "Hello?"

"Hey, Dad, I thought you were coming home?"

TWENTY-SEVEN

Lieben und Arbeiten?

Anders paused a moment, swallowed a mouthful of cold air, and braced himself as he entered the house.

The boy had run out into the driveway to open the taxi door, had reported that the photographs would be blown up by tomorrow morning and delivered to Conyers & Dean; he now stood back watching his parents greet each other in the downstairs hall. Caroline looked grave. Her short black hair shone as if she had just come from the hairdresser. She wore a gray silk suit, a white blouse and pearls, and she saw instantly that something was wrong.

"I just got home myself and I haven't changed," she said sounding breathless, moving into the living room. "Sit down right here, Graham." Awkwardly, not knowing quite what to do, Anders touched her elbow, kissed her lightly on the ear, and sank into the sofa.

"Been an interesting trip. Boatie, you want to fix some drinks for us?"

The boy left the room.

"Take your shoes off," said Caroline, frowning as she sat on the edge of the wing chair beside him.

"Caroline, did you sign the agreement with Hyde? I don't understand why Rosemary couldn't find you when I called, it's terribly important —"

"Are you going to take those shoes off?"

"Caroline, for Christ's sake!" but he did take off his left shoe and the black wool sock. She reached down and pulled his pink naked foot into her lap. "*Ouch!* Don't press like that."

"It's come back! You're going to see George Stevens in the morning."

"I can't, Caroline, I've got to be with Boris in New York tomorrow, I should have gone directly from the airport but Boatie showed up and I didn't know what you decided. . . . Look, if you've agreed to sell your stock to Francis Hyde you don't want Boris to find out from the tape, do you? Hyde will announce that the minute he files your agreement with the SEC."

"I spoke with Boris on the telephone after I talked to you, so Boris knows about Mr. Hyde's offer. Is your knee swollen too?"

"*Boris knows?* What did he say?"

"Well, he said it *is* a lot of money, he understands I might have reasons for wanting to sell now and he wouldn't blame me if I sell at this price, if I take this opportunity, but he thinks that Mr. Hyde misunderstands the whole situation, Mr. Hyde mainly wants the Siegler business and the Siegler family just will not work with somebody who was in Hitler's SS, they will simply pack up and go to General Electric or somebody like that, so he thinks that your plan is the best plan for keeping Boatwright together, essentially to have the company borrow enough money to buy all the stock in public hands — and that would include the shares that Mr. Hyde and Mr. Gesstler's Germans have bought, but not Boris's shares — and not mine. Is that right?"

"That's right," said Anders. "If we take Boatwright private, the only stockholders would be Boris, Boris's employees, Waldstein and Hammerbrook's clients — and you. Of course, a few years down the road you might decide to go public again, but for the time being you'd be locked in. And until they get the loans paid off, you wouldn't get much in the way of dividends."

Caroline looked at him but didn't say anything.

"We'd have to live from my income at the firm, I guess, but I have to tell you that they're going to cut me back," he said, and then, avoiding her eyes: "Ordway tells me I'm to be replaced by Tommy Sharp as head of the department."

He felt Caroline's steady eyes. He felt her cool hand still holding his foot.

"Well, that doesn't sound like the end of the world," she said quietly. "You always hated the administrative side, and Tommy Sharp is better suited to that kind of thing anyway," and Boatwright Anders came back carrying a wooden tray with three tinkling glasses.

In the dining room, Anders opened a bottle of California Beaujolais and was pleased to see Caroline drink her share. He told them about his trip, concentrating with genuine fascination on the story of Waldstein, Hammerbrook & Co. Caroline served lamb chops and succotash and vanilla ice cream with frozen strawberries, and said very little. Boatwright Anders watched his parents carefully. When dinner was over he said: "I've got some reading to do. It's nice to have you home, Dad!" and disappeared.

They looked across the table at each other. Here it comes, thought Anders.

"What time is it in Germany now?" she asked.

He looked at his watch. "Quarter to two tomorrow morning, and I'm fading fast. I should have stuck to soda water on the plane, like Otto Waldstein, but I didn't."

"Go on upstairs, I'll just put these things in the sink. Mrs. Wallace can do them in the morning."

"Upstairs? Do you want me to stay in the guest room?"

Caroline was clearing the table, looking down at what she was doing, not looking at him. "Who said anything about the guest room?"

He had unpacked, put his dirty laundry into the hamper, and was stepping out of the shower when Caroline came in, wearing her white slip, and the sight of her in the steamy heat of the bathroom, bulging plump and pink in the tight white slip with a black curl hanging in her eye suddenly made him lightheaded with desire. "My suit has to go to the cleaner," she said quickly. "The cleaner comes tomorrow — Wait a minute, Graham, we've got to talk, we have got to talk about this thing because — Graham, I can't brush my teeth when you're doing that!"

The water was running in the sink. They stared at themselves in the mirror.

"I love you," he said. "I don't want to live without you." He turned the water off. "Caroline, please don't sell your stock to these guys! You don't need that much money! Nobody needs that much money. That much money destroys people. Look around. Look at the girls you grew up with. Look at your sister, for that matter. Three hundred thousand a year after taxes! Loneliest person in the world. Divorces. Depressions. Nervous breakdowns. Kids on drugs. Kids locked up in loony bins. Do we need that? We're doing fine. Our kids are doing fine —"

Caroline swallowed. "We're doing fine?"

"Do you really want the whole world begging you for money — morning, noon, and night?"

"But that's what I do now! I raise money for the Orchestra —"

"You are a paid professional, doing a professional job — *arbeiten und lieben!*"

"What's that?"

"That's what Freud said. He said we must work and we must love. You've got your work, I've got my work —"

"I thought he said it the other way around. I thought he said *lieben und arbeiten*, didn't he put love first? And now you're the one that wants to talk about work and money and Francis Hyde and my goddamned Boatwright stock. . . . Graham, I can't *think* when you're doing that to me! . . . You're going to break my pearls, Graham. . . . Please, you know I'm too short for that without heels on and I want you off your feet! . . . Look, *all right!* Will you please lie down and let me finish brushing my *teeth?*"

Later, in the dark: "You know, it *isn't* sexual jealousy! I always had this feeling deep down inside a lot of men don't really *really* like to do it . . . but you do, you just love to do it, I knew that from the minute I saw you, and you sort of have to do it all the time, so why does it have to be with me all the time? I understand that, and you know I haven't made a fuss about that — but this is different, this one still wants to *supplant* me, still wants to get rid of me!"

"Can't happen," he mumbled, his face against her back. She still wore her slip and her brassiere. "Are you going to take your money and run?"

"Can't you please, *please* forget about my money?"

"And run?"

"Go to sleep," he felt her say. "It's over and done with. I'll tell you about it in the morning."

His body clock was still on Hamburg time, so he woke up at 4:38 in the morning according to the digital clock in the darkness, and he knew exactly where he was because he heard the newspaper truck grinding and clinking down Juniper Lane. Snow chains? This late in March? No, this is April now. Snow in April? He heard the silence outside, the silence that meant snow on the ground. Wet spring snow falling through the trees, falling into the winding suburban roads, falling into the rolling lawns and the covered swimming pools and the boxed boxwoods all around him. Adjusting his legs slowly and carefully in the smooth warm sheets — the slightest movement hurt like hell now — he tried to remember what the silently falling snow reminded him of, but then his mind switched to that big, white, chlorine-smelling room on the top floor of the University Hospital where they give therapy to the arthritis patients — hot whirlpool baths and ultrasound massages and he couldn't remember what else they did up there but he could never forget what those people up there looked like, some of them with terribly deformed and twisted hands or spines or knees or feet — and some of them were not so old, either, but then he managed to wrench away from that because he just didn't have time to see Stevens because Stevens would put him right into the hospital whereas he had to go over to New York, he should have gone to see Boris directly from Kennedy, this whole thing was slipping away from him, but how could he get over there if he couldn't walk? *Over and done with?*

Sleeping silently, she shifted the weight of her body and rolled against his back. His soul swooned slowly. . . . That was it! The falling snow, the bed warmed by their bodies, the silently falling snow made him think of the most beautiful sentence, the last words in the last story of Joyce's *Dubliners* where the guy is lying in bed with his sleeping wife thinking about the boy who loved his wife, the boy who is dead, thinking that pretty soon we'll all be dead so what difference does it make? and the snow is falling softly upon the Bog of Allen and, farther westward, softly falling into the dark mutinous Shannon waves, and how does it go on? *His soul swooned slowly as he heard the snow falling faintly through the universe and faintly falling, like the descent of their last end, upon all the living and the dead.*

TWENTY-EIGHT

Pennington's Day

— Hi, George, where are you calling from?

— Listen, I apologized to Mary for calling you so late at night, but somebody's got to tell me what the fuck is going on down there!

— Where are you, George?

— *Where am I?* I am still in the goddamned Hyatt Regency Hotel in Cambridge, Massachusetts, where I was sent the day before yesterday to contact old Walther Siegler or one of his sons or *somebody* at Siegler with authority to talk to us, but nobody up here will talk to me and now I've been *forgotten*, is that what you're telling me, for Christ's sweet sake? Whose idea was it to send me up here, anyway — Nobody at Siegler will see me or even talk to me on the telephone and I have to find out what's going on by reading *The Wall Street Journal* — What kind of a way is this to run —

— Oh God, George, I'm sorry, just come on home on the first plane tomorrow —

— I called you but they said you were downtown. I called Pennington but they said he was in a meeting, they've been telling me that *all day long!* He doesn't return —

— This hasn't been Bill Pennington's day, George. Come on home.

— Charlie, would you mind telling me what the hell —

— George, I hardly know where to begin!

— Are we going ahead with this harebrained Seagull deal?

— No, the Seagull is dead in the water. Jesus, you wouldn't believe —

— Then why is their price up? Why did Boatwright close at 31 today, if we're not buying? Who's buying?

— Apparently they're going private, doing an LBO. They haven't announced it, but the rumor is on the Street, First Hudson called us about it yesterday, and there are Conyers & Dean lawyers all over Boatwright's offices on Park Avenue, their people have been running back and forth on the train for days, and so the arbs are buying the stock again.

— What happened with Mrs. Anders? I thought she was going to sell. . . . Pennington got up in the middle of the night to write the agreement —

— Pennington got up in the middle of the night to write the agreement, they brought the agreement over to Mrs. Anders to sign, she signed it —

— She did sign it?

— She did, the lawyers had the amendment to Seagull's 13D all ready to go down to the SEC, in fact the messenger is on the train to Washington when Pennington gets a call from Mr. Hyde: don't file the agreement, we can't go ahead with this deal, we've got to find Caroline Anders and persuade her to *tear up* the agreement!

— *What?*

— Look, I didn't know a goddamned thing about all this. Not one goddamned thing! I'm only trying to run the Company. This is all from Pennington. Today. I get to hear all this *today!* We're having lunch at the Union League, me and Ed Finnegan and two guys from the Italian company. I mean we *are* still trying to run a business, trying to sell products in thirty-five countries, we've got other things to do besides worry about Boris Fleischer and Walther Siegler and Boatwright's price every fifteen minutes and the goddamned investment bankers and lawyers day after day after day, so Bill Pennington comes by the table and says "Charlie, I think it would be a good idea if you walk across the street for a few minutes when you've finished lunch, I've got something you'd better look at," so I did that. I sent the others back to the plant and I went up to the Openshaw firm and Pennington took me into his office and he shut the door and then he uncovered some newspapers that were spread out on his work table and here were these two great big photographs blown up. . . . I don't know, maybe the size of a newspaper page, huge, big pictures, and one of them shows this guy in a Nazi battle uniform sitting on top of a tank or something and pointing a machine gun right at you and grinning! And the other one has all these guys sitting in rows, you know, like prisoners? With numbers hung around their necks, and I said what the hell is all this about, Bill, and he shows me a letter from Graham Anders, Conyers & Dean stationery, dated yesterday, hand-delivered this morning. Anders says he thought we might be interested in a couple of photographs of Gottfried Gesstler, taken in connection with his military service and then he goes on to explain that the first picture is Gesstler during the Battle of the Bulge in 1944 and the second is Gesstler in 1946 on trial for shooting American prisoners. War crimes trial!

— Jesus Christ!

— Jesus Christ is right. Can you imagine what happens to our business —

— Could the pictures hurt us?

— Could *kill* us!

— Really?

— Kill us!

— You think it's true?

— Sure it's true! You know how this whole thing began, don't you, this whole unbelievable mess? Mr. Gesstler, our partner in Seagull, is the stepfather of you-know-who!

— But Pennington only got the pictures this morning? How did the Old Man —

— Already knew about them! When you-know-who got back from Germany — day before yesterday, I guess — she told him the story and she told him Anders has the pictures and that's when he called Pennington and told him to reverse the whole thing about Mrs. Anders's Boatwright stock.

— Well, why should she do that?

— At thirty-five bucks a share, why indeed should she do that? She could buy the whole town —

— Good Christ, Pennington must have put some conditions in it —

— Yeah, you would think so, wouldn't you! I guess they were so afraid she wouldn't sign, or that she'd take it over and show it to Conyers & Dean . . .

— Well, my God, even so, she'd have to bring a lawsuit, we could make all kinds of arguments —

— You think the Old Man wants a lawsuit about all this? He doesn't want one goddamned *word* about all this —

— Okay, I can see that, all right. . . . Are you going to tell me what happened?

— Well, they call around to look for her. First they can't find her. Panicsville! Then they find her right in her office, Orchestra Association. Pennington asks can he come over and see her. No she says, she hasn't got a lawyer herself, but she'll see Mr. Hyde.

— I thought he was in the hospital.

— No, turns out he's okay, doesn't even need an operation, he's home in his apartment, she says if he wants to discuss this subject any more he had better come over and see her. So he did.

— What happened?

— Well, this is all from Pennington, who wasn't there either, but Pennington got his marching orders right after this meeting. Caroline Anders sounds like a cool cookie. An iron lady. She let the Old Man tell his story about these goddamned pictures and he couldn't tell if she already knew about them —

— Hadn't Anders told her?

— I don't know, I guess the Old Man couldn't tell, but anyway she listened to his story and then she told him she had to make a telephone call and she would give him his answer after she made the call, would he please excuse her? So the Old Man had to sit out in the waiting room there —

— Calling Anders!

— No, she told him Anders is in Germany or on the way home or whatever. Can't reach him.

— Calling somebody else at Conyers & Dean.

— No, he didn't think so. He thinks she called Boris Fleischer. Old Man sits in the waiting room. Finally she asks him in again, she says okay, she'll tear up the agreement, she and Fleischer will take steps to eliminate the SS pictures if the Seagull project is dismantled and the Boatwright stock that Seagull has bought will be sold to Boatwright when, as and if Boatwright makes an offer to all its public shareholders — that's the LBO, of course. Documents to be prepared by Conyers & Dean within twenty-four hours. The Old Man says sure, agreed, I guess he's relieved, he stands up and wants to shake hands, but Mrs. Anders says there's just one more thing.

— Just one more thing?

— Mrs. Anders is sorry that she's got to involve herself in such a personal matter, but she knows that Mr. Hyde will understand if she asks what's happening about his prenuptial agreement with Karin Bromberg.

— Oh my God! What *is* happening about that?

— What can the Old Man say? Apparently she's now agreed to the marriage settlement and he's going to take her on a trip, he's thinking of buying an island off the coast of Georgia, in fact he's flying down there today . . . hell, George, I don't want to make this up, I can't imagine exactly what he told Mrs. Anders, I really only know what Pennington was told.

— What was Pennington told?

— You know the old Hyde Place, Conroy's castle out in —

— Yes, of course I know it, I've been there, he promised to give it to her —

— Yeah, well she ain't going to get it! Mr. Hyde is going to buy it from Conroy under their agreement, and then he's going to make a gift of it to the Philadelphia Orchestra Association, documents to be prepared within twenty-four hours by Pennington and reviewed by Conyers & Dean!

— I don't believe this!

— Isn't that generous of the Old Man? I never knew he had such an interest in music!

— Are you saying he's going to marry that woman, after she . . . after she —

— He's besotted!

— He's *what?*

— That's what Pennington said. Pennington's voice was shaking. *Besotted in the woman!* Had to have Sandra look that up when I got back. Means stupefied, means stupid or foolish, means infatuated or obsessed.

— *Jesus-K-Christ!*

— Know what I think? I think he was so relieved that his prostate is okay. . . . He's almost seventy, how much time has he got? And this girl knows how to charge his battery. . . . He's hooked! He's just plain hooked on this particular piece, never mind what else she does, simple as that!

— But the Hyde Place, my God! Iron lady or not, does the Old Man roll over for that kind of money? How many acres is it, anyway?

— Well, I agree, it isn't like him, but he knows he stubbed his toe on this whole thing, his personal project from beginning to end, and he doesn't want people to find out, I guess. . . . Anyhow, that's the reason you couldn't get through to poor old Pennington, he's got his hands full. He's got this whole mess to clean up now: he's got to dissolve this Seagull deal with the Germans — after advising them that nobody would care about their military service forty years ago; he's got to close on the Hyde Place with Charlie Conroy so that the Old Man can give it to the Orchestra; he's got to start all over again with that miserable prenuptial agreement . . . and he doesn't even know the rest of it!

— What rest of it? You don't mean there's more?

— This can wait 'til you get home, George. Come on in to see me tomorrow — or even next week, there isn't any hurry —

— About what? There isn't any hurry *about what?* Come on, Christ Almighty, Charlie, has this got something to do with *me?* Don't you leave me up here to —

— *All right!* But you're not going to like this. Unfortunately there's a telephone on that damn island. I wish he would concentrate on his sex life, but he called this afternoon and he wants you to think about moving some of our legal work from Pennington's firm to Conyers & Dean. He thinks maybe the trademark litigation work, for starters. You know they did lose that case last year —

— I don't think I heard you right, Charlie.

— You heard me right, all right. This is the second time Mr. Graham Anders has derailed something around here —

— He's out to get Anders? He's out to get Anders so he wants to move legal work to Conyers & Dean?

— If C & D makes certain changes. One certain change.

. . . .

— You there, George?

— I'm here.

— What do you think?

— Well . . . I think that's pretty cute. . . . But they won't do it. No way! He's the grandson of George Graham. Well, maybe that doesn't matter, but he's been there twenty-five years. At least. And if they really do take Boatwright private, he'll have a bigger lock on Boatwright than before. He has other clients. He's a department head. . . . I don't see it, Charlie.

— What did we pay Pennington's firm last year? Round numbers?

— A million two-hundred fifty. Or sixty.

— Lot of money!

— But that's everything! He's going to take *everything* away from

Pennington? It makes no sense, Charlie. And C & D won't do it. Will they? They *can't!* How will it make them —

— I guess not. Apparently he tried it out on Ordway Smith the other day, and he didn't get very far. I'm supposed to ask what you think.

— I think . . . I'm not sure I dare . . . All right, Goddamn it, we've always been level with each other! I think the Old Man is beginning to . . . You'd better not quote me on this! I mean it wasn't Anders who stuck it to him this time; it was the women! One of whom he still plans to marry! Besotted? *It's worse than that!* Listen, our fees to outside law firms would be twice as much if I hadn't taken the routine work inside, if I didn't go over every bill they submit with a magnifying glass, I make them justify *every fucking minute* of billable time, who worked on what how long —

— I know you do, I know you do, George, nobody is questioning —

— I think this is a bunch of shit, Charlie, I really do! I don't think Bill Pennington is Jesus Christ and his people have made mistakes, everybody makes mistakes, but they've done a good job for us for a long time, and this kind of behavior . . . I mean this is a public company, you know! Is this how you run a public company? I mean don't we have a board of directors? I mean *Christ!* After all —

— Come on home, George. Come on home and help me run this public company! And have another drink before you go to sleep. I'll see you tomorrow.